# RED MOON

## Ralph Cotton

BERKLEY
New York

**BERKLEY**
An imprint of Penguin Random House LLC
penguinrandomhouse.com

BERKLEY and the BERKLEY & B colophon
are registered trademarks of Penguin Random House LLC.

ISBN: 9780451240101

Signet mass-market edition / July 2013
Berkley mass-market edition / April 2023

Printed in the United States of America
7   9   11   13   15   14   12   10   8   6

For Mary Lynn, of course . . .

# PART 1

# Chapter 1

_Badlands, Arizona Territory_

The young Ranger Samuel Burrack lay atop a mammoth boulder overlooking a stretch of spiny hills skirting the Mexican border northwest of the Nogales badlands outpost. A storm was hard blowing. Through the lens of an outstretched telescope, he studied three watery figures while raindrops crawled sidelong across the circling lens. To his right lightning twisted and curled in a gunmetal mist on the distant curve of the earth.

_"Tormenta mala de viento—ciclón!"_ an old stable hostler had warned him two days earlier when the sky over Nogales had taken on a pallid yellow-gray and the hot desert wind began sucking southward like some terrible demon drawing in its breath. "Here is the stillness before the terrible storm," the man had warned in stiff English, raising a crooked cautioning finger. "The longer the stillness, the more terrible the storm," he'd added, lowering his voice as if such information were privy only to himself and the Ranger.

Sam had simply nodded in reply. Storm or no

storm, he had a job to do. Weather was just a factor to acknowledge, but not a factor to concede to.

He'd thought of the old man when the stillness lingered throughout that day and part of the next as he'd pushed on. He'd kept watch on the sky for what good it did him—watched it gather and loom until at last a roiling blackness rose from the bowels of the earth and robbed the morning of its light, falling upon the earth as if in vengeance.

"Good prediction, hombre," Sam reminded himself with no real surprise, reflecting on the old hostler's conversation from two days ago.

Before leaving town he had said *gracias* to the old man for his warning as he unrolled his brown rain slicker and put it on. With his big Colt resting on his hip, protected beneath the slicker, he'd tied down his bedroll atop his saddlebags and stepped up into the roan's saddle, spreading the tails of his long rain slicker down the horse's sides. He'd reminded the hostler that *bad* weather did not stop *bad* men, and the old Mexican had shrugged his thin shoulders either in sympathy or resignation and stood watching as the Ranger turned to ride away.

"Go with God," the old man had whispered in Spanish, seeing the Ranger's headstrong surplus roan balk and sidle and shuffle on its hooves.

"Always," the Ranger had replied, tipping a gloved hand as he'd gathered the unruly roan beneath himself and chucked the animal forward. The roan snorted and grumbled in protest, but did the Ranger's bidding all the same. And so their journey had gone.

*Bad men and lawmen . . .* , Sam thought now in retrospect, holding a tight focus on the three faces beneath their wet wind-bent hat brims. They tugged and tightened their drenched hats down against a hard blow of wind, the loose tails of their rain slickers wagging and flapping wildly, like the tongues of a gaggle of lunatics. He might say that times like this neither lawman nor outlaw had sense enough to get in out of the rain. But that wasn't being fair to his own profession—his brothers in arms.

Lawmen endured bad weather because their work required it.

Outlaws, murderers and rogues of the kind he pursued played out their hands fast and loose, with no regard for weather or anything else. He suspected that deep down the lawless realized the broad possibility of each day being their last, and he understood their thinking. It gave lawmen like himself little choice but to follow the lead set forth by their miscreant prey, no matter the climate, no matter the trail.

*And that's the whole of it. . . .*

He drew a closer focus and moved from face to face on the subjects in the small round frame of the wet lens. He could see their lips moving. An arm pointed off toward the trail rising and falling out of sight across a sandy stretch of squat cactus and scarce patches of spindly wild grass standing cowed beneath the gray blowing deluge. The arm belonged to the group's leader, Wilson Orez, and had Sam not known it already he would have deduced it, seeing as how these other two appeared to listen to the man, nodding in agreement, checking the wet rifles in their hands while Orez raised a wadded bandanna and mopped blow-in rain from the side of his neck, his beard stubble.

*Wilson Orez . . .* From what the Ranger had learned of the man, Orez was tough, smart and fearless: a former cavalry scout, desert seasoned, a man trained to keep a cool head while sudden death lurked all around him. Sam ran down a mental list he'd compiled on him. Wilson Orez was part Scots-Irish, part White Mountain Apache. His skill with a rifle was unsurpassed. He was both fast and accurate with a handgun—an expert with a knife. He had faced the feared Apache warrior TaChima from the Compa clan, brother to the dreaded Apache leader Juan Compa.

*You know your history when it comes to killing,* Sam reminded himself grimly.

In a straight-up knife fight, toe-to-toe, *mano y mano,* Orez had killed TaChima graveyard dead. Sam considered it, finding it noteworthy how these sorts of facts sprang so readily to his mind.

*Part of the job,* he decided, dismissing the matter, going on with his thoughts.

TaChima had earned the alternative calling of Red Sleeve, a title originated years earlier by the famed Mimbreño Apache leader, Mangas Coloradas.

Being a Red Sleeve Warrior put TaChima at a high position of respect among all the Chihenne warriors in the Animas Mountain Range. TaChima had not been a man to take lightly, Sam acknowledged. Yet, according to the story generated among Captain Edmond Shirland's California Volunteers,

Wilson Orez tracked TaChima into the heart of Apacheria, the People's stronghold.

Standing alone, naked save for a loincloth and a knife in hand, Wilson Orez had cast a challenge of honor for the sake of blood vengeance—a matter of powerful medicine among the killer elite of the Apacheria alliance. Thereupon he had calmly, methodically gutted and all but quartered the dreaded blade-man as if he were some sacrificial steer.

*And that's the man you're after today.*

*But he's older now,* Sam thought in reply. He lowered the lens from his eye in the heavily blowing rain and thought about it as he wiped a wet gloved hand across his face. At the end of this storm, there wouldn't be a hoofprint left to follow between here and the border. He raised the telescope back to his eye and homed down onto the three figures. Thunder split the sky high above the low-hanging blackness.

*Stay close,* he told himself. Whatever moves these men made, he'd have to be prepared to make it with them. *No matter the climate, no matter the trail . . . ,* he repeated to himself. Stay close and at the same time try to keep a man as trail-savvy as Orez from knowing he was there. Lightning glittered as he looked closely back and forth at the faces of the other two men. There was something at work between these two—something secretive. He could see it in their eyes. Were he in any way a friend or an associate of Wilson Orez, he would have to warn him to watch out for these two. But that was none of his concern.

Another thing, forget Wilson Orez's reputation,

he reminded himself. Having too much respect for a bad man's reputation was as dangerous as having too little. Either would get you killed. Besides, if there was one thing he learned *quick* out here, it was that a man's reputation was almost always larger, more powerful than the man. Leastwise, enough so that the prowess of the man lived on long after the man himself had gone to dust.

*But not Wilson Orez*, a voice cautioned inside his head.

*Stop it*, the same voice rebuked. His hands tightened around the lens.

As he grappled with his thoughts, he saw Orez step into view, blocking the face of one of the men. No sooner had Orez stepped into sight than he stepped back out. When the Ranger saw the other man's face again, he saw the red line of gushing blood spewing from the man's sliced-open throat.

*Whoa!* He hadn't expected that.

Sam tensed, watching through the circling lens as the man's wet gloved hands clamped up over his throat attempting to stay the flow of arterial blood. But the reflex didn't help. The dark blood jetted from between his gripping fingers as he staggered forward into the mud and blowing rain. His wet hat came loose and flew from his head in a spiraling spray of water.

Sam watched; the surprise of the brutal act was gone now, yet the intensity of it held him captivated until he swung the lens onto Orez to see what was coming next.

Gray rain blew howling across the land between the Ranger's lens and the grizzly scene of silent carnage. Wilson Orez had moved fast. By the time the sheet of rain had blown on and the Ranger had Orez back in focus, he saw the other man had bowed forward at the waist. Orez gave a hard sidelong jerk on the handle of his big knife and Sam saw the blade slip out of the man's abdomen where Orez had just then buried it to the hilt. At the man's side, a big Remington revolver fell from his wet hand into the mud at his feet. The man sank to his knees, then flopped forward, face-first with a muddy splash.

Orez stepped back, red blood washing from his knife blade, turning lighter, thinner in the rain. Sam turned and scanned the telescope to where ten feet away the man with the gaping throat had struggled along as far as he could and appeared to melt down into the ground.

*Two down, one to go.*

Marking the spot in his mind with a close-by stand of rain-whipped juniper, Sam closed the telescope between his wet hands and slipped it inside his slicker. Picking up his Winchester from beside him, he slid back on his belly to the edge of the boulder and down its side to where the surplus roan stood waiting. The horse appeared annoyed and restless, hitched to the spiky remnants of a weathered piñon. As Sam shoved the wet rifle down into the saddle boot, the roan grumbled and nickered and tossed its head against its tied reins. A forehoof splashed down hard in a puddle of water.

"Hope I haven't kept you from anything pressing," Sam said wryly, unhitching the exasperated animal. The roan was one of three horses making up the Nogales outpost's surplus riding stock he'd had to choose from. His personal stallion, Black Pot, was still recovering from a pulled tendon he'd picked up during their previous venture across the Mexican border.

The roan snorted and raised a threatening rear hoof. Sam ignored the gesture and patted its wet withers.

"I know," he said quietly. He stepped up into the saddle as if they were longtime friends. Before the roan could organize itself enough to offer resistance, he'd backed it a step, collected it firmly beneath him and nudged it forward through the mud. "I know," he repeated. "You're a tough fellow. Now let's go."

The roan settled as if satisfied it had made its position clear and went on, taking up a steady gait, the Ranger riding easy, his hand drawn loosely on the reins. With the horse's head lowered sidelong against the blow of wind, he'd only managed to get halfway across the rolling terraced land before the constant slam of wind and water and the lack of visibility forced him to step down from his saddle, draw his rifle and lead the roan the rest the way.

When he did reach the place where the killings had taken place, he came upon the spot all at once, the powerful thrust of the storm waning for a moment to reveal the juniper bush. The slant of the rain corrected itself and fell straight and steadily. He stood in the silver-gray mist like some supplicant to the dark sky churning above him. Rifle in hand, he stared through a braided stream of water running steadily from the lowered front brim of his sombrero.

Fifteen feet in front of him the juniper bush was stooped and dripping. Beyond the juniper, pipe organ cactus stood erect like lean apparitions in a low swirling mist. Sam looked around at the sodden ground expecting to find the bodies of the two men. Yet, only mildly surprised, he found no sign of the hapless thieves except for the dropped Remington and two watery pink puddles lying in the indentations where the two had fallen and the rain had not completely washed the blood away.

He looked at the watery hoofprints, barely visible now in the falling rain. Each set showed signs of equal weight on their backs. Stooping, he picked up the black-handled Remington and inspected it. The initials *TQ* were carved into the right side of the handle.

"You loaded the bodies up and sent them off." Sam spoke to himself as if he were speaking to Wilson Orez. "Wise move, Orez." He shoved the Remington under his slicker into his gun belt. "You're a cautious man," he murmured, still searching the rolling land while the wind rebuilt and groaned and came hurling back across the land in a low, menacing roar.

Even in a storm Orez had lowered any pursuer's chances of following him, no matter how briefly, from a sure thing to the slimmer odds of one-out-of-three.

The wind passed and started to build again as he noted the three sets of hooves disappearing in three separate directions before being lost to the pounding deluge altogether.

Standing behind him, the roan grumbled and sawed its head against its reins, feeling the rain lashing sideways once again. Lightning sprang up anew and writhed in place, followed by another deep rumble of thunder. The roan whinnied and shied.

"Easy, boy, easy," he said to the horse, jerking firmly on the reins, settling the animal. He stood staring out into a distant swirl of silver-gray until the rain slashed in horizontally again and obscured even that.

Still he stood with his slicker tails twisted and flapping sidelong, the brim of his sombrero pressed straight up on one side. He considered Wilson Orez, trying to sketch out a better picture of the man, this man he was sent to stop—*to kill*, he corrected. He'd seen enough to realize *killing* was the only thing that would stop Wilson Orez. He'd watched two men fall in their own blood as the silent scene played itself out beneath the rumble and roar of the storm. Orez was cautious and deadly, a man who killed quick, kept moving and left little behind to follow.

"So, this is how it is with you," he said quietly out to the dark swirling firmament. In reply, lightning and thunder cracked and exploded all along the far curve of the earth.

"All right, then," he said, clearing all slates, settling all accounts past or present in preparation for what lay at hand. He felt the big Remington, cold and wet on his belly beneath his slicker, as he pushed forward against the wind, pulling the roan behind him. "You best stay up with me, horse," he cautioned over his shoulder. "Orez might just eat you before it's over."

The roan sawed its wet head in protest, but followed, mane and tail wind-whipped, slinging water.

# Chapter 2

Four miserable souls inside a mud-locked stage-coach huddled together as the storm ruled sky above and earth below in the breadth of its fury. In the mud outside, a strongbox and another larger leather-bound valuables crate lay with their lids gaping open. Rainwater had long filled both open containers, forming small waterfalls down over their sides.

"I've never seen it blow so bad or rain so hard," said Dan Long, the stagecoach driver. "And this is a desert," he mused, and shook his wet head with irony.

"I've seen it blow on and off like this as long as ten, twelve days in a row," said Maynard Dawson, the shotgun rider.

"Do tell," said a soft, feminine voice from the seat facing opposite the coachmen.

"Oh yes." Turning from the canvas-draped coach window, Dawson dug his fingertips spider-like into his thick gray beard as he warmed to conversation. "I've seen a hard turn of weather set in like this. No telling how long it might last." He looked at two sets of watching eyes and continued. "Once when I was just a boy growing up in—"

"Damn it, Maynard," said Dan Long, seated beside him. He growled in exasperation. "Remind me to never ask you nothing, ever again."

"What'd I do?" Dawson asked.

"All's I asked was has it let up any?" said the driver. "You took off with it like we asked you to give us a speech."

"I was explaining myself for the lady's sake, Dan'l," Dawson said evenly.

"Yes, but I'm betting the lady would appreciate not hearing all your blather," Long said. As he spoke, his eyes softened as he and the shotgun rider turned in unison to the young Southern dove seated opposite them.

"It's quite all right, fellows," said the dove, Jenny Lynn Beaumont, most recently from Atlanta, Georgia. "I enjoy taking in knowledge at every opportunity." She gave the two a thin, enduring smile. She sat nursing an unconscious hardware drummer, his battered head resting in her lap. She kept the bleeding on his brow minimized by dabbing the swollen cut with a wet length of cloth she'd torn from the hem of her petticoat.

The two coachmen looked at each other. Maynard Dawson almost sighed with pleasure at the sound of her soft Southern accent.

"I could listen to you talk all day about *thimbles* or *coal buckets* either one if you was a mind to," he said. "With all respect, that is, ma'am," he added quickly, jerking his wet hat from his head in afterthought.

"Lord, Maynard, you couldn't keep your mouth shut to save your life," Long said.

"What'd I do?" Dawson asked again.

"You've gone and embarrassed the young lady," said Long.

Jenny Lynn gave the two a demure look and lowered her eyes to the battered drummer. She dabbed gently at a trickle of blood. The drummer came around a little and rolled his eyes.

"Are—are we there yet?" he asked through thick swollen lips.

The two coachmen looked at each other. Dawson shook his head, grimly forecasting the wounded man's chances.

"Shhh, you lie still, Mr. Weir," said Jenny Lynn, still dabbing at his cuts and welts. "Everything is going to be just fine." She paused, then said, "Do you hear me, Mr. Weir?"

"We're almost . . . there, you say?" the drummer murmured sluggishly as he drifted back to sleep.

Still shaking his head, Dawson stared at the knocked-out drummer and said under his breath, "Miracle he ain't dead already, a licking like that. I never seen such a pistol whipping. For a minute there I was wondering if—"

"Hold it. What was that?" said Long, sounding hushed all of a sudden.

Dawson gave him a curious look. "That was me saying I never saw such a licking."

"No, you fool," said Long, throwing back the long canvas window cover against the lashing rain. "*Out there*. I heard something out there."

Dawson looked up at the sound of rain ripping across the thin veneer and wooden rib coach roof.

"I don't know if you heard anything for all this racket," he said. But even as he spoke, he fished the two-shot derringer from his vest pocket, twisted around in his seat and looked out with Long from behind the rain-pelted canvas.

"Back there," Long said, rain blowing in their faces. "Is that a rider?"

They stared through the sheets of rain and a silvery mist looming along the trail.

"Maybe it's one of our horses come back to us," Dawson offered.

"Not a chance," said Long. He stared long and hard, then changed his mind and said, "But it might be."

"Sit back, let me out," said Dawson, raising his wet hat, placing it back atop his head. He started leaning, making his way past Long toward the door.

"What are you doing, Maynard?" Long said, sounding shaken at the prospect of a rider showing up on them.

"While you make up your mind if it is or ain't one of the horses come back, I'm going to see for myself," Dawson said, throwing open the door into the blowing rain, splashing down into the muddy water covering the trail. Holding his hat down in place with his left hand, the small derringer in his right, he pushed forward, struggling to stay upright against the crushing wind.

"What do you see out there, Maynard?" Long shouted through the raging storm.

"Not a blasted thing," shouted Dawson in reply. "A horse—No, wait. It's horses. I see some horses, is all."

"Are they ours?" shouted Long. "I surely hope they're ours."

"Wait," said Dawson. "There's a man leading

them, on foot." He raised the derringer arm's length and called out to the obscure figure leading three horses toward the coach, "Hold it right there, mister, or I'll shoot you dead."

Lightning licked and glittered; a hard clap of thunder seemed to break the sky in half and drop part of it to some lower level.

"Don't shoot," called a voice. "I'm Ranger Sam Burrack, sent from Nogales."

"Says he's a lawman, Dan'l," Dawson called out toward the flapping window canvas. He lowered the derringer a little and tried squinting through the harsh silvery swirl of rain and wind. Sheet upon sheet of rain lashed against him.

"Ha!" Long said, pulling the canvas back a little. "*Now* they send a Ranger?"

"Come on in slow and easy. Let me see you good," Dawson called out. "We're armed to the teeth here," he bluffed. "I'd better see a badge stuck on you."

The Ranger walked in closer, both he and the roan bent against the storm even as wind and rain slackened for a moment. When he stopped five feet from Maynard Dawson and looked at the small derringer pointed at his chest, he slowly raised a short-barreled shotgun and held it out butt first to the coachman. Lightning twisted again, casting a wide rose-blue streak beyond the black horizon.

"My badge is under my raincoat. But here, I'm guessing this is yours," the Ranger said, his voice lowering along with the storm's intensity. "I found it in the mud alongside the trail."

Thunder slammed off the unseen walls of heaven.

Dawson took the shotgun as a thin braid of water ran the gutter between the barrels.

"Ranger, we are dang glad to see you," he said as the wind seemed to draw a deep breath and blow even harder. He pocketed the derringer and wiped a hand down the shotgun barrel. "I thought I'd never see this baby again. I'm much obliged." He gestured the Ranger toward the stagecoach door. "Coming in, Dan'l," he said to the canvas window cover. He swung the door open.

Stepping in out of the blow, Sam looked around the dark, confined coach. He saw two sets of wary eyes turned to him, and the bloody man's head lying in the young dove's lap.

"Howdy, Ranger, I'm Dan Long," said the stagecoach driver in a raised voice. "This is Miss Beaumont. You couldn'ta got here soon enough to suit us. I hope you have some strong thread and a good sharp needle." Thunder exploded like cannon fire. Long flinched, then continued. "We need to get this fellow's head sewn up in a few places."

"I believe I do have some supplies for that purpose," Sam said above the rain's gravelly roar. He tipped his wet sombrero to the young dove, then eyed the knocked-out drummer's head on her lap.

"It made no sense, beating this man so bad, Ranger," said Long. "It was the leader who did all the beating. His men just watched him do it."

"That was Wilson Orez doing the beating," Sam said. "Orez had his own reason."

"Wilson Orez?" said the coachman. A fearful look clouded his brow. But he swallowed a tightness in his throat and put his fear aside. "Still, they made nearly fifty thousand here today, gold coin and cash greenbacks. They had nothing to be upset about."

"Fifty *thousand*?" Sam said. He gave the coachman a look.

"I know it sounds crazy, that much money traveling by stage in a strongbox," Long said. "But Keyes City Bank said they needed the money. I knew they'd be better off breaking it up over five or six runs. But bankers only listen to other bankers. So there it is." He shrugged. "I still can't figure Orez pistol-whipping this man like this."

"Orez wanted to make sure you'd get busy taking the wounded man back to Nogales instead of following him and his men wherever they're headed."

"I can see his reasoning when you put it that way, Ranger," said Dawson, squeezing into the coach behind him. "Not that we could have gone chasing after them anyway, them driving all our horses off in front of them. Our search party could've when they come and found us, but not us."

"Us with no guns to boot," Long threw in, beginning to see the outlaw's purpose in beating the drummer senseless.

On the dove's lap, the drummer groaned, coming around a little and trying to raise his head.

"This man needs attending to," said Jenny Lynn. She pressed the man's head back down firmly and wiped the wet cloth back over his forehead. "I fear his head may be cracked deep inside."

"I'll just get the thread and medical supplies from my saddlebags, ma'am," Sam said.

"Poor fellow," Maynard Dawson put in, looking down at the bloody drummer, knowing it was only by the luck of the draw that it was not him lying there beaten senseless. "I'll check around up under my seat. I just might have a bottle of rye some passenger left by accident." He caught the stern look Dan Long gave him and added, "You have to admit, it comes in handy, times like this."

Without answering him, Long said to the Ranger above the roar of the storm, "While you're taking care of this one, Maynard and I will go search for the other four horses. Looks like this blow ain't going to let up any time soon."

The Ranger only nodded as he backed out the door in a crouch into the hard, pelting rain. Once he was outside, the two coachmen hiked their coat collars up and stepped out behind him.

"You're going to be just fine, Tunis Weir," Jenny Lynn said quietly to the bloody man cradled in her lap. Her words fell away beneath a hard slam of incoming thunder.

The storm continued to rage outside while, in the light of an oil lantern, Jenny Lynn held the dazed man's head still as the Ranger closed and stitched shut a half dozen deep cuts on his battered head. Before Sam started his work with a needle and a length of coarse thread, the young dove poured several good stiff belts of rye into the drummer's gaping mouth, which he drank eagerly.

Sam sat watching, waiting, needle at ready.

"All set, Mr. Weir?" the dove asked. The man looked up almost contentedly through bleary eyes

at the lovely young face and the bottle of rye looming over him.

"Yep, sew me on up," he managed to say in a
thick, slurred voice.

The young dove poured a final swig of rye into
the drummer's mouth and watched him swallow
it. When he let out a whiskey hiss and settled down
with his eyes closed, Jenny raised the bottle to her
lips and took a large swallow. Lowering the bottle,
she handed it to Maynard Dawson and wiped a
thin wrist across her mouth.

"Sew him up, Ranger," she said firmly as lightning flashed around the edges of the window
cover, and she sat looming over the drummer, her
weight ready to press him down if need be. Thunder split apart like stone in the sky above them.

# Chapter 3

A full hour later as the storm continued to rage its way past them like an army at war, the Ranger finished drawing the last stitch taut beneath his blood-stained fingertips. When he leaned back and gave the young dove a nod, she patted the man's trembling shoulder and sat back against the coach seat. Across from her the two coachmen sat staring, soaking wet from having searched without success for the other four horses.

"We're all done, Mr. Weir. You're going to be good as new," she said quietly down to the swollen, battered face in her lap.

"I know it," he replied in a halting, trembling voice. He managed to reach a hand out in search of the rye bottle. Dawson leaned forward and gave it to him. "I expect I'll be leaving now?" he asked.

"He's out of his head," Jenny Lynn whispered to the Ranger. Patting Tunis Weir on a shoulder, she said, "You poor dear man, you won't be going anywhere. Lie still now."

"The stitches have stopped you from bleeding as bad," Sam said to the wounded man. "But we still need to get you back to Nogales and have the doctor look at you—make sure nothing's broke."

"Obliged, Ranger," he murmured through swollen lips. He took a shorter drink from the bottle and handed it to Jenny Lynn, who in turn gave it to the shotgun rider. Dawson took it as he continued staring down at the drummer, engrossed.

"I once sewed up a dog's neck," he said as if in awe.

"It ain't the same," Long said sarcastically.

"I know it," said Dawson. "I'm just saying, is all." He started to raise the bottle to his lips, but Long yanked it from his hand, corked it and placed it on the seat beside him.

"Keep your head clear, Maynard," Long said. "We've got plenty to do without you getting *wallowing drunk* on us."

"Wallowing drunk?" said Dawson. "When did I ever get—"

"Will those two horses pull this stage back to Nogales?" Sam asked Long, cutting Dawson short.

"They'll do it, but they won't be fit for nothing for a week afterward," Long said.

"We can go search for the others again if you want us to," said Dawson.

"The longer we sit around here wiggling our toes, the worse the flooding is going to get in every direction," Long reminded his shotgun rider.

"Don't leave on my account," Tunis Weir blurted out mindlessly in a half-conscious whiskey stupor.

"Shush now, Mr. Weir," Jenny Lynn whispered down to him, carefully stroking his lumpy, stitched-up forehead. "You go on to sleep—let them talk."

The Ranger and the two coachmen had turned

at the drummer's sudden outburst. Now they huddled together at the closed door, the rain lashing at the window cover and pounding sidelong on the wooden coach door. The thunder and lightning quieted down for the moment.

"We can search for the other horses as we go," Sam said, picking the conversation back up where they'd left it.

"What about that roan? That cayuse of yours?" Long asked the Ranger. "Will he back to a load?"

"I expect he'll do it, but he's not going to like it one bit," Sam said. "Neither will I." He looked back and forth between the two sopping-wet coachmen. "I'm going to need him rested and ready."

"You can stall him there at our relay station a day or two," Long offered.

"Huh-uh," Sam said. "Soon as we get to Nogales, I'm heading back out."

"Out in all this?" Long said as if in disbelief.

"Yep, that's my plan," Sam said. "This can stop any minute. I'm not that far behind. I don't want to quit his trail."

"Quit his trail? There's no trail," said Dawson. "It wasn't raining this hard when Moses built his ark."

Sam and Long just looked at him.

"Moses?" said Long.

Dawson's face reddened in the candlelight.

"I *know* who it was," he said. "Anyway, this whole stretch of desert is going to be mud soup for the next week, and that's if this gully washer plays itself out in the next few hours."

Without reply, Sam crouched and backed out of

the stage door. While the wind lulled, he held his bloodstained hands in front of him and washed them in the cold, falling rainwater.

Fifty thousand dollars was a lot of money for a stagecoach to be carrying, all in one run, he considered to himself. But his thoughts were taken from the matter as he noticed the empty strongbox and valuables crate lying in the mud. Strung out a few feet behind the coach were a women's carpet travel bag and a larger man's leather satchel lying half-sunken in a brown puddle of water.

He walked to the two cases, picked up the woman's thinly loaded carpetbag and clamped it up under his arm. Picking up the man's leather satchel, noting a clasp open on one end and the cover flap turned back, he couldn't help seeing the butt of a bone-handled Colt standing in a holster, the gun belt wrapped around it. He glanced through the rain toward the stagecoach, then reached into the satchel, lifted the Colt from its holster and turned it in his hand.

The big Colt glinted in the grayness of the storm. Sam noted the clean, well-oiled feel of the gun as he pulled back the hammer and turned the cylinder with the ball of his thumb. He found the gun's action smooth and firm like that of his own—a well-attended tool of the killing trade. He saw that the gun's front sight had been expertly removed from its barrel, making for a snag-free draw.

*A drummer, huh?*

He glanced again toward the coach as he slid the gun in and out of its custom low-cut holster, noting how easily the holster gave it up. All right, he reasoned, a drummer might carry such a gun. It wouldn't be the first time he'd seen a man carry more gun than he needed, especially a man who spent much of his life traveling the frontier on business.

He slid the gun into its sleek-fitting holster and shoved the whole rig farther down into the satchel. He carried both wet pieces of luggage back to the coach.

When he opened the coach door and climbed in, Sam pitched the luggage on the floor and looked at Weir and the young dove. Weir sat slumped where Jenny had helped him sit up a little on the seat and leaned him against the backrest. He managed to hold the wet cloth to his forehead.

"I found these in the mud," he said as the two looked at the dripping luggage, then at him.

"Oh! Thank you, Ranger Burrack," Jenny Lynn said. "I don't know what I would have done had I left my bag here. It has everything I own in it, modest though that may be."

"The thieves must have let them fall from on top when they untied the strongbox," Sam said. He gazed evenly at Weir as he spoke.

Weir returned his gaze, the wet cloth cupped against his battered face.

Finally he said in a strained, halting voice, "Too bad I didn't have this . . . with me. I have a . . . gun in there."

"Oh?" Sam said flatly.

"Yes, a fierce piece of equipment . . . I won it off a fellow a while back," Weir said through split and swollen lips.

"Won it, huh?" Sam said with a questioning look.

Jenny Lynn sat quietly, watching with interest.

"Poker . . . ," said the drummer. As he spoke, he lowered his hand from his head and made a gesture as if dealing cards.

Sam only nodded and stared at him.

"It might be a blessing you didn't have it on, Mr. Weir," Jenny Lynn cut into the looming silence. "It may well have gotten you killed."

The drummer breathed in deep and closed his eyes in reflection.

"Yes, that may well be," he said, raising the wet cloth back up to his head.

The three turned as the door opened and the shotgun rider stuck his face inside, rain running from the guttered brim of his hat.

"We've got both the coach horses hitched and ready, Ranger," he said. "But your roan is acting ugly about the whole deal."

"I'll take care of it." Sam stood crouched and stepped toward the open door. But as he started to step down, he picked up both the carpetbag and the man's satchel. He handed them to Dawson. "Here," he said, "tie these on top, give these folks a little more room in here."

As Sam spoke, he turned and looked at the drummer to check out his reaction.

"Much obliged, Ranger," the drummer said without hesitation, raising the wet cloth back to his face. "I feel safer you carrying a gun than I do myself, the shape I'm in."

As Sam shut the stagecoach door and he and Dawson walked forward, huddled against a new round of blowing rain, the shotgun rider shook the leather satchel.

"You mean this hardware drummer has himself a gun in here and wasn't even wearing it?" he said to the Ranger. He shook his head. "Why do you think he'd do something as stupid as that?"

"I don't know," Sam said, staring ahead to where the roan and Long stood in a driving sheet of rain. The roan reared and whinnied and pulled against the reins in Long's hands. "But I'm working on it."

Night seeped into the black sunless sky almost without notice. The three horses pulled the coach upward onto a higher trail, skirting around a low hillside fraught with deep-cut ravines, sunken boulders and sparse piñon. In front of the two big coach horses, Sam sat atop the roan and led the team and the heavy coach upward. The roan had balked against stepping into the traces, but had finally settled and turned surly and silent as it pulled forward.

Heavy rain fell dart-straight around the Ranger, horses and rig, while on the black horizon the wind had drawn its breath inward, beginning to circle and fashion itself into a funnel, ground to sky. The sky itself roiled atop the mad twisting wind like some mighty beast picked at with a stick, until at length the taunting would once again send it raging mindless across a hapless drowning land.

"You're doing good," Sam murmured down to the roan's dripping mane. His hand sloshed inside his glove as he patted its steaming withers. Looking behind him, beyond the team of likewise steaming coach horses, Sam saw the silhouettes of

Long and Dawson standing blacker than the silver rain-threaded night around them, each coachman driven to occupy his seat only out of one's respect for the other.

In a paler flash of lightning, the two coachmen saw the Ranger half-turned in his saddle looking back at them.

"There's the wide cut right ahead, see it?" Long called out as distant thunder rumbled.

"He sees it," Dawson grumbled beside Long. "He's been seeing it. We can't miss it 'less the trail's washed out."

"Don't even say that, joking," Long replied under the pouring deluge.

"I *ain't* joking," Dawson said in a lowered voice.

"I see it," Sam called out in reply, turning forward, his sombrero low and dripping water. As he spoke he saw the wide black void flash on and off again, turning purple-blue in the fleeting ribbon of light. Closer now he caught a glimpse of the gray grainy cliff sprawled jagged and shiny against the night high above them. From inside the black void, he heard the steady crushing roar he'd heard for the past half mile.

*A runoff,* he told himself; and no sooner had he recognized the sound than Long had called out this very thought from the driver's seat.

"A big one at that," Long had said. "I know this cut. A high ledge runs all along this side of it."

*Good enough. . . .*

They had sighted the wide cut in the trail forty minutes earlier in the streaks of light. From there, as they had neared the wide break in the hillside, the roar of hard-rushing water had guided them through blackness between intermittent streaks of lightning as surely as all sound guides the blind.

*Watch the edge*, Sam reminded himself, catching a glimpse of the rocky outer trail edge as lightning blinked on and off teasingly. The sound of the hard runoff grew closer, more intense as he rode the roan forward. Knowing now that the roaring sound guiding him would mislead him if it resounded above any washout lying closer across the flooding trail, he slowed the roan and felt the team horses and coach slow down behind him.

"By dang, he's gotten us there," Dawson said in relief, seeing the wide break ahead of them in the recurrent flash of light. Feeling a cold silence from the seat beside him, Dawson added quickly, "The two of yas, that is."

"Hmmph," said Long, water running freely from the guttered front brim of his drooping hat.

"Brake them while I check ahead," Sam called back to the coach seat.

"It's set," said Long, as soon as he'd pulled back hard on the brake handle and hitched the team's reins around it.

Stepping down from his saddle in a flash of lightning, Sam caught a glimpse of one of the missing coach horses standing in the trail, its eyes locked on him, its back and nostrils swirling steam upward in the downpour.

"Another horse up here," he called back, keeping his voice measured and above the rain to keep from spooking the animal.

He walked back to the roan, took down a coiled rope and moved forward in the darkness, catching another glimpse of the animal in the next flash of lightning. When he reached the horse, he heard its iron-rimmed hoof take a wary step away from him, closer to the raging water below the ledge behind it.

"Easy, boy, you don't want to go that way," he whispered soothingly, moving forward slow and steady, not stopping to ask the horse's permission.

By the time the horse took another step away, the Ranger had his wet gloved hand flat on its neck, a loop uncoiled and ready to slip over its head. The big horse was calm enough. But the animal wasn't taking up with him, and Sam knew this was no place to argue the matter. He lowered the loop away from the horse; the horse tossed his head away from his hand. Sam watched him shuffle off through the pouring rain. A few feet away, the big animal stopped and looked back from the mouth of the ledge Long had told him ran around the length of the deep, narrow hill canyon. The horse blew a nose full of steam, turned and walked out of sight.

"All right, you lead," Sam said, unheard in the pouring rain. He followed the horse onto the ledge and walked out twenty feet, judging the width of the ledge against that of the stagecoach, seeing the edge, seeing the rain flicker silver, falling out of sight into the black raging water below.

Turning from the edge, he saw not one but two dark steaming horses in the next flicker of light. Then he saw a third as he turned and walked closer.

"Well, now, look at you," he said, low, evenly as he let out three coils from the wet rope and stepped forward slowly. "I'm betting all three of you would like to get out of here . . . get back with your pards?" Lightning flashed. He stopped and stood in the pouring rain, rope in hand. The horses gathered and start walking to him.

"That's what I thought," he said quietly as the rain turned sidelong on a rising gust of wind.

# Chapter 4

───

By the time the Ranger led the three coach horses around the mouth of the ledge onto the trail, the wind had come back howling and strong. Gray lashing sheets of rain blew the tails of the Ranger's slicker sideways along with the horses' manes and tails as man and animals struggled toward the stagecoach, where the other two team horses and the roan stood in the howling darkness, their heads ducked low.

Hearing the sound of the horses' hooves clomping toward them beneath the howl of wind and the rip of rain across the coach roof, Dawson pulled the window canvas back an inch with his hand and squinted into the squalling storm.

"I'll be dipped in duck fat," he said, seeing the black forms of the Ranger and horses against the gray sheets of rain.

"What's wrong?" Jenny Lynn asked from the other seat, the sleeping drummer's head on her lap.

"Nothing at all's wrong, little lady," said Dawson with a beard-shrouded grin. "Ranger Burrack has gone and found our horses for us!"

"You must be crazy," said Long, leaping over to the window beside him. The two stared out through the turbulence for a second. Then they looked at each other. "No, you're right, Maynard!" he corrected quickly.

"Dang right I'm right," said Dawson, pulling his wet hat down tight and hugging his collar up around his cheeks.

"I've got to . . . get up from here," the sleeping drummer said through blue swollen lips. "Papers need signing. . . ."

"No, you don't, Mr. Weir," said the young dove. She pressed him back down as his arms flailed aimlessly. "You stay right there and go back to sleep." She leaned down close to his battered face and spoke sternly. "Do you understand me, mister?"

"I do . . . now," said the groggy man. "Wake me in St. Louis. . . ."

"He's babbling like an idiot," said Dawson, the two wet coachmen looking down at the purple swollen face in the woman's lap. They both shook their heads in sympathy.

"Come on, pard, we've got a job of work to do," Dawson said finally. He threw open the door and splashed down into the mud to help Sam with the horses. Long noticed the concerned look in the young woman's eyes.

"Don't you worry, ma'am," he said. "With our horses back, we'll lie low till first light and get on up out of here."

"But—but will we be all right, I mean, up here on the hillside?" the woman asked. "What if the trail washes out from under us?"

"We're better off up here, for now, ma'am," said Long, tugging his wet hat down tight around his head. "Lower lands are already flooded out down there. "No, we'll be all right here." He gave her a smile that looked strained as he backed out of the coach in a crouch, splashed down into the mud and forced the door shut behind him.

"The hell is . . . he talking about?" the battered drummer asked in a half-conscious voice. He swung his head back and forth on the young dove's lap.

"Shhh, easy, Mr. Weir, don't worry about that," Jenny Lynn said soothingly.

"Who—who am I . . . ?" he asked, his words trailing as they left his poorly performing lips.

"You are Mr. Tunis Weir," Jenny Lynn said evenly, distinctly, as if teaching a slow student. "Remember . . . ?" She pressed a hand on his chest. "It's important you remember as much as you can—your name, who you are, where you're from."

"I am Tunis Weir . . . ," the drummer recited groggily. "I am Tunis Weir, from . . ." He stopped, a blank expression on his face, his mental capacity failing him.

*Jesus. . . .*

Jenny Lynn bit her lower lip and held back a tear. Patiently she took a deep breath and started all over.

"Illinois, Mr. Weir," she said. "You are Tunis Weir from Chicago, Illinois. You sell hardware supplies across the Western frontier."

"And we . . . know each other, then?" he asked.

"No. I read a letter from inside your coat pocket," Jenny Lynn replied.

"Oh yes, I do . . . I remember now," the drummer said, his recall coming back at her prompting. He managed to pat a bruised hand on his lapel pocket. "I'm a *hardware drummer*." He tried to open his swollen eyes a little wider. "And you are a dove?" He tried to form a smile, but his swollen lips wouldn't allow it.

"Yes, I am a dove," Jenny Lynn said acceptingly.

"Then we could . . . ?" His words trailed again, but his hand tried to reach her bosom.

"Please don't, Mr. Weir," she said, pressing his hand down away from her. "This is no time to be fooling around. My only concern this night is to get you back on your feet. We're on a bad spot here." She scooted around beneath him and tugged upward on his shoulders. "Since you are coming around some, maybe it's best you sit up on your own for a while—clear your head a little?"

"I—I believe you're right, Jenny Lynn," he said, sitting up with her help and slumping against the back of the seat. "I certainly took a bad beating, didn't I?" He let out a long sigh.

"Yes, you did, Mr. Weir," the woman said. "I'm glad you're starting to remember that much, at least."

"Things will come back to me," the drummer said, closing his swollen eyes.

"I know they will sooner or later," the woman said, straightening her dress on her lap where he'd been resting his head.

Outside in the wind-whipped rain, the Ranger and the two coachmen began hitching the three horses back into their places. Sam unhitched the roan and led it aside so he could rehitch it in the front spot. From there he could sit atop it and lead the coach forward around the mouth of the ledge. Along the ledge he'd find a place close up against the rocky wall that would provide some shelter from the hard brunt of the storm.

In a lingering flash of lightning, Sam stared into the two coachmen's wet dripping faces as they hitched the fifth horse into position.

"Ready for your roan, Ranger," Long shouted through the wind and rain. Thunder crashed loud and hard up above them in the flooded ravine. The earth shook hard beneath their feet.

"Holy cats!" Long shouted with a start. "That one had some muscle and claws in it!"

Sam stood still, listening intently beyond the roar of wind, rain and rushing water. Even in the raging storm, the horses grew skittish at the feel of the earth trembling violently.

"Easy, now, easy," Dawson said, settling the animals. To Sam, he shouted, "How'd you manage to find these boys anyway?"

"I didn't find them," Sam shouted in reply. "They found me."

"Still, you must've done something right," Dawson said as the Ranger pulled the reluctant roan over into place.

"Just lucky," Sam said, listening in the direction of the last hard slam of thunder. The sound seemed to be holding on, still grumbling far up the ravine atop the raging runoff water.

"If it's luck, I hope you don't run out of it," Long shouted.

"Here's hoping," Sam replied, still listening, not

liking the sound of whatever was going on up in the ravine.

With the roan in place, the two coachmen started to turn and trot back to the coach. Sam had stepped up in the stirrups and started to swing his leg over the roan's wet saddle when he heard the rumble he'd been listening to grow louder, deeper. As he stopped and stood in the stirrups, another hard crash caused the earth to shake violently beneath them. But this time there was no thunder, only the hard slam of earth against earth, followed by the same terrible sound resounding far up the ravine.

"Hold it!" Sam shouted, stepping down from the frightened roan's side.

The two coachmen had heard and felt the same thing. They froze in place.

"What in God's name is that?" said Long, almost to himself.

No sooner had he spoken than the three heard a terrifying ripping and breaking of trees and rock barreling toward them down the ravine ledge. As they stared into the black darkness, twenty feet away they saw the black rocky edge of their trail rip away and fall crashing into the raging flooded ravine.

"Holy *God*!" shouted Dawson, he and Long staggering to keep from falling, seeing even in the rain and darkness the trail width lessen by a full five feet as if carved away by some large unseen saber. "The trail's washed out on us! The whole cut's collapsing!"

Seeing quickly that the trail had suddenly become

too narrow to turn the coach, Sam shouted, "Get the people out! We've got to make a run for it!" Even as he spoke, he stooped and jerked a long knife from his boot well. With no time to unhitch the spooked and rearing horses, he sliced wildly, freeing them from every tether he could find. As the team of horses reared and stepped in place in spite of their fear, the roan tried to turn and bolt away. But Sam held its reins tight.

Looking back toward the coach through the blowing rain, Sam saw the coach door fly open and the man and woman spill out into the mud just as the two coachmen made it to them.

"Hurry!" he shouted back at them as the two coachmen helped Weir and Jenny onto their feet. "Get a horse, get yourselves out of here, fast!"

Even as Sam spoke, another hard cracking sound ran along the crumbling edge of the trail. Two more feet of trail dropped thunderously out of sight. The roan whinnied and reared as the woman came running, the two coachmen right beside her supporting the drummer between them. Sam held the roan by its reins as he shoved the woman up onto one of the coach horses. Sam reached for the drummer as the coachmen approached.

"Get out of here yourself, Ranger!" shouted Dawson, he and Long shoving the man up over a coach horse's back. Dawson turned the big horse and slapped it soundly. Water splashed on its rump. As soon as the man took off right behind the woman, Dawson turned to the Ranger and shouted, "Long and I are gone, Ranger! Don't worry about us! Get out of here!"

Sam saw the two of them jump atop two coach horses and turn them quickly. As they rode away through the blowing rain, Sam slapped the fifth coach horse on its rump and sent it running along behind them. Farther up the ravine, another loud ripping of wood and crack of rock resounded. A hard surge of roiling black water splashed high in a powerful spray above the ravine cut.

"Let's go, horse," he said to the roan, jerking its head down sharply enough to get control and jump up into the wet saddle. The roan spun two full circles before Sam got it focused and straightened and racing away alongside the high slapping spray of water rising above the edge of the washed-out trail. Twenty yards along he heard the hard wrenching sound of earth tearing away from the hillside.

Looking back over his shoulder, even in the gray rain-whipped darkness, Sam saw a wide swath of trail fall away from beneath the stagecoach. As the coach fell out of sight, he saw the ledge trail crumbling, falling away, the jagged edge drawing closer behind him and the roan. In the black, angry darkness ahead of him, he heard the terrified whinny of one of the coach horses and the long, deep-toned scream of one of the men. Yet he saw a trace of neither as the roan raced along ahead of the crumbling trail that appeared determined to consume them.

As wind and rain seemed to stop and collect itself for another hard round, beneath the Ranger the roan suddenly made a terrified and enraged sound like none he'd ever heard. He felt the horse attempt to stop by backpedaling, sliding, lowering onto its rear shanks, its rear hooves still pumping and kicking against the broiling floodwater replacing the crumbling land behind it.

To their front, rear and right, the trail was gone except for the few yards breaking away beneath the roan's wildly flailing hooves. The Ranger saw the only way to go. In desperation he jerked the roan's reins hard, putting the animal onto the rising rocky hillside to their left. The animal whinnied in fear and rage, but followed the Ranger's demands.

Sam slapped his reins back and forth on the horse's withers; he pounded his boots to its side, goading it upward, the horse belly-crawling, digging, Sam feeling the rock ground at his boot toes. The horse bawled loudly but kept climbing, inch by inch, up the steep wet hillside, the floodwater raging, licking at them from behind.

As the horse turned quarterwise onto its side, Sam saw his chance to roll free of the saddle onto his feet and keep climbing forward beside the animal, pulling on its reins until the horse righted itself on its belly and half rose on its hooves.

"That's it, get up, climb! Climb!" the Ranger shouted, seeing the roan begin to make headway on the hillside. Yet no sooner had the horse started to gain its footing than the water and dirt at its hooves fell away. Sam felt one rein break in his hand, the other slide from his grasp. He saw terror in the roan's eyes as the horse reared high in a broad flash of lightning, spilled backward, pawing at the black sky, and whinnied loud and long as the raging water swept it away.

Sam looked on, shocked.

The roan was gone; there was nothing he could do about it. All he could do was try to save himself. The sound of the roan's tortured whinnying grew distant, soon overcome by the roar of water and the rumble of more thunder overhead. With the water still blasting against the crumbling hillside, Sam climbed, wallowed, dug and pulled himself upward through a downsurge of mud and rain. At times he rose half-crouched only to be knocked back down. Other times, he pulled himself upward on his belly until at last he found a jagged rock summit and threw himself over onto it.

He lay spread-eagle for a moment a torrent of muddy runoff water passing over him on its way over the edge of the hillside. Near exhaustion, he lay gasping for breath, his face cocked away from a hard-blowing rain.

*All right . . . all right, I'm going,* he reasoned with himself, his instincts and will insisting that he get up, keep moving, free himself of this perilous place. Yet, as he tried to push himself to his feet, the same crushing force of wind and water hammered him back down, reminding him there was still no letup.

He crawled on, upward across deeply stuck boulders, while the rushing water ate away at the ground holding them in place. When he reached one that was wide enough to cling to for a moment, he lay across it like some human sacrifice until he'd gained enough strength to continue crawling.

Nearing the top of the hill, he felt a hard pounding of water across the back of his shoulders as he pushed forward through a wide, short waterfall. Then suddenly, when the downfall of water had moved back across his hips, he stopped and felt a dry, warm breath of air from a deep black hole in the earth lying before him.

*An overhang,* he thought, feeling a sudden grate-fulness toward this merciless terrain.

"Thank *God*," he managed to say aloud, drag-ging forward until he freed himself from the cold slice of the waterfall. There he lay flat-faced on the dry musky-smelling ground. *This will do, this is good. . . .*

Yet, even as relief and hope kindled a glow inside him, his thoughts were interrupted by a low, menacing growl from the blackness lying in front of him.

*Oh no! A panther. . . .*

Now it came to him, the muskiness he smelled. It wasn't just the smell of earth. It was the scent of cat. He had crawled inside a panther's lair. He should have recognized it sooner. *But you didn't,* he told himself.

As the growl continued strong and steadily, only a few feet from his face, he reached a wet hand slowly down his side and to his disheartened surprise felt his empty holster. All right, the Colt was gone. Still, he wasn't leaving here. *Not on a night like this,* he through wryly . . . *not without a fight.*

Before trying to reach farther down to the knife in the well of his boot, he realized in that second that not only his knife but his boot itself was miss-ing; and he stopped cold.

*I'm not leaving,* he said silently to the growling cat. Knowing the cat could see him, but he could not see that cat, he slowly searched with his hand along the ground up and down his side until he grabbed a rock the size of a large apple. He gripped the rock tight as the cat's growl grew, then fell. It sounded as if the animal had moved closer to him. He heard deep rattling in the animal's breath as he imagined it looming over his body. Yet he managed to lie as still as death, the rock in his hand offering little hope should the cat decide to kill him.

In the night behind him, lightning twisted long and sharp in the sky, giving only a thin shadowy outline of the big cat. Thunder followed, erupting like cannon fire as if besieging earth and all lying above and below it. The Ranger caught a glimpse of the shadowy outline as it shrank back farther into the heavy blackness.

*All right, then,* he thought, again speaking silently to the cat, trying to calm himself. *We can get along here, you and me. We can get along.*

He kept a firm grip on the rock and lowered his face to the dry, musky ground. In front of him, the big cat continued to growl, but the sound fell from a threat to more of a continuing warning. To his relief, he heard a slow brush of padded paws as the animal crept farther back into the overhanging blackness. He imagined that somehow the cat had reconciled itself to him being there, and why. Neither was the hunter here, and neither was the hunted. Outside, man and cat shared a common enemy. Until that enemy passed, they had to allow for each other no matter how combative and begrudging their attitude.

He wasn't welcome here, he understood that. Yet here was where fate had landed him. He lay silent and still in the blackness, clenching the rock in his fist, while the sound, the presence, the fear and at length the essence of the big cat fell away into a deep empty darkness.

Outside, the storm raged.

# Chapter 5

In the midst of that electric night, a dreaded sleep forced itself upon him. It was a thin, icy sleep from which he awakened sharply with the slightest sound or supposed imaginings his exhausted mind could conjure. More than once he could feel the panther looming over him, staring down quizzically like a house cat at a wounded rat. He felt its breath on his neck, but each time his eyes sprang open and his hand gripped a rock, he realized the cat was not there. All that loomed above the mouth of the cave was the damp, heavy night, its dark presence divided only by intervening streaks of silent lightning.

At some point near a flat gunmetal dawn, the Ranger instantly tensed as he felt the cat's paws touch down on his back, first at his shoulders, then at his hips as the animal raced across the length of him. This time it was real, he realized. He hadn't managed to raise the rock an inch when he heard the cat dart through the diminishing veil of muddy water behind him and run off into the flooded terrain.

He let out a breath and rested his forehead on the dirt for a moment, realizing that none of this was a dream, not the cat, not the storm and not the roan washing away from him on the crumbling hillside.

*What a night.*

He caught a glimpse of the big stagecoach sinking out of sight on a rolling sweep of floodwater. Then he thought about the people—the driver, the shotgun rider and the two passengers—and he pushed himself up onto his elbows. Feeling the rough overhang on his sore shoulders, he backed out through the cold muddy waterfall and down three feet onto the rocky water-cut hillside.

He waded—one boot, one sock-covered foot—across a knee-deep flume of runoff filled with twigs, a cache of dead scorpions, floating berries and chunks of cactus. Across a rock, a bull rattlesnake was in its death throes, flattened and bloody across its middle. Its head was swinging and thrashing aimlessly. Seven feet across the natural rock-lined flume, he stepped up on a foot-high rock edge and looked down on the sporadically flooded land below. In the cold windless rain he felt strangely that the night was still upon him. In the gray-black distance, lightning flicked on and off as it had throughout the night.

Through the silvery downpour he looked back and forth across the width of the rolling flatlands, where hills had turned to islands overnight and where lower hills lay submerged to their peaks, strewn randomly about like wet wrinkled backs of surfaced whales. At the bottom end of the ravine, the heavier run of water had gone on, leaving behind it a wider half-circling gravel pan that had drained downward, flattening acres of wild grass in a swirl and spilling over a ledge of rock worn bare from thousands of years of such deluges.

On the other side of that drowned grass plain, he spotted the dark lump of one of the stage horses lying wet and still in only inches of muddy water. For a moment he continued to only stand staring through a curtain of streaking water, taken by the enormity of the flooded land. When the day's first thrust of wind peppered rain against his side, he took a deep breath, let it out with resolve and pushed himself forward toward the dead horse.

"Start there, and hope it gets better," he told himself solemnly, holding his wet hand on his brow as a visor against the rain. He made another long sweep with his eyes, before stooping and climbing down over a slick wet boulder and down the wet slippery hillside.

He stopped at the bottom of the hill and saw one of the stagecoach's doors lying busted, wedged in a bed of rock. A thin stream of runoff water still rippled across the shattered door; the remnants of a canvas window cover floated in place like the sails of some ill-fated ocean vessel.

He stood for a moment over the coach door, looking farther down a shallow-running current. A tangle of coach reins, traces and tacking was bobbing in the water, trapped in a small pool against a large sunken boulder that had managed to not give itself up to last night's angry torrent. Farther down he saw a wet hat lying in mud where the receding current had left it.

Not his hat, but a hat. . . .

He stepped into the shallow current and made his way toward the hat like a man who sought a great treasure and did not want to appear too anxious to claim it. When he reached the mud where the hat lay, his feet sank to his ankles with each step. But he continued to that spot, picked up the soaked hat, shook it and slapped it against his thigh, then pulled it down onto his forehead against the pouring rain.

"Obliged," he murmured to anyone or anything who might be listening.

He examined himself, taking stock of what the storm had snatched from him. He was short one boot, with it his boot knife, in addition to his Colt, his rain slicker and his sombrero—now replaced *temporarily*, he told himself, adjusting the soaked hat. Already he felt better, the cold rain no longer beating down on his bare head.

As he stood assessing himself and his predicament, he heard the sound of a horse whinny in the distance where the shallow runoff ran out of sight over another rocky ledge.

"All right, talk to me," he said aloud to the unseen animal.

He walked back into the cold water where countless other storms had worn the bottom to solid rock—rough, he reasoned, but better and stronger footing than the mud his feet had sunk in—and he followed the direction of the horse's single whinny for nearly an hour with no other encouragement until he stopped and sat down midstream on a rock. He slumped there in the falling rain, tired, wet and dejected. Then he perked up and rose to his feet when he heard the horse again, this time much closer, he thought. Drenched, cold, his lips blue and tight from the chilling rain, he pushed himself forward with only the thinnest thread of hope and walked on.

A half mile farther along the path of the receding floodwater, he stopped and stared down at a fresh set of hoofprints sunk deep and clear in the soft gravelly mud. His eyes followed the hoofprints backward to the muddy water, then forward out of sight around a stand of rock. As he tracked the animal's path, he heard another long, loud whinny resound from the rocks.

"I hear you," he said quietly, quickening his pace. "I'm coming."

Following the sound of the horse and its hoofprints for the better part of an hour, he left the flooded desert floor and climbed halfway up a rocky pyramided hillside. From there he looked back down on a thin, muddy ocean drifting serpentine through cactus, rock and standing scrub. He saw more pieces of the shattered stagecoach lying in the mud below him.

Farther downstream he saw the woman's carpetbag and the man's satchel lying on their sides, both of them open wide, articles of clothing trailing in the mud and draped over rock and spiked to the broken trunks and tendonlike roots of unearthed cottonwood and piñon.

As he looked down at the articles, a slight movement and the sound of a hoof clop drew his eyes to his right where, as if from out nowhere, the roan had stepped into sight and stood staring at him blankly.

"My goodness," the Ranger whispered in awe. "What are you doing alive?"

The roan blew out a breath and scraped a hoof

on a rock. Sam saw the saddle hanging beneath the horse's belly, the leather stirrup skirts mud-covered and upside down, flared slightly like some strange new wind guides. The roan's bit was out of its mouth, its wet bridle twisted sideways down its jaw, a piece of the broken rein still hanging there, dripping rain. Blood oozed from a cut under the horse's chin.

Sam took a step toward the roan, but the horse backed away, as if having vowed to choose its company more wisely after last night's foray.

"Easy, now," Sam said, not stopping his slow advance until he took the horse by its hanging bridle and rubbed a hand down its wet muzzle. "I know it was a hard night. I was there, remember?" As he spoke he straightened the bridle and checked inside the horse's lips and teeth before slipping the bit back into its mouth.

"I don't even know how you managed to do this," he said, looking at the bit as the roan adjusted it with a twist of its jaws and a curl of its lower lip.

The horse stood still for him while Sam reached atop its back, loosened the saddle cinch and dropped the muddy, wet saddle to the ground.

"Well, look at this," he said, bemused, seeing first his saddlebags hanging, still tied in place and covered with mud, then the broken stub of his Winchester butt sticking out of the saddle boot. "I suspect we're both due a turn of luck this morning."

He reached down under the horse and dragged the saddle out, righting it on the ground. He tugged on the broken rifle and found it jammed deep into the saddle boot. Picturing the floodwater as it rolled the roan over a hard roll across rocks, he saw how the rifle got jammed down hard enough to break the butt stock.

Untying the wet, tight rawhide straps on his saddlebags, he rummaged inside until he found a small pocketknife. He opened the knife and cut at the saddle boot until he had enough room to get his hand down inside and grip the metal chamber of the stockless Winchester. With the carefulness of a preacher handling gold, he twisted and pulled on the rifle until it slipped free of the wet leather and came out in his cold blue hand.

"Now let's see if it works," he murmured up to the roan with some measure of satisfaction. The horse stood with its head cocked, looking down at him curiously as Sam levered a round out of the chamber and caught it. He let out a sigh, then stepped back from the roan and pointed the rifle into the air and pulled the trigger. The rifle bucked; an orange-blue fire streaked from the wet barrel. "All right, we're armed," Sam said, standing, looking the rifle over in his hands. Smoke curled from the wet barrel. "Let's see what that shot brings in."

The shot caused the roan to jerk back a step as the rain turned on the rising wind and blew in hard against them. Sam took the short stub of the rein and held the roan in place.

"We're getting down out of these rocks," he said. "There's a big cat up here prowling around for breakfast."

The roan turned its head against the cold rain and chuffed and stood pawing at the rocky ground.

"I don't like it either," Sam said. "Get some rest.

I'll be needing a ride out of you before the day's over." The weather was getting worse, but he knew he couldn't let it dictate terms to him. Orez was out there using the weather to whatever advantage he could. Sam knew he could do no less himself, not if he wanted to put an end to the man once and for all.

The roan grumbled and jerked on the broken rein, as if it understood the Ranger's proposition and would have none of it.

Sam checked the horse over for any injuries, then stooped, picked up the muddy saddle, saddlebags and all, and hefted the load onto his shoulder. Standing, he took the short broken rein and turned in the rain. He weaved and sloshed his way down through the wet rocks, the roan at his heels. In the gray-black distance thunder rumbled out behind a sharp streak of lightning.

When the Ranger and the roan descended the rock hill and crossed a muddy plane of swirled flattened wild grass, Sam stood the reluctant horse at the edge of a sloping gravel pan. The horse started to venture a step forward, then stopped short, drew back and stood, head lowered in the blowing rain, watching the Ranger walk the last forty feet out through the soft mud to the water's edge.

Broken Winchester in hand, Sam stood above the man's wet leather shoulder satchel and flipped it over in the mud with his rifle barrel. He had hoped beyond logic that the wrapped gun and gun belt were still there, but no such luck. He looked all around until he knew for certain the gun was not lying nearby, then followed the muddy edge to where a long black swallow-tailed dress coat lay spread on the ground, partly covered with settled gravel, silt and mud. But he didn't care.

He picked the drenched coat up, shook it out, wrung it between his hands, shook it again and put it on. He buttoned it, feeling it cold across his wet chest. *It'll have to do*, he told himself, knowing his body heat would serve to warm it a little.

He turned and walked a few yards along the muddy edge, noting that the roan also turned at the edge of flattened grass and walked along with him. When he stopped, the horse stopped; it stood once again pawing the wet ground with its head lowered against the rain.

Sam looked all around among the strewn articles of clothing and spotted a man's pair of leather braided gallows linked at the middle and a short dress boot lying sole up in the mud. He picked up the gallows on his rifle barrel and stuck them down in his coat pocket. He turned the boot over with his rifle barrel, picked it up and slung mud and water from it. Shoving it under his arm, he turned and walked back to the roan. There he put the wet boot on and cut the link holding the gallows together. He tied the two gallows end to end, then tied one end to the roan's broken rein. Rain blew harder, whipping the swallow-tailed coat around his thighs.

"Let's get out of this mud," he said. "Go shoot this rifle one more time."

But almost before he got the words out of his mouth, a shotgun blast resounded from farther down the stream of runoff water. The roan pricked its ears; the Ranger froze for a second, staring in the direction of the shot.

*Maynard Dawson, the shotgun rider?* Sam thought.

"Come on," he said to the roan, grabbing the saddle and throwing it up onto his shoulder. He led the horse away from the mud and onto the gravelly apron below a short stretch of low hills. Not wanting to spare another bullet, especially now that he knew someone had heard his shot, he walked to the high end of the gravel apron, where he could see beyond a low rise to another lower land break.

"And there you are . . . ," he said, seeing Maynard Dawson struggling forward, his short-barreled shotgun hanging from his hand, Dan Long draped over his shoulder. Footprints led snaking back out of sight along the path of last night's flood runoff.

Sam whistled loud and long through the blowing rain, but was unable to make himself heard from so far away.

"All right," he said, as if giving in. "One more bullet."

Before firing his rifle in the air, he looked all around and walked to a place where he knew he was free from shadows, provided Dawson could see him at all through the harsh weather.

Waiting until the wind and rain lulled for a moment, Sam raised the rifle, fired it and began waving it back and forth slowly over his head. He saw Dawson stop at the sound of the shot and look all around in the right direction.

"Now see me up here," Sam said, still waving the broken rifle. Beside him the roan watched curiously.

The Ranger had all but given up when suddenly he saw the shotgun rider lift his shotgun above his head and wave it back and forth slowly in reply.

Sam stopped waving the rifle and pumped his arm up and down in the rain. Before losing sight of the man in the rain, Sam saw him lower Long from his shoulder, look up and pump his shotgun up and down, mimicking Sam's movements.

"Good for you, Dawson," he said as if the shotgun rider could hear him. Wind and rain lashed harder than it had all morning, washing the shotgun rider from sight, but Sam had seen enough to know they had spotted each other. That was good enough for now, he thought.

"Stay where you're at, Dawson," he said aloud to himself, causing the roan to prick its ears again and stare at him quizzically. "We'll come down to you as quick as we can."

Thunder rumbled again, this time louder, moving closer. The roan tensed and chuffed and tried to toss its head. But Sam held the makeshift rein firmly. Once again rain slammed in sidelong, sharply, like a handful of darts. Overhead the sky blackened.

# Chapter 6

By the time the Ranger reached the shotgun rider on the lower terrace, the brunt of the present storm had passed on. The wind had fallen off; the rain had dissipated to a fine, cold mist. Yet, on the low, dark horizon, another front had already begun forming up, gathering itself like some vengeful army ready to mount another assault. A low rumble of thunder resounded along the curve of the earth. The roan chuffed and grumbled as if cursing the thunder and rode on at a labored gait with kicked-up mud clinging to its belly and legs.

Atop the roan Sam studied the dark sky and guided the horse around a muddy basin that had receded overnight only to begin rising again throughout the morning. As he rode closer to the shotgun rider and the body of Dan Long lying on the wet ground, the old coachman stood up where he'd seated himself on a rock and stared grimly toward him.

"I never expected to see you or your horse again, Ranger," the shotgun rider said as Sam brought the roan to a halt and stepped down from the saddle.

"Nor I you," Sam replied, leading the roan closer.

"When I heard your shot, I had to think long and hard before I fired my last load," Dawson said.

"I'm glad you did fire it," Sam said. He looked down at the muddy shotgun leaning against the rock, then at Long's body on the ground at Dawson's bare, bloody feet. "I see your driver didn't make it," he added respectfully.

The shotgun rider's eyes grew watery as he shook his head and spoke.

"I found him adrift and pulled him out of the floodwater," he said. "It wasn't the water that killed him, though." He gestured a nod down at Long, showing Sam the deep wound in the coach driver's abdomen. "He had a piece of iron railing from the top edge of the coach stuck through him." He paused and added, "I pulled it out so's I could carry him better—couldn't stand looking at it sticking in him anyway." He took a deep breath.

Sam looked at the long trail of bare footprints weaving across the wet desert long behind the shotgun rider. He looked down at Dan Long's wet boots. Then he looked at Dawson's bloody, mud-smeared feet.

"Oh, I know what you're thinking, Ranger," Dawson said. "Why didn't I leave him there and come back for him later? I couldn't do it, leave ol' Dan'l that way. This desert is full of lobos and coyotes. Dan'l would never have let me hear the end of it if I let them eat him."

"I understand," Sam said quietly, knowing the old man was deep in his grief. "I was just wondering. . . . Think your pard would mind if you wore his boots? You can see he's got no more need for them, can't you?"

"Oh yeah, I can see that," Dawson replied. "I know he's dead and all. But Dan'l was a strange one when it come to his stuff. I can see him not liking the idea of me wearing his boots." He looked down and wiggled his thick bloody toes. A cactus needle stood stuck atop his mud-streaked foot. "The thing is, I couldn't bring myself to take them off him." He looked off northeast. "Anyways, Nogales will be sending somebody out for us any time. They always do when a storm like this hits and they have a coach out in it. Especially when they know there's passengers."

Sam nodded and looked off in the direction of Nogales for a moment.

"What about those passengers?" he asked. "Did you see what become of them?"

The old coachman shook his head.

"Not a sign," he said. "But it was so dark, they could have drowned right beside me. I'd never seen it unless lightning flashed on them." He shook his scraggly head again, reliving the night's experience. "I'll tell you what. That's the closest to hell I'll ever be until the real hell comes along."

"They have to be down along there somewhere," Sam said regarding the two passengers.

"I'd say so too," said Dawson. "But I never seen them. I found dead coyotes, dead lizards, dead coach horses—even found a foreleg of one where the poor thing must've got it wrenched off between some rocks. But no passengers, not yet anyway."

"How long do you suppose before somebody will come looking for you?" Sam asked.

"They could already be on their way," said Dawson, picking at the seat of his wet trousers as he looked off toward Nogales. "That is if the weather ain't as bad in that direction."

"We're a far ways off the trail," Sam said, considering things. "It could take them some time finding us."

"A situation like this, they'll look for smoke or fire all up along the rocks," Dawson said. "Trouble is, where are we going to find any dry wood, except under some overhang higher up?" He looked up the steep rocky hillsides. "You like to climb as much as I do?" he added wryly.

"Come on," Sam said, noting the gray-black sky moving closer overhead. "Let's get your pard across the horse's back and get on up there. It looks like this blow's not finished with us yet."

"Blasted damn desert," said Dawson, standing in the rain. "One minute a man's ready to sell his soul for enough water to wet his tongue. Next minute he's fighting for his life to keep from being washed off the earth." As he spoke, lightning twisted white-gold in the black sky; thunder rumbled in closer and exploded overhead.

"I've got his feet," Sam said, stepping over to Long's body on the ground and stooping down to pick him up.

Dawson scooped Long up carefully beneath his wet limp shoulders, and the two lifted the body and laid it over the roan's wet saddle, Sam taking pains to be extra careful owing to the shotgun rider's feelings toward his fallen comrade.

As the two prepared to leave, Dawson stood beside the horse and patted Long's wet back.

"I believe you would like Dan'l had you two got to know each other, Ranger," he said quietly.

"I'm sure of it," Sam replied. Before the shotgun rider could say any more on the matter, Sam pointed off toward a long shelf of rock halfway up a rocky hillside.

Dawson only stared at him curiously.

"Once we get up there and get a fire going, we'll both feel a lot better," Sam said. "You can tell me all about him."

The old coachman chuckled gruffly and drew his shoulders up against the rain, the wind starting to rebuild.

"I know I talk too much, Ranger. Dan'l tells me that—I mean he *told me* that all the time," he said, correcting himself. "Sometimes I get to talking and just get carried away in it. Dan'l always said I'd make a good politician, preacher or such—"

"I understand," Sam said, gently cutting him short. He took the roan by its single rein and turned it toward the hillsides, his shortened rifle in hand. "We can talk while we're walking. We don't want to get caught in this blow that's coming."

"I'm with you on that," Dawson said, following alongside him, limping a little on his bloody feet. "I've had enough rain and wind to last me a lifetime."

They walked on as the rain and wind grew more intense, the storm moving up onto the far edge of the earth, ready for another hard round.

It was midafternoon when the two sloshed upward among the rocks through a hard, wind-driven rain no less violent than the one they'd survived the night before. Thunder and lightning moved up close on their trail as they reached the ledge running along the hill line and stepped into shelter beneath it. Beside the Ranger, the roan hugged close to the inner rock wall of the overhang and slung his wet head. Long's body lay draped across the saddle. Water ran down and dripped from his purple fingertips.

"It looks like it falls back deeper up there," Sam said, gesturing ahead of them along the stony overhang. Water drained from his drooping hat as he spoke. He took the hat off and slapped it against his leg and put it back on. Beside him, he couldn't help noticing how Dawson eyed the hat with close attention.

"Is this your hat, Dawson?" Sam asked. "If it is, you're welcome to it. I found it alongside the flood-water."

"It belonged to the drummer," Dawson said. "He was wearing it when Orez started working him over with his pistol barrel—poor sumbitch." He winched just picturing the incident. "I never saw it after that."

Sam took the hat off and looked it over. It didn't look like the sort of hat he usually saw traveling drummers wearing. It looked more the sort of Western wide-brimmed hat a man wore in open country to keep the sun from frying him. He turned it in his hand and put it back on and fun-neled the front of the wet brim as best he could. Lightning caused the roan to flinch and nicker warily under its breath. Sam held its rein firmly and rubbed its muzzle to calm it as thunder crashed, shaking the whole hillside.

"Let's keep moving, keep this horse settled," he said to Dawson, stepping forward, leading the ner-vous roan.

Dawson picked up twigs and small weathered tree branches from along the dry inner wall as they moved on, the overhang widening for them as they went.

"I know Orez pistol-whipped Weir to make you and Long take him back to town," Sam said. "But why him, you suppose? Why not you or Long?"

"Good question," Dawson said. He was stooped down on the ground, picking up more scraps of pine needles, small branches and twigs blown in over time off the desert floor. "Must have been the drummer gave him some sass, I reckon. Dan'l and I watched him walk over to Orez bold as brass and start talking to him. Don't know what he said, but Orez commenced using his head like a piñata." Dawson shook his head recounting the matter. "Orez's own men tried to stop him, but he wouldn't hear of it—kept beating Weir until he was on the ground, still as death. I thought sure he'd killed him."

Sam only shook his head, recalling the drummer's face, how badly beaten it was. "Orez could have beaten the poor man half that bad and still served his purpose," he added, thinking out loud.

"I don't know how lucky Weir was after all, Ranger," Dawson said, a nice pile of twigs and needles forming in the crook his arm. "I'd as soon died from the beating than get my head sewed together just in time to get washed away in a flood. Would have saved him a lot of pain, and the rest of us some good whiskey."

"Yeah, I suppose it would at that," Sam said, looking back down at the rushing floodwater rising again on the desert floor.

They walked on in silence, the overhang deepening into the hillside, until they came to a spot where the roan stopped all of a sudden as if to say he would go no farther.

"What's happened to him?" Dawson asked, giving the roan a peculiar look.

"Wolves," Sam said. He pointed at the ground with the tip of his rifle barrel. The faded paw prints of many wolves ran back and forth on the dusty stone shelf beneath them. Atop the faded prints, new fresh prints stood out. The fresh prints appeared to stop abruptly, circle short and turn back the way they came.

"I hate wolves," Dawson whispered, his voice lowering with caution. "I expect the storm's got them stirring about in the daylight." He glanced around at the gray-black overcast pall, the shadowy blackness beneath the overhang. "If you can call this *daylight*, that is."

Sam looked out and around through the heavy silver-threaded rain, the gray endless sheets of it spraying, swirling and spinning away in the wind. In the direction of the trail leading back to Nogales, he saw nothing. But he knew the trail was there, and he knew that between these passing storms a fire and its smoke could be seen should anyone be searching for the stagecoach.

"We're as good here as anywhere," he said to Dawson.

Dawson warily eyed the ledge farther along in front of them, and fresh tracks of the wolves leading away.

"I couldn't agree more," he said. He stepped farther back under the overhang and dropped the gathered pile of fire kindling in the dust. "I always say, if you can't trust your horse . . ." He grinned stiffly and let his words trail.

Moments later the two sat side by side near a small fire made with a flint striker and some gunpowder from one of the Ranger's rifle bullets. Beside the Ranger lay a creased and unfolded sheet of thick beeswax-coated paper that surrounded an open cartridge box. Beside the box sat a small battered four-shot pocket gun. As Dawson rubbed his sore, raw feet in the heat of the fire, Sam took the bullets from his rifle, checked them and put them aside. He replaced them with rifle bullets he kept stored in waxed paper for just such an emergency. The Winchester had performed well when he'd signal-fired it earlier, but with wolves prowling, he didn't want to risk a misfire.

Dawson watched a small, battered coffeepot sitting in the low flames. In the pot a modest palmful of crushed coffee beans from the Ranger's saddlebags began to boil in rainwater they'd caught running down from the ledge lying above them. The shotgun rider fanned the aroma of the coffee into his face and breathed deep.

"I wish this coffee was just waiting to wash down an elk steak smothered in onions," he said.

"Let's not talk about food," Sam replied. He levered the rounds through the short rifle to make sure it worked properly, then reloaded. Picking up the pocket gun, he stood up in the heat of the small fire.

"Sorry," said Dawson. "I'm used to Dan'l shutting me up all the time."

Long's body was leaning against the far wall in

the tall afternoon shadows. A few feet away the roan stood with its head bowed, resting nearly asleep, a rear hoof tipped. Beyond the edge of the cliff overhang, the thunder and lightning had passed on, leaving a heavy rain falling in its wake.

"It'll be dark soon," Sam said. "I'm going to take a look ahead, see if I can find any more scrap wood," he said. "Are you going to be all right here?"

"Right as a man can be, under these circumstances," Dawson said, looking at his dirty, bloodstained feet as he rubbed them.

"Here," said Sam, "I found this in my saddlebags." He held the pocket gun down to the shotgun rider, butt first.

Dawson looked delighted. He snatched the gun quickly.

"Much obliged, Ranger," he said, looking the gun over. He looked up. Sam saw the question in his eyes.

"I wanted to check it over first," Sam replied. "I'm still not sure of it. It was awfully wet. The heat has dried it some. It's only four shots."

"Four shots, huh?" said Dawson, opening the gun's chamber and reclosing it.

"It beats nothing," Sam said quietly. "If it's not too damp to fire."

"Yes, it beats nothing," Dawson said, gripping the gun by its barrel. "If it won't fire, I can always wallop a wolf in the head before it gets the better of me."

"I won't be gone long," Sam said. "If you need me back here, yell out."

"Don't you worry, Ranger, if a wolf sticks his nose

around this ledge, you'll hear me sure enough—*hell*, they'll hear me all the way to Nogales."

As Sam turned to walk away along the ledge, the roan, standing unhitched, stepped forward to tag along with him. But the Ranger stopped and took the rein dangling loose from the horse's muzzle and led him back. Still, he did not hitch the animal. Instead he patted the roan's withers and left it standing in place. From the fire, Dawson watched curiously.

This time when Sam walked away, the horse leaned forward a step but stayed where the Ranger had put it.

"You picked a peculiar time and place to be training a horse, Ranger," Dawson called out, the battered pocket pistol lying in his lap.

"I didn't pick the *time* or the *place*, Dawson," Sam called back over his shoulder. "This horse has proved he wants to stay alive. The least I can do is teach him how."

Dawson shook his head and looked back into the fire, rubbing his aching feet.

Sam looked back at the roan as he walked away along the ledge, seeing the animal staring back at him.

# Chapter 7

---

Before the Ranger had gone fifteen feet along the ledge, when he stopped and picked up a short length of dry weathered pine lying at the bottom edge of the inner stone wall, he saw scrapes of bones from small game strewn around. Clamping the wood up under his arm, he walked on, the short rifle in hand, another twenty feet, where he found another short scrap of pine, this one with rough bark still clinging to it.

*More bones*, he told himself, looking all around. Countless paw tracks, some old and some recent, leading back and forth along the ledge path. The flooding had the night predators up and on the move. This looked like a trail they frequented heavily in foul weather. Wolf packs ate their larger kill wherever they took it down. But any wolf, especially a lone male, seldom passed up a chance to bed down and eat in a nice dry place.

Judging from the amount of tracks, Sam knew that a good size pack of Mexican *lobos* must be living here. Like the men he hunted, the wolves of the Sonoran Desert recognized no border. They followed their needs and their instincts. Anywhere there was a large pack, there would be lone males tagging along nearby hoping to gain acceptance. This low rocky line of desert hills belonged to *El Sonora lobos*, no doubt about it, he told himself.

For the next twenty minutes he busied himself gathering dry wood scraps until upon rounding a turn he stopped where the overhang ended in a falling rain and a steep, narrow path swung upward onto the slick, wet hillside. A flash of blue-white lightning blossomed and disappeared. Thunder exploded.

*This is as far as you're going,* he cautioned himself, seeing at his feet a thick round piece of deadfall. Even though it rested out from under the overhang in the falling rain, he knew he could bank it against the fire and dry it out enough to burn, maybe to last throughout the night. Thinking about the coming night, he looked around at the rain and at the darkening, misty land below. Yes, this was as far as he could risk going. Negotiating this path back through the moonless dark would be treacherous, wolves or no wolves, he warned himself.

Stooping down, he grabbed the wet log and placed it atop the other wood he now held cradled in his left arm. But when he rose halfway to his feet, he froze, seeing the bared fangs of a large wolf standing up on the slick narrow path, staring down at him with a low growl. Lightning lit the big animal's snarling face.

He kept calm, reached his thumb over the rifle hammer and cocked it slowly, the big leader watching him intently. As he cocked the rifle he saw a second wolf, then the dark outlines of a third and fourth, standing farther up the trail in the shadowy darkness. Recognizing more silver-black images up the trail and alongside it, he took a step backward, slowly, not about to drop the armload of wood, not about to do anything sudden that could cause a commotion or trigger an attack.

One firm pull of the trigger and he knew he had the lead wolf dead in its tracks. The others would scatter, but for how long? And how many others were there? No matter, he thought. This was no place to take on a pack of wolves. A high narrow ledge like this, even with his Winchester levering shot after shot, the pack would soon overpower him. He would go to the ground beneath a flurry of claws and fangs, or off the edge down a steep cliff hillside of jagged rock. Either way he would be dead.

*Easy, boy. . . .*

He noted the lead wolf's growl grew quieter as he took his steps backward. The animal made no move forward, nor did he lower into a crouch in preparation for an attack. The fact that the lead wolf hadn't immediately sprung upon him and brought the others with it gave him reason to think they weren't ready to take him as prey—not right then anyway, he told himself, his rifle ready to explode at the slightest sign from the big pack leader.

They had found the scent of man and horse on their trail and had ventured forward to take a look. Man they could do without, but warm horseflesh under a dry overhang on a wet night like this would be too much for the carnivores to pass up. Still, this was a curiosity call, he decided, backing away one cautious step after another without the lead wolf stalking forward.

Had he turned and run or made any sudden move at all, the wolf's natural instincts would have been to pursue him, to take him down. But he wasn't about to show fear if he could keep from it. After all, he'd spent the previous night holed up with a panther, he reminded himself.

*So far, so good.*

He moved backward slow and steadily and made his way around the turn in the narrow ledge without the pack leader following. Once he'd put the turn between him and the leader, he breathed a little easier. He knew predators were visual, no species more so than wolves. The fact that the wolf had let him out of its sight was a good sign. Now to keep the big leader back.

Before he had gone ten feet, he saw the tip of the wolf's nose appear around the turn in the ledge path. With a loose, quick aim, he squeezed the trigger and watched a spray of rock fragments jump in every direction as the explosion resounded. The wolf's muzzle vanished; a yipping cry went up as the animal spun in pain and fear and raced away.

All right, he'd had a good turn of luck. Now it was time to clear out, he thought. He retreated as the wolf's cry grew farther away, out from under the cliff overhang and up the hillside. Unable to lever a fresh round into the rifle chamber without dropping his load of firewood, Sam hurried back toward the campsite. The firewood was too important to leave behind. When the wolves came back, as he knew they would, fire would be the only thing to hold them at bay throughout the night.

Now it was time for him to take the upper hand and keep hold of it however he could, he told himself. Clutching the armload of precious firewood to his chest, he hurried back to where Dawson and the horse waited for him. But before he'd gone a hundred feet, Dawson met him on the darkening ledge, limping along toward him on his blood-smeared feet. Rain sprinkled in under the overhang as lightning flashed and stood as if suspended for a moment.

"I—I heard your shot, Ranger," Dawson said, gasping for breath, the battered pocket pistol clasped tight in his thick hand. "I came running." He stared warily past Sam into the darkness along the ledge path. "Wolves, I figured?"

"You figured right," Sam said. "Here, take this." He held the armload of wood out for Dawson, who took it quickly. "I need to pull one up."

"How many?" Dawson asked. He stacked the wood over into his arms, aware of its importance if they were going to stay alive through the night.

"Five or six, maybe more," Sam estimated, levering the shortened Winchester. "I scared one of them back, but they won't stay away for long. The darker it gets, the more they're going to want to come for the roan." The Ranger looked back along the ledge and saw the horse standing there, watching them in the shadowy darkness as lightning blinked on and off.

"Don't worry, Ranger," said Dawson. "I didn't leave him behind. I couldn't have left him even if I'd wanted to, unless I had a log chain on him."

"Good, I've got him," Sam said, stepping over to the nervous roan, taking the makeshift rein in hand. "You get ahead of us with the wood. We'll follow you to the fire."

"Looks like we're in for a long night of it," Dawson said. He glanced back along the dark ledge as he walked past the roan and the Ranger and hurried along ahead of them with the firewood.

As soon as the two men and the tense roan returned to the campsite, Dawson laid out the wood in a row, surveying each piece closely, speculating which logs would burn the longest before they would need to rekindle the small fire.

"If you get another shot at the pack leader, I hope you'll do us both a favor and blow his danged head off," Dawson said as he examined their supply of firewood on the ground.

"I don't know that it was the leader I got a shot at to begin with, but I'll kill whichever ones I have to kill to break up the pack and get us out of here alive," Sam said. He stood holding the roan by its single rein, his arm looped up under its head. He rubbed its muzzle soothingly.

"Had I killed the wrong wolf up here on this tight ledge, there's no telling what the rest of the pack would have done," he said quietly.

"If it's a small pack, four of five of them, they'd have broke up right then and got out of here," Dawson put in.

"What if they're not a small pack?" Sam asked flatly. "What if that wasn't the leader?"

Dawson didn't answer. Instead he looked back along the ledge in trepidation.

"I knew a buffalo hunter who told me a lot about wolves, from living in the high north country. He said a good pack leader keeps a loyal *segundo*, a number two who does his fighting for him."

"I've heard that too," said Dawson, keeping a wary watch on the ledge in both directions as wind-whipped rain howled and hammered across the hillside. He took a deep breath and shook his head.

Sam just looked at him, seeing how rattled he was.

"Don't mind me, Ranger. I know you know what you're doing," he said. "I'm just running my jaw is all . . . nerves, I reckon. Two things I've always feared something awful is wolves and rattlers. Here I am so hungry, if I saw a rattler, I'd eat it before it stopped wiggling. But wolves, that's a whole other thing."

"I understand. Try to get yourself some rest," Sam said. "They know we're here. We'll be hearing from them soon enough."

"What about you, Ranger?" Dawson said. "You're needing rest as bad as I am."

Sam ignored his question, looking off along either end of the stony ledge path, knowing the wolves had access to them from either direction. He lowered his arm down from the horse's head and saw it lower its head and relax. Then he sat down quietly with just enough rein hanging down for him to hold on to it at shoulder level.

The roan stood above him, dozing lightly, while the Ranger sat with the shortened Winchester across his lap, staring out into the darkness through the pouring rain. Moments passed; the storm raged. Two feet away Dawson sat in rigid silence, ready to tend and stoke the fire at a second's notice. When the first long howl resounded along the hillside to their right, Dawson looked up, startled, gripping the pocket pistol.

Sam stared at him and nodded, feeling the roan snap awake and jerk at the rein in his hand. Rising to his feet, Sam stood close to the roan, settling it. He stroked its muzzle, rein in hand.

"They've thought it over," he said quietly to the worried shotgun rider. "Sounds like they're going to test us awhile." He ran a hand along the Winchester, stopped his thumb over its hammer and cocked it.

"You going to take a couple of potshots at them—turn them back before they work up their nerve?" Dawson asked, looking back and forth in each direction as another howl rose from the other end of the ledge.

"Let them howl awhile," Sam said. "It'll give us an idea how many we're facing."

"The longer they howl, the bolder they'll get," Dawson cautioned.

"And the more surprised they'll be when they find out we're not helpless here," Sam said. As he spoke, he stepped back and guided the roan a few feet from the fire. Dawson watched him reach behind his back with his rein hand and come back with a half dozen .45-caliber pistol bullets he'd popped from the band of his gun belt.

For the next hour they stood, ready and alert, hearing the howl of the wolves grow closer, bolder, more intent. The howling helped the Ranger draw a mental image of the pack's numbers, the sound resounding across either end of the ledge path and along the hillside atop the overhang.

"Step back, Dawson," Sam said, judging the pack to have worked itself into a killing frenzy.

With a short torch he'd made burning in his hand, Dawson stepped back away from the fire as the Ranger reached forward and pitched the six pistol cartridges into the red, glowing embers.

"Here they come!" Dawson said, hearing the sound of running padded paws on the stone path to his left.

Almost before he'd spoken his words, a flurry of fur, fang and claw spilled around either end of the path into their wider camp area.

Sam turned loose of the roan's rein and threw the shortened rifle into play. At hip level he fired, levered a fresh round and fired again. His first shot picked up a big wolf in full leap and hurled him out over the edge of the overhang. His second shot sent a young wolf rolling backward in the dirt, causing others to have to leap over him to continue their attack.

The sound of shots alone turned back the less courageous animals. But there were plenty left to tear two men and a horse apart. On Sam's left, the roan whinnied in terror, but its hind legs pumped like pistons into the writhing, snarling wall of fur that had set its sights on horseflesh.

Sam levered another round, hearing the pocket gun explode in Dawson's hand. He caught a glimpse of a wolf falling back, yipping, screaming in pain. Seeing that he himself had no time for a third shot, Sam swung the Winchester barrel around just in time to crack a wolf across its open, snarling mouth.

The animal flew into its pack mates, but it rolled

onto its paws again and charged forward. This
time a bullet from the Winchester nailed it backward in a twisting bloody ball of fur. But now
other wolves were upon him; Sam felt fangs sink
deep into his shoulder as he struggled too late to
lever another round into the rifle chamber. He felt
himself going down, the wolf's jaws holding his
shoulder in a powerful grip.

But at that second the bullets in the fire began
exploding amid the charging pack. Bits of fiery
coals sprayed up and filled the air like angry
fireflies. Wolves panicked, not only at the roaring cacophony of gunfire and the spray of burning
coals, but also at the feel of hot embers burning
deep through their outer fur and sizzling on their
skin.

*Just in time.* . . .

The wolf had dragged the Ranger to his knees,
the rest of the pack ready to leap in, join the take-
down and the kill. But now with the pack breaking
and scurrying away from the bullets and exploding campfire, Sam managed to swing the Winchester around and lever it. As the wolf slung its head
back and forth trying to get the Ranger flattened
beneath him, Sam jammed the tip of the barrel into
the animal's lower guts and pulled the trigger.

The animal flew away, but he did not turn loose
easily. The Ranger felt the skin and muscle atop his
left shoulder rip as the fangs raked and sliced away
from him. He swayed on his knees; this was no
time to fall, he told himself. Shaking the pain and
dizziness off, he struggled to rise, levering another
round into the Winchester.

The pack had scurried away, yelping, their tails tucked, all except for three of them. These three were atop the roan, taking it down. The roan struggled down on its front knees, a wolf astraddle its neck, its fangs trying to take a hold there, but the horse's thrashing head managing to dodge the fangs, for now. Another wolf snapped viciously at the horse's exposed muzzle but hadn't yet caught it. A third, younger wolf clung by its fangs to the horse's front shoulder.

With all his strength, Sam drew the rifle around one-handed by its barrel and swung it, his left arm hanging at his side. The heavy rifle chamber hit the wolf at the base of his skull and sent him flying from the roan's back. The roan, whinnying, snorting, threatening rose, still fighting for its life. Sam swung the rifle again at the young wolf on the horse's front shoulder. But the animal saw what was coming, releasing its grip on the roan and darting away. Sam heard it yelp as a shot from Dawson's pocket gun hit it in its rump.

The wolf at the roan's front turned tail at the same time and disappeared in a flash of fur, paws and lowered head. Sam grabbed the roan's rein. His right hand still holding the rifle, he gripped the rein and held firm, lest the horse in a panic run away along the same path as the wolves.

"Easy, easy . . . ," Sam said, trying to hold the roan steady, offering his hand to its muzzle to calm it. But the roan was wild-eyed with fear and fury and would have none of it. The horse reared and twisted and kicked. Sam held firm and turned down Dawson's offer to take the rein when Dawson stepped in beside him, the smoking pocket pistol in hand.

"I'll take him, Ranger. You're bleeding," he said.

But Sam held on for a moment and felt the roan begin to settle. He let the horse cut back and forth, snort and blow and scrape a hoof as he looked it over. The roan was bleeding from claw and fang marks, but nothing that couldn't be dressed and attended to, he told himself with relief.

"You're bleeding, Ranger," Dawson repeated, out of breath but sounding stronger, more confident than he had earlier.

Sam looked Dawson up and down.

"So are you, Dawson," he said.

Dawson saw the questioning look and gave a thin smile.

"I dread a fight coming worse than anything," he said. "But once it gets here and gets started, I'm into it up to my neck."

"That's good to know," Sam said. "Because I've got a feeling they'll be back most any time. I don't think I saw the leader."

"Let them come," said Dawson. He raised his voice and called out into the storm, "I hope they *do come back!* We'll be ready for them!"

He took the roan's rein and helped the Ranger over to the fire and seated him. He looked at the wound and grimaced.

Sam took the roan's rein in his right hand, his rifle across his lap.

"There's no time to do anything but to wrap it good and tight," he said to Dawson. "I want to be on my feet when they come back for the kill."

"Maybe they learned their lesson," Dawson

said, carefully peeling the swallow-tailed coat back off Sam's ripped shoulder, seeing exposed muscle and tendon.

"Maybe," Sam said, looking at the wound with him, "but I'm not counting on it."

# Chapter 8

A new round of storms rolled past the hillside with the same hard-blown intensity as before. The outer edge of the cliff overhang lay draped behind a waterfall. Yet, seven feet behind the veil of runoff water, men and animal were dry and warm. With the fire fed and stoked a little brighter than it had been earlier, the Ranger sat with his ripped swallow-tailed coat and shirt off, lying on the ground beside him. The roan stood wearing a loop of rope from the Ranger's wet saddle that Dawson had fashioned into a hackamore. Sam sat on the remaining coil of the rope while Dawson tore the sleeve off his bloody shirt and ripped it into strips for a bandage.

On either side of the ledge and on the hillside above them, the howling had begun again. Sam and the shotgun rider looked at each other with dread in their eyes.

"Sounds like I'd better hurry some," Dawson said, even though he had been working quickly all along.

Sam nodded, his free hand over the broken Winchester across his lap. He turned his head sideways and looked down as the shotgun rider cupped his hand under a large flap of meat and carefully turned it over and smoothed it back into place atop the Ranger's left shoulder.

"I hope I cleaned that good enough," he murmured, second-guessing his medicals skills.

"So do I," said the Ranger. He watched as Dawson picked up strip after strip of the torn shirt-sleeve and circled them snugly under Sam's armpit and up around his shoulder.

"I'm thinking if everything heals down into place, this is just as good as getting sewn up," Dawson said. "What do you think?"

Sam just looked at him for a moment, realizing the shotgun rider had decided they weren't going to come down from this hillside. Their bones, and the bones of the horse, would join the other bones he'd seen lying scattered along the inside of the ledge.

"I don't have enough thread anyway," Sam replied. "The drummer took it all."

Dawson nodded and went back to bandaging.

"Just as well, then, I reckon," he said.

A twisting bolt of lightning lit their stony lair; the roan flinched and nickered under its breath. Sam took his hand off the rifle and gripped the rope running beneath him, preparing for the coming clap of thunder. But the roan handled the thunder better than he had before, and Sam turned the rope loose and looked back at the bandaging going on.

"I'm out of bullets, you know," Dawson said quietly as he worked.

"I figured you were," Sam replied.

On either end of the ledge, the howling continued in spite of the storm.

Dawson shrugged and didn't look up as he

wrapped the last of the strips around the Ranger's shoulder.

"It don't matter, though," he said. "I just don't want to go down without making a good showing." He paused, then added, "I expect no man does, huh?" As he asked he picked up the Ranger's shirt— now a one-sleeved shirt—and held it down and open for the Ranger to slip his left arm into.

Sam didn't answer. Instead he looked his bandaged shoulder over and carefully lifted his arm and slid it into the shirt. His hand was stiff and numb; a deep, dull pain radiated from his upper arm up into his neck. But both arm and hand were working.

*Good enough for now,* he thought.

"Did you and Long know the young dove?" he asked quietly, as if they had been discussing her all along.

Dawson, looping a length of cloth over Sam's neck for a sling, stopped and gave him a quizzical look.

"I swear, Ranger," he said. "At a time like *this,* whatever made you ask something like *that*?"

"Just curious," Sam replied quietly, slipping his left arm into the sling. He gestured for the shotgun rider to hand him the swallow-tailed coat. "Did you, know her, that is?"

Dawson shook his head as he picked up the coat, holding the sleeve open for the Ranger's right hand; he only draped it up over his wounded left shoulder.

"Jenny Lynn?" He seemed to have to consider it first. "No, I can't say I did." He closed the coat enough to button one button in the middle.

"What about Long?" Sam asked.

"He didn't either," Dawson said. "Leastwise, if he did, he never let on like it." He grinned and cut a glance toward Daniel Long's gray-faced body leaning against the wall. Then he lowered his voice as if Long could hear him. "Dan'l ain't a man who liked speaking much about his private goings-on."

"I understand," Sam said, listening, noting that the howling wolves had moved into a closer circle around them. Outside the overhang, the storm raged and flashed and pounded. What kind of wolves came out in this kind of weather? Sam considered the question while adjusting his coat. He placed his hand back on the shortened rifle. *Loco lobos . . .* He quoted a saying he'd heard an old Mexican mutter regarding the habits and peculiarities of the wily Sonoran Desert wolves.

"*Mas loco lobos . . . ,*" he repeated, murmuring in a trailing voice; and in spite of the howling and the hard passing storm, he closed his eyes for a moment and felt himself begin to drift.

*Whoa! None of that,* he scolded, throwing his eyes open quickly, looking all around.

"I was going to let you sleep awhile longer," Dawson said beside him, feeding another piece of wood into the fire. "They've quit howling. I've heard no sound of them."

Sam shook his head, confused.

"I've—I've been asleep?" he asked.

"Yep, nearly an hour," Dawson said.

"I . . . didn't mean to," Sam said, trying to clear his mind.

"You might not have meant to," said Dawson,

"but you did all the same. I expect you must've needed it."

Sam looked all around, noting an odd stillness to the night, the water from overhead no longer rushing down, only dripping steadily. The wind had died down, leaving only a light, falling rain—more of a mist. The roan stood over him, seeming more at ease as he looked up at it.

Taking the rope from under him, Sam handed it to Dawson and stood up stiffly.

"What about you?" he asked. "How long's it been since you've slept?"

"Ha! I don't do much sleeping, Ranger," Dawson boasted. "I never did." He held the roan's rope and gestured out across the night. "Storm's gone too. At least for now anyway . . . maybe for good," he added hopefully.

"Maybe," Sam said idly.

He walked close to the edge and looked out across the night. The sky still lay low and swollen, black and moonless overhead. The wind had turned to a barely noticeable breeze. In the distance, where the storm had moved off to, a low rumble of thunder threatened new terrain. Lightning flicked like dim candlelight.

"Figure we could make ourselves a run down from here come morning?" Dawson said.

"Yes," Sam said, "wolves or no wolves."

Winchester in hand, Sam looked down at the rolling flatlands below them. He saw only a gray shroud of fog banked and hanging in low spots between the lower hills.

"Now we're talking," Dawson said. He fished a

railroad pocket watch from inside his trousers, slapped it on his palm and opened the case. He studied the round face of the watch in the firelight and said, "If the water didn't ruin this thing, we've got near two hours before sunup."

Sam looked at the ledge in each direction.

"I can't figure what happened to those wolves," he said, sounding concerned.

Dawson stepped closer, the roan right behind him. The horse pawed at the ground and chuffed, getting nervous again.

"*Mas loco lobos*," Dawson said with a grin and a shrug. "Crazy wolves," he translated, "like you kept whispering in your sleep."

But Sam didn't return the grin.

"It's too quiet. I don't trust it," he said.

Dawson's grin went away as suddenly as it appeared. The roan reared and whinnied loud.

"No, I don't either!" he said in a hushed tone, holding on tight to the horse's rope. He gestured a nod toward the ledge leading off to their left, where in the outer glow of the fire stood a large wolf staring at them from the turn in the path.

Sam swung the rifle up one-handed, cocking it.

*The leader, or his second-in-command?* The thought raced through his mind as the tip of his rifle followed the wolf, trying to get an aim at it, seeing it race straight for the roan as if he and Dawson weren't even there. Then it was too late. The wolf was too close to the roan for him to take the shot.

Dawson had to give the roan slack. When he did, the roan took it. The horse reared high, wild-eyed, and came pawing down savagely at the wolf with a lot of fight in his blood. The Ranger saw it;

at the same time he saw three more wolves slip into sight at a run, as silent as smoke, straight at him and Dawson.

His shot lifted one of the wolves off the stone path, sent it sprawling backward and off the ledge. The other two swerved around their fallen pack mate and kept coming. The Ranger levered the shortened rifle one-handed and fired again. One of the wolves rolled away. The other circled and ran back around the turn in the trail as if something had fouled their attack plan.

Sam turned quickly to help the roan. The horse, holding its own, swung around, kicking hard and fast, still holding the first wolf at bay. Sam saw his chance and shot the first wolf as it leaped up for the roan's rump.

As he saw the wolf slam against the stone wall and fall, he turned stunned at the sound of rifle shots exploding from the other side of the overhang.

"What the hell!" Dawson shouted, turning with him. "Who's out there?"

From the other side of the ledge, another shot exploded. A wolf rolled into sight in a spray of blood and slid pawing for its life off the rock ledge and into the bottomless darkness.

The two saw the blaring glow of a lantern coming into sight along the ledge path.

"Don't shoot at us, Dawson!" a gruff voice shouted. "It's me and Doc Simmons. We come to rescue you two stagecoach bummers!"

"Thank God," Dawson murmured. "It's all right, Ranger. Here's our rescue party."

Sam breathed in relief and turned his cocked

rifle to the other side of the ledge path. Seeing no more wolves, he stood slumped and uncocked his Winchester as the lantern-bearer stepped into sight.

"Ranger," said Dawson, "this is Clevo Strait." To Strait he said, "Ain't it just like you to show up once we got everything under control?"

Strait, a large full-bearded man in a set of wet buckskins behind an open rain slicker, looked Sam up and down in surprise. He held a smoking Spencer rifle over his right shoulder.

"I thought it was you and Long up here, needing help," the man said, touching his hat brim toward the Ranger as he spoke to Dawson.

"It is," said Dawson, "except Long is dead." He gestured toward the body lying against the stone wall. "This is Arizona Ranger Sam Burrack."

Strait looked first at Long's gray-faced body in the shadowy glow of lantern light. He shook his head with regret, then turned to Sam.

"Howdy, Ranger," he said, touching the brim of his wet hat respectfully.

Behind him, a younger man wearing a long frock coat and carrying a medical bag and a rifle walked into sight. He stared at Long's body and also shook his head in regret. Then he noticed Dawson's bloody feet, then Sam's arm in the sling.

"I'm Dr. Simmons," he said efficiently. "Who needs attending first?" He held on to his leather bag but slipped a haversack of supplies from his shoulders, dropped it at his feet and leaned a shiny new Winchester against it.

The night remained calmer save for the rumble of distant thunder and the diminishing sound of runoff water running down all around the hillside. Beneath the overhang, the oil lantern glowed white-gold in the moonless night. The Ranger had turned down a bottle of rye whiskey Doc Simmons offered him. He sat sipping hot coffee made from the ground beans the young doctor took from a package inside his haversack while he treated the Ranger's shoulder wound.

Dawson and Clevo Strait each ate from heated tins of beans taken from the same source, the two of them having taken position at either side of the campsite watching the ledge path in both directions. The roan stood to the side chewing and appearing to savor a handful of grain that Strait had poured on the ground for him.

Halfway through sewing the Ranger's shredded shoulder back together, Doc Simmons looked over at Dawson taking a long swig of the rye, washing down a mouthful of warm beans.

"Almost finished here," he said to Sam. He stared at Dawson from above his wire-rim spectacles. "If you're going to change your mind about the whiskey, Ranger, you'd better not wait long. Dawson's got the manners of a pig when it comes to rye."

"I heard that, Doc," Dawson called over to him. The doctor ignored him.

"I'm good, Doctor," Sam said. "Beans and coffee was plenty for me." An empty tin plate he'd eaten from lay beside the fire. The doctor looked at it and shook his head.

"I don't know that I ever saw a man eat while I was still sewing him up," he said. As he spoke, he ran the half-circle needle through the Ranger's flesh and made another stitch. Sam clenched his teeth but otherwise ignored the pain.

"The Ranger don't fool around, Doc," Dawson said, the bottle standing on a rock beside him while he spooned more beans. "I've learned that about him."

"How long on this wound, Doctor?" Sam asked, glancing down at his shoulder while the doctor drew the thread snug and began looping it with the point of the needle, tying it off.

"Three or four days you'll be using your arm without it feeling like it's on fire," the doctor said. "It'll have to heal awhile longer, but you'll be able to use it well enough." He clipped the thread and prepared it for another stitch, his fingertips bloodred to his second knuckles.

"On your way here, Doctor," Sam asked, "did you see either of the passenger's bodies, or any coach horses?"

"No, Ranger, we didn't see either of the passengers, which is most upsetting," the doctor said. "But we did see a couple of dead horses. One had a harness on it. I presume they were the coach horses."

Sam nodded and fell silent. The doctor eyed him above his wire-rims.

"Of course you can check closer on our way back, during the day. Perhaps it won't be storming then—we'll see better."

"I won't be going back with you, Doctor," Sam said flatly. "I have to be getting on."

"What?" The young doctor looked at him, bemused, and almost smiled. "But of course you will. We may still have bad weather coming."

"What are you talking about over there?" Dawson asked, stepping over from his position.

"Ranger Burrack thinks he's going to be *getting on*," the doctor said, almost mocking the Ranger.

"What are you talking about, Ranger?" Dawson asked. "You can't go nowhere, the shape you're in."

Strait put in, "If you get out there and get a case of the fever with that shoulder wound, what'll you do?"

Sam only stared at the three of them.

"I think we all know what I'll do if I come down with the fever, don't we, Doctor?" he said.

"Yes," the doctor said. "You'll die. If it were an arm or a leg, it could be removed. But a shoulder . . ." He shook his head. "There'd be little chance of saving you."

"So it won't matter if I'm out here on the trail or back in Nogales," Sam said. "If I catch the fever, I'd likely die wherever I am."

"But in Nogales someone could take care of you, make you comfortable," the doctor reasoned.

Sam and Dawson looked at each other; Dawson grinned and took a long swig of whiskey.

"Obliged, Doctor," Sam said. "But I'm not looking to catch the fever, or to be comforted. I'm looking to bring in the man I'm trailing."

"Do you not hear what I'm telling you, Ranger?" the doctor said, getting exasperated. "You cannot go on the trail until your wound is better, and that is that."

"I'll be on the trail either way, Doctor," Sam said, "whether I'm going backward to Nogales or forward in pursuit. That being the case, I'll choose forward every time."

Dawson and Strait both chuffed.

"He's got you there, Doc," Dawson said, tipping the rye bottle toward the Ranger in salute.

"Indeed," the doctor said skeptically. Speaking to Strait he said, "Clevo, gather what the Ranger needs. We're turning back when I'm finished here." He looked down at the broken stock on the Winchester across his lap. "You can take my new rifle. It's been fired very little—but mind you, I'll expect it to be returned to me, *unharmed*," he emphasized.

"I'll do my best, Doctor," Sam said. "You have my word."

The doctor only nodded as he looked back down at his work. He put the sharp tip of the needle against the torn flesh on the Ranger's shoulder. Piercing the sore and damaged flesh, he pressed it through.

Sam sat looking at Dawson and saw the grim look on his face. He raised the tin cup of coffee to his lips as the doctor drew the thread snug.

Dawson finally shook his head and looked away toward the feeding roan.

"I'll get your horse readied up for you, Ranger," he said. "If you're crazy enough to go on in this weather, I'm crazy enough to help you get started."

"Obliged, Dawson," Sam said quietly as the doctor continued his work.

# PART 2

# Chapter 9

———◆———

*El Pueblo de Armonía, Old Mexico*

Hard rain had hammered on the battered tin roof throughout the night, finally easing up, the wind diminishing from a roar to a whisper. Water burrowed in beneath the eaves and cut itself a channel. Now, even though the rain had stopped, the water still ran down the adobe's rear wall and guttered in a stream across the dirt floor. One of the new Texan gunmen, Evan Hardin, stepped across the stream toward the front window. Rifle in hand, he looked out through one of the gun port crosses that had been carved in the center of each of the adobe's ancient window shutters.

"I had a feeling deep in my guts," he murmured, raising his rifle to his shoulder and taking aim through the gun port at the rider coming up into sight. He eyed down his rifle sights and centered on the rider's chest, allowing for the short rise and fall of the galloping horse.

"*Bang!*" he said. A grin came over his scarred, beard-stubbled face as he continued looking down the rifle sights for a second longer. Then he lowered the rifle and brought the tip of the barrel out of the gun port. "Guess what, Freeman. I just shot our new boss," he said over his shoulder. "If I'd had a mind to, that is," he added.

"Yeah?" Behind Hardin, Freeman Manning— the other new Texan gunman—threw his worthless poker hand down on the battered wooden table and stood up, adjusting his gun belt and the gun standing in its holster. He shot a guarded grin across the table to another gunman, Rudy Roach. A young Mexican woman, Rosa Dulce, was perched on Roach's lap, her hand moving around inside Roach's half-buttoned shirt.

"If Evil Evan here so much as *dreamed* he shot Wilson Orez," Hardin said, "he'd wake up with this whole place stinking."

Rudy Roach chuckled under his breath. He shoved the woman's hand away.

"You're right in my way, Rosa Dulce," he said, reaching out and pulling in the few dollars and coins lying in the middle of the table. To Manning he said, "Your pard wouldn't be the first gunman Wilson ever caused to soil himself—not the last either, I'm willing to wager."

Evan Hardin stared at the two of them, his rifle hanging in his right hand. He switched it over to his left. His right hand opened and closed near the Colt on his hip.

"No man's yet to make me soil myself," he said. "I'm looking right now at the two least likely to ever bring it about."

As always, Manning couldn't tell if Hardin was serious or not. Instead of replying, Manning picked up his damp Stetson and placed it on his head.

"Since he's here, just as well we go out front and greet him." He adjusted his big revolver in its holster. "If you can stand up yet, that is," he said to Roach.

Roach looked embarrassed. He gave the young woman a stiff little nudge.

"Step up, Rosa, darling," he said quietly. "Let's go see what Wilson Orez's got to say when he meets you."

"Do you think he will like me?" Rosa asked shyly.

"Darling, he'd be a fool not to," Roach replied.

"Ummm, Wilson Orez!" Rosa Dulce's eyes brightened as she stood and shook her full peasant skirt out and let it fall down below her calves. "Always, I want to meet this man *so* much."

"Oh, and why is that?" Rudy Roach asked, a little piqued by her words.

"Because I always hear that he is an *hombre malo*," she said, her voice turning hushed and excited.

"Oh? Because he's a *bad man*, eh?" Roach said. He gave Manning a wry look.

"*Sí! Hombre muy malo*," said Rosa Dulce, appearing even more excited than before. "*Muy, muy malo*," she added, smiling seductively, cupping her hair at her neck.

"Hear that, Rudy? Your bride says that Orez is a *very, very* bad man," Manning chuckled, looking at Roach with an arched brow. "And how long did you say you two have been married?"

"Damn, darling," Roach said to Rosa Dulce, looking deflated, ignoring Manning's question.

Rosa's smile fell away as suddenly as it had appeared.

"What I say that is wrong?" she asked. She looked back and forth at the faces of the gunmen nervously.

Manning chuckled again.

"I expect you're able to stand up now," he said to Roach.

Still seated at the table, still ignoring Manning, he looked up at Rosa Dulce for a second and shook his head slowly.

"Darling, no man likes to hear his wife carry on about another man that way," he said quietly to Rosa. He stood up, adjusted his gun belt and the crotch of his trousers.

"*Sí*, I know this," Rosa Dulce said, still uncertain what she had said that had been so poorly taken. She tried to make up for her uncertainty with a bright smile, realizing from experience that she was among dangerous men.

"You *know* this?" said Roach, eyeing her quizzically.

Manning and Hardin only passed each other a look. They had met Roach and his bride only a few days earlier on their way here to ride with Orez.

"*Sí*, I know this. I know that men are jealous," Rosa said, smiling, twirling her skirt back and forth playfully. "I am not so stupid, you know."

Roach, his brow wrinkled, was having a hard time understanding.

"You know it, but you say it anyway?" he asked, trying to get it straight in his mind.

"There, you *are* jealous, no?" she said. She started twirling her skirt more briskly side to side. She cocked her head and said teasingly, "You are a jealous, jealous man."

"I'm not jealous," Roach denied flatly.

"Yes, oh yes, you are," she taunted, flipping her skirt up at him like some matador goading a sullen bull. "You are a jealous, jealous man."

"So, then . . . you said it just to make me jealous?" Roach looked at her, confused, feeling embarrassed under the gaze of these two new gunmen.

"No, I only said that *always I want to meet him*," Rosa replied. "It is you who make yourself jealous."

"Oh, then you . . ." Roach tried to consider her words. But he had to stop, bewildered, unable to even get so much as a starting grasp on what she was talking about. Finally he shrugged as the other two gunmen walked out the door and left it open behind them. "We'll talk more about all this some other time," he said quietly between the two of them. "We've got some things that need sorting out."

Following the two Texans out front, Rudy Roach and Rosa stood back against the front of the adobe out of the peppering rain and watched as the rider dropped below a low hill and in a moment bounded back into sight. Roach stood watching as Orez rode closer, seeing the easy way he let the horse take in the wet ground beneath its hooves, splashing up mud-silvery water and leaving a mist of it suspended for a moment in its wake. The money from the stagecoach hung in two canvas bags on either side of Orez's saddle.

*A very, very, bad man? What the hell is wrong with her?* he asked himself. What kind of bride had he chosen for himself?

He cut a guarded glance sidelong at the beautiful young woman without her seeing it. He noted the look in her dark eyes as she stared toward

Wilson Orez, and he didn't like it. He saw her
secretive smile as she watched Wilson Orez draw
his horse quarterwise, then straighten it at the
front hitch rail and stop. Orez swung the canvas
money bags over his shoulder and stepped down
from his saddle into the mud, his rifle in hand.

*The hell's wrong with this woman?* Rudy Roach
asked himself again. The two weeks she'd been
with him, he'd never seen her act this way. Of course
they hadn't been around anybody until yesterday
when they arrived here to meet Manning and Hardin. Wait a minute, maybe it wasn't her. Maybe it
was him, getting himself all worked up for no reason. Maybe he was just being jealous—*you jealous,
jealous man,* he pictured her saying. Maybe that's
what she was trying to tell him. He considered it,
but then dismissed the matter. There was nothing
wrong with him. He watched Orez step under the
front canvas overhang and slap his wet hat against
his thigh.

"What are you doing here?" Orez asked Freeman Manning bluntly, looking at each man in turn.
His eyes lingered on the woman for a second, but
only for a second. Then he looked back at Manning.

Manning appeared surprised at Orez's question.

"We're here to take up with you, like we agreed
to, Wilson," he said. His eyes went to the canvas
bags, then quickly back to Orez's face. "You said
meet you here, to ride with you, remember? You
said you needed us to keep watch on your back
trail, lag back and shoot holes in them for you if
need be."

Orez looked at him for a moment.

"There's nobody trailing me," he said. He gestured back into the distant rumble of thunder and swirl of black-gray sky above the desert hills and basin. "If there had been, I shook them off a long time ago. Nobody tracks in this kind of weather."

Manning and Hardin looked at each other.

"Then you want us to go on," Manning asked, "or cover your back like we said?"

"Do what suits you," Orez said. "While my trail has disappeared, I'm going up there to lie low among my people, the Red Sleeves." He gestured in a direction of a line of taller hills not even visible from where they stood.

*His people?* Manning said to himself. He and Hardin looked at each other. Neither had heard of the Red Sleeves kicking up any dust in years.

The three gunmen knew better than to ask for clarification. They knew he was talking about Apache renegade country, the Twisted Hills at the foot of the Mexican Blood Mountains, a rugged place where rebel warriors on the run holed up, away from both the Mexican *federales* and the American cavalry.

"What would suit Evan and me," said Manning, speaking for the two of them, "would be to get on a looting spree while this weather has everybody hunkered down. Seeing them bags hanging over your shoulder makes me hungry for some myself."

"Yeah, me too," said Hardin. "I always say if a man ain't robbing something, what the hell is he doing?" He smiled thinly.

Orez considered it. He looked back and forth between the two of them, then moved away as if in thought. After a moment, his caged eyes went to the young woman.

"Where did you take this one captive?" he asked

Roach, looking Rosa Dulce up and down appraisingly.

"Captive . . . no, Wilson," Roach cut in. He gave a thin, stiff smile. "This here is no captive. This is my brand-new *wife*." He took Rosa by her arm and pulled her forward. "Rosa Dulce, this is Wilson Orez."

"I am pleased mostly to meet you," Rosa said, excitement and fear in her eyes as she stepped forward, managing to wiggle her arm loose from Roach's hand. "Rudy tells to me everything about you."

"He does?" Orez gave Roach a hard look. "What do you tell her?" he demanded.

"No, she doesn't mean that," Roach said quickly.

Wilson Orez settled some. He looked the woman up and down again, then looked back at Roach.

"She's a captive," he insisted.

"No." Roach shook his head. "I swear she's no captive."

"She is a captive," Orez insisted. As he spoke, he took the woman by the arm and led her inside.

"Jesus!" Roach murmured. He gave the other two gunmen a worried look. They followed Orez and the woman inside. "I've got to make him understand, this is my wife. This ain't no made-up deal here," he said quietly.

The two Texans just shot each other a quizzical look.

Orez seated the woman at the table and looked around the crumbling old adobe, the muddy floor with its interconnecting rivulets of water. Rifle at the ready, he stepped across the floor with his rain slicker dripping water. He inched a heavy wooden door open and looked in the adjoining room, seeing a blanket spread on a pile of dry straw. He walked back toward the woman and looked down at her, taking her by her chin. She smiled with fear in her eyes as he turned her face back and forth, inspecting her.

Seeing Orez handle his woman, Roach started to take an angry step forward. Manning grabbed his shoulder, stopping him for his own good.

"*Huh-uh,*" Manning whispered.

Roach clenched his teeth and his fists. But he stood still, knowing Manning was right.

"She is a captive," Orez said. He turned quickly and stared hard and accusingly into Roach's face. "If she's not a captive, what's she doing with you?"

Roach only stared, not knowing how to respond.

Manning cut in trying to change the subject.

"Say, Wilson, where's Tom Quinton and The Slider?" he asked, looking around as if he had missed seeing the two men. "We expected to see them here." It was Tom Quinton who'd introduced them to Orez. Maybe Quinton could remind Orez, since he seemed to have trouble realizing why they were here.

"They didn't make it," Orez replied, without taking his eyes off the woman. "Have you eaten?" he asked her.

"Yes, I have. Thank you," Rosa Dulce said, fluttering her eyelashes a little.

"Tom Quinton and The Slider didn't make it?" Manning said.

"What did I say?" Orez said bluntly.

"Where does that put us?" Manning asked.

Orez didn't reply. He continued staring at the

woman. "Come with me," he said to her. He pulled her to her feet even as she started to stand on her own. He moved toward the other room with her.

"*Whoa*, now, hold on!" said Roach, stepping forward, grabbing Rosa's other arm before Orez pulled her away. "Damn it, what do you think you're doing, Wilson? I told you, this is my wife! This ain't like the times before. This is the real deal. We just got married!"

"Congratulations," said Orez. He gave a yank on Rosa's arm and pulled her away from Roach toward the doorway to the other room. "She's going with me," he added bluntly.

Rosa Dulce gasped.

"Like hell, she is!" said Roach. He slapped a hand on the butt of a Colt holstered on his hip. Orez's hand came from behind his back with his large knife gripped in his fist.

"A man doesn't fight over a woman with a gun, Roach," he said in a cool, lowered voice. "This kind of fight calls for cold steel."

"I'm not fighting you with no knife, Wilson. I'm no damn fool." He started to lift the Colt. "But you ain't taking her in there, that's a fact."

"I warned you for the last time, Rudy," said Orez.

Manning and Hardin took a step back, both knowing from Orez's reputation that at any second the big knife would whistle through the air and plant itself deep in Roach's chest. They doubted that Roach would even get the Colt clear of its holster.

"Wait. Stop, Rudy! It is okay!" Rosa said, pivoting around between the two men. "I'll go with him. It is okay! I do not mind so much."

*Do not mind so much?* Roach stood stunned. What was this?

"Really, it is all right with me," Rosa said. "We will only be a while. I do not want you to fight over me."

"But, Rosa, darling! I can't let him take you in there. You're my wife. . . ." Roach let his words trail.

"But I want to go," Rosa said. "Don't you see? I want to go with him. It is all right."

"Let's go," Orez said gruffly, jerking on her arm.

*Son of a—!* Roach slumped and watched as Orez and his wife disappeared through the doorway. Rosa smiled and blew him a kiss. Then a dirt-frayed canvas fell closed over the doorway. Roach heard Rosa giggle and let out a little squeal. He turned and looked around at Manning and Hardin.

"She's a good-natured one, I'll say that for her," Manning interjected. "Has she got any sisters?" He stepped over, looped an arm across Roach's shoulder and he and Hardin ushered the stunned outlaw out the front door. In the falling rain, he unhitched Orez's horse and the three led the wet muddy animal to a small plank and adobe barn.

"I—I can't believe she wanted to go with him," Roach said brokenly, stopping outside the barn, staring back toward the adobe.

"It does seem peculiar, I'll give you that," Manning said. Hardin nodded his head in solemn agreement. "Are you sure this woman knows you two are married?" Manning asked.

"That's a hell of a thing to say," said Roach. "Of course she knows it."

"No offense intended," said Manning. "The two of you are indeed *legally wed*?" he pressed.

"Damn it, *yes*," said Roach. Then he paused and recanted. "We didn't stand before a preacher or nothing like that, but we both made promises."

"Oh . . . ," said Manning.

He and Hardin looked at each other.

"Everything was on the level?" Manning pried. "No trouble of any kind?"

"No, hell no," said Roach. "Well . . . " He paused. "I did sort of, more or less, shoot her pa. But it was nothing. We were trying to leave. He was stopping us—"

"Whoa, now, back it up there," Manning said, cutting him off. "You say you *shot her pa*?"

"Jesus," said Hardin, standing listening, holding Orez's horse by its reins.

"I was drunk, all right?" Roach shrugged.

"Let me ask you this, Rudy," said Manning, holding up a finger for emphasis. "Before you *sort of more or less* shot him, was she willingly leaving with you? Or did she only become *willing* after you shot him?"

"Like I said, I was drunk," Roach repeated with a shrug. He paused again under their accusing stares. "She seemed more willing afterward than she was before, but that's only natural, I think—"

"There it is," Hardin said abruptly. "He stole her. Orez was right, she's a captive."

"I never stole her, *damn it!*" Roach said. "She's no *captive*, she's my wife!"

Manning looked off at the adobe through the cold pouring rain, then back at Roach.

"Not right now, she's not," he said.

"Damn Wilson Orez for taking her, and damn her for going with him," said Roach. He raised his Colt from its holster, cocked it and started to walk toward the adobe. But he melted to the wet ground in a splash of water and mud as Manning stepped in behind him and soundly smacked his rifle butt into the back of Roach's head.

"Damn, you've killed him," said Hardin.

"No, I didn't. But Orez most likely would have," said Manning. "He hired us on to watch his back. We're watching it. Help me get this knot-head up and out of the rain."

Shaking his head, Hardin dropped Orez's horse's reins and stepped around to take Roach by his muddy feet.

"This right here is the very reason I'll never get married," said Hardin.

"They're not married, damn it," said Manning, the two of them stooping to pick up the unconscious gunman. "You heard him—he stole her just like Orez accused him of doing. Sounds like it's not the first time he's ever done something like this."

"Yeah, but still. Married? Captive? I've seen it go both ways," Hardin said, shaking his head.

Manning just stared at him as they carried Roach inside the barn. Orez's horse walked along behind them, its reins dragging in the mud.

# Chapter 10

In the afternoon, the storms returned. Rosa Dulce had opened her eyes at the sound of thunder slamming down hard overhead, causing the adobe to tremble. She lay still for a moment, gathering her waking thoughts. When she saw lightning flare on the darkened adobe walls, she turned over quickly and looked toward the open window, knowing she had closed and bolted the shutter earlier that morning.

A feeling of dread and fear came over her as she saw in another flash of lightning Wilson Orez standing naked in the open window. His big knife hung in a fringed and beaded sheath down his right shoulder.

But in an instant she shed her fear of him and relaxed in the soft, blanketed straw. There was nothing to be afraid of, she reminded herself, recalling their earlier encounter. He had not harmed her. He had forced himself upon her as she had expected. She had surrendered herself to him, if not wantonly, at least not unwillingly, having found out even as a mere child that this was the best way to survive. And yet this man, Orez, had not taken her. When the time came for him to do what she saw his body was prepared to do, he had stopped himself. He had moved away from her and across the darkened room.

Recalling it, she pulled a corner of the single blanket over herself and lay staring at him. In a flash of lightning, she saw Orez's big gun lying on the pallet beside her. The canvas money bags sat on one corner of the pallet. But she only glanced at them, feeling a sharp chill of excitement run through her as she realized the gun hammer was already drawn back, fully cocked. God, did he not know the gun was there? she asked herself. If he knew, did he not think she would grab the gun, point it at his back and pull the trigger? He knew she was a captive. Didn't he realize what an escape opportunity this gun gave her? She decided to make her move.

Orez stood with his arms outstretched across the open window, his hands on either jamb. He was an older man, and he faced the storm as if he were in some way its supplicant, in other ways its commander. Looking at him, she noted, conjured a coppery taste of blood in the back of her mouth. She saw there was great pain in him.

She could raise the gun and kill him, and be out the window and on a horse—shoo the other horses away in the storm. She closed her hand around the big gun butt. But after a moment she released it and gasped to regain her breath.

"What's stopping you?" Orez asked flatly, staring out at the black, swirling sky. His hair fell silver-black to his shoulders and stirred on an offshoot of wind. In the lightning flicker, deep scars on his left shoulder and lower right side were illuminated, stark and gruesome. They were painful to look at. She winched, knowing her hands would have had to touch those places had he remained atop her and done what he'd first intended to do.

"Go back to Rudy," he said, as if he was disgusted that he had not done what he could have done so easily. He sounded disappointed, she thought.

She fell silent beneath another slam of thunder, and waited as it rolled off the other end of the earth.

"Rudy is not my husband," she said. "I only say it because it is what he says."

"I know," he said, speaking to the passing storm. "Rudy steals women and thinks they're his wives." He paused and continued staring out into the blackness. "Go to him. I'm done with you."

She lay silent. She never wanted to see Rudy again.

Orez paused and listened for the rustle of her departure. Not hearing it, he let out a long breath, staring deeper into the rain and its gray, all-consuming darkness.

"Go on, now, there's nothing here for you," he insisted, closing his eyes for a moment.

She started to speak, but thought better of it. She sighed and reached for her clothes on the corner of the straw pallet. But when she started to stand and dress, Orez turned from the window and stared at her.

"Wait," he said.

She stopped and held her clothes gathered at her breasts, waiting to hear what he'd say next.

He stood looking down at her, the front of him wet from the blowing rain. Another deep scar across his chest, another on the front of his left thigh.

She looked up at him questioningly, and she parted her knees slightly to him.

"No," he said. He picked up his shirt and dried himself, while from the other room the two of them heard the men's voices speaking back and forth across the wooden table.

"Did he kill your family?" he asked her matter-of-factly, in a lowered voice.

"I have only my papa," she replied in a whisper. "Rudy shot him, but he still lives, or so it was when we left."

"You came with him to take him away from your father, to keep him from shooting him again," he said. It wasn't a question.

"I lie down for him, I say I am his wife," she said quietly. "For you I will say the same thing . . . if you want me to."

He stood silently and stared toward the sound of the men's voices beyond the closed door, as if considering her offer.

"No," he said. "Get dressed."

She continued staring up at him, her clothes in hand, making no attempt at dressing. She preferred any man to Rudy Roach.

"Why did you not take me?" she whispered secretively. "As badly as I saw you wanted to."

"I said, get dressed," Orez said firmly. "I told you I'm done with you." He hooked his thumb in the knife belt hanging down his shoulder. "I thought I wanted you. I changed my mind."

She looked almost hurt by his words.

"Then—then why did you want me to begin with?" she asked.

"I don't know," he said, dismissing the matter. He stopped, then said, "Because you look like somebody I knew a long time ago."

"Oh. . . ." She lay silent.

"Because in the dark I saw myself with her," he said. "You looked like her, you felt like her . . . you tasted like her—" He stopped himself short. "But you're not her."

She looked at him with interest, sensing there was more to come.

"No, that's not why I did it," he said. "I did it because I felt it might be my last time. All right?" His voice had a ring of finality to it.

She only stared at him in silence. Lightning streaked and flashed purple-orange on the wall and across his face. Thunder slammed down overhead.

"Your last time?" she whispered. "What do you mean . . . ?"

He stared at her without answering.

Was it death she saw in his face, heard in his voice?

"Come down here," she said softly, on an impulse. She patted a hand on the pallet beside her.

He shook his head *no*. Yet, as if on second thought, he stooped down and laid his clothes aside. He uncocked the big gun and placed it on his clothes.

"Perhaps this is the last time," she whispered. "Perhaps it is only the first of many times to come. Or perhaps we only lie here in each other's arms until the storm passes."

Orez didn't reply. Instead he stretched out beside

her and looked up at the crusty mud and timber ceiling. Above the ceiling, rain spilled like iron nails pitched across the tin roof.

"Think of me as her if you need to," she whispered. "I do not mind so long as she is someone you love, someone you are tender and gentle with."

"She's dead," Orez said bluntly. "Everybody I know is dead."

"Oh." She paused, but only for a moment. She softly touched a hard terrible scar on his chest. "Even so, tonight I will be this woman, and you will not be alone," she whispered.

When the storm had let up a little, the rain no longer falling at a slant, Freeman Manning and Evan Hardin sat at the wooden table playing poker. They had left Rudy Roach half-conscious and sulking in the barn with the horses.

"What kind of fool is this Rudy Roach? He goes around stealing women, thinking they're *his wives*?" Hardin pitched in three cards, then drew three more and tucked them one at a time into his hand.

"I won't even try to guess," said Manning, also straightening his card hand.

"Maybe that smack to the head you gave him will straighten his outlook a little," said Hardin.

"I don't know," said Manning. "Alls I know is Wilson Orez hired us both for our shooting ability. If he wants us to shoot Rudy, that's within my makeup. But as for knowing why an idiot does what an idiot does . . ." He let his words trail. "That's not in my range of understanding."

"Well, anyway," Hardin said under his breath, "it looks like Orez has turned out to be the benefactor of Rudy's *marriage*." He grinned and nodded toward the closed door.

"I don't want to even picture what's going on in there," said Manning. "It would only serve to make me sorely aware of how some men have all the luck and others of us don't even get the shavings off the stick."

"Amen, I hear you," Hardin said with a slight chuckle. He laid his cards down and fanned them. Three kings and two sevens stared up at Manning. "This might not boost your attitude any." He gave another grin. *"Casa llena!"* he said, beaming.

"Full house . . . ," Manning translated bitterly. "Son of a bitch. See what I mean?" he growled, throwing his cards down in disgust.

Both gunmen turned in surprise when the front door flew open so hard it banged against the wall and stayed there. Roach stepped in, his gun hanging in his right hand, cocked and ready. The two gunmen froze, seeing Roach staring straight at the closed door to the next room. Manning already had his hand on his Colt lying on the table. Hardin's hand rested on the table edge, ready to drop to his holstered Colt.

"I can't stand it!" Roach shouted at the closed door. "Come out, Wilson. I'm going to kill you!"

"Easy, Rudy," cautioned Manning. "We talked about all this earlier. Mine and Evan's job is to cover the man's back. We can't let you do this. Why don't you go on back and try to cool down before—"

"Both of you stay the hell out of this, unless you want to die with him!" Roach shouted, cutting Manning off. "I ain't forgot that one of you busted me in the head." He quarter-turned toward them, his gun still hanging in his hand.

"All right, Rudy, it's all your show," said Hardin, hoping to pacify the enraged gunman until he got a chance to go for his own gun. "We've not been riding with you or Orez long enough to go taking sides. Ain't that right, Freeman?"

"You're damn right it's right, Evan," said Manning, knowing what was up. "You and me are newcomers here. We need to keep our noses out of it." He didn't have to give Hardin a look. It was understood, they would both chop the gunman down as soon as his attention strayed from them.

Roach turned back to the closed door as fresh thunder rumbled in the distance with a promise of more storms to come.

"You heard them, Wilson!" he shouted at the closed door. "It's between you and me! You're not taking this woman from me. I aim to kill you and take back my wife!"

Seeing Roach's wild eyes fix on the closed door, Manning and Hardin started to make their move. Manning's hand closed tight around the butt of his gun on the tabletop. Hardin's hand dropped and closed around the holstered Colt on his hip. Both guns started to swing toward Roach at the same instant. But both stopped and froze for a second, seeing Roach buck an awkward step forward. A red spray of blood misted in the air in front of him as a bullet whistled through the open front door and punched a large hole through the middle of his back.

"Orez?" said Manning. The two stared toward the open front door. But whatever thought they might have formed on the matter vanished as a heavy barrage of rifle fire ripped through the open front door and thumped into the thick wooden window shutters. Bullets zipped in, knocking over chairs, dinging and ricocheting off the large iron pots in the hearth. Splinters flew through the air.

The two gunmen dropped and took cover, turning the thick wooden table over between themselves and the wide-open front door.

"Get that door shut, Evan," Manning shouted, reaching his Colt around the edge of the upturned table and firing.

Without hesitation, Hardin belly-crawled from behind the table to the front corner of the room. He stopped long enough to peep out through a crack in the front wall from where he spotted four gunmen crouched behind cover in the falling rain, pouring rifle fire at the adobe. Beyond the gunmen, a Mexican peered out around the corner of the barn door.

"Damn it," Hardin said in a harsh tone beneath the roar of the rifles.

"What have we got out there, Evan?" Manning said, hunkered down in a corner, having managed to grab his Spencer rifle and a bandolier of ammunition from against the table. He popped a handful of bullets from the bandolier and dropped them one after the other down the open loading tube of the Spencer as he spoke.

"Looks like we've got ourselves a bounty posse, Freeman," Hardin called out beneath the roaring gunfire.

"Bounty posse?" said Manning. He winced slightly. "That's what you make of it?"

"Yep, that's what I'm seeing," said Hardin, speaking loudly over the gunfire. "Leastwise I've seen no badges out there. I've heard no offer of surrender."

"Jesus," said Manning. "I knew riding for Orez would be tough, but damned if this don't try a man's patience." He cocked the Spencer and called out to the closed door were Roach now lay dead, his limp body jerking, fresh gaping wounds still appearing from the relentless rifle barrage.

"Are they all right in there?" Hardin called out to Manning, beneath the heavy firing.

"I don't know," Manning replied. "Are you two all right in there, Wilson?" he relayed to the closed door.

"No answer," he called out to Hardin when he heard no reply from the other room.

Turning, Manning ran in a crouch to the front wall and kicked the front door shut as bullets thumped into it. Then he peeked out the window, poked his rifle out through the gun port, found a target in the cloud of burnt gun smoke and falling rain and fired.

"Keep them busy, Evan." Manning crawled over to the other closed window where Hardin had stood up and began pumping steady fire through the gun port.

"That's the very thing I'm doing, Freeman," Hardin called back in reply.

"Let's see who we've got out here," Manning whispered to himself, gazing out through his gun port, looking for a target through the silver-gray deluge. "One thing for sure," he said to himself. "They won't be burning us out of here."

Manning took close aim at a brown derby bobbing behind the cover of a stack of weathered and broken barrels. Even as the gunfire thumped into the window shutter all around him, he waited until the derby rose fully into sight and squeezed the trigger. Shots homed in heavier on his position, but before ducking away he saw the red cloud of blood appear as the bowler hat flipped crazily away in the rain.

"You got him, Freeman!" shouted Hardin as the gunfire waned a little. "Nailed that dewberry dead as hell!"

Inspired, Hardin took close aim and blasted out a shot that struck an exposed shoulder and sent a man flipping backward from behind the cover of a broken-down wagon, his yellow rain slicker tails spinning end over end.

"These gun ports are the only way I'm fighting from now on," Hardin called out with elation. "I believe we're going to beat these bastards."

"Pay attention over there," Freeman Manning called out, seeing a bullet zip through a crack at the edge of Hardin's closed shutter and send up a spray of wood and stone chips. Hardin had to jerk back a step from it.

"Hold your damn fire!" a loud gruff voice called out from the cover of a stack of seasoned firewood.

The rifle fire stopped.

"Who are we shooting at in there?" the voice called out to the adobe.

"Little late to be asking," Manning replied arrogantly. "Are you giving up?"

A tense pause ensued. Then the voice called out, "The only man we've got paper on is Wilson Orez. We know you're in there, Orez. We figured you would be showing up here. These others don't have to die with you."

"Bounty hunters, huh?" Manning called out. "How do you know we don't have money on *our* heads?" As soon as he'd spoken, he eased backward across the room toward the closed door. Hardin kept an aim out through the gun port.

"Whoever you are, we'll cut you loose in exchange for Wilson Orez," the voice said. "Alls you've got to do is back out of the way so's we can have at him. That's all I'm asking. You've got five minutes to think it over."

Manning knocked softly at the closed door.

"Are you hearing this, Wilson?" he called out to Orez. "This bounty hunter thinks we're going to Judas you up to him. I'm just letting you know that ain't going to happen. Me and Hardin don't neither one play that way." He waited and when he heard no reply, he said, "Wilson? Do you hear me?" He paused, glanced at Hardin. "Wilson . . . ?" he said again.

"Jesus," said Hardin. "He's gone, Freeman! He has run the hell out on us, leaving us fighting to save him!"

"Damn it all, I ain't ready for this," Manning said in stunned surprise. He took the door handle and swung the door open, revealing the empty room.

Out front, behind the broken-down wagon, the bounty hunter leader, Sterling Warner, checked the gold railroad watch in his wet, gloved hand and put it away under his rain slicker. A stream of water ran steadily from the front-guttered brim of his tall

Montana-crowned hat. He tweaked the point of a white walrus mustache in contemplation.

"You've got two minutes left," he called out to the adobe through the falling rain. The wind had begun to rise again, turning the rain at an angle. Distant thunder began creeping closer. "*Galdamned* if it's ever going to quit raining," he murmured to himself. "A man's a fool being out here."

"Wilson Orez is not here, Mr. Bounty Hunter," Hardin called out in reply. "Now where do we stand?"

"He is, you lying son of a bitch. There's no way he could've got away 'less he's swum off. I've got men guarding the barn."

A shot roared from the adobe window's gun port and thumped into the side of the wagon.

"Do not call me a lying son of a bitch!" Hardin shouted.

"I called you a lying son of a bitch because you are a lying son of a bitch!" said Warner. "You need to understand that it's only going to make things worse on you when we ride roughshod through that mud hut and trample it down. You hearing me, Wilson Orez?" he shouted even louder for the benefit of Orez, who he was still convinced had to be listening. "Are you going to put your men through this?"

"He is not here, damn it!" shouted Manning. "What do you need to hear from us?"

Warner jerked his watch back out from under his slicker, checked it and put it away.

"Time's up," he called out with finality. "You've had your chance to be on the level. You chose not to. Now we're going to—" He stopped and turned suddenly when his nephew, Madden Warner, came splashing through the mud from the barn. "Damn it, Madden! You nearly got yourself shot, running up on me all of a sudden."

"Sorry, Uncle Sterling," the young gunmen said, sliding to a halt in the mud, out of breath. His rifle barrel almost jammed into his uncle's eye. Warner swatted it away. "I checked the barn like you told me to do. Jack Heaton is dead. His throat's been cut from ear to ear!"

"Damn it," said Warner, gripping his rifle tight. He looked off through the rain to the adobe, then back to his nephew.

"What about the horses?" he asked quickly. "Are there any horses gone?"

"There's two horses gone, uncle," Madden said solemnly. "Darcy's in the barn too. Said he mistook Haco for one of them and shot him in the head and belly—Haco crawled up on his paint horse and lit out of here. Darcy's going to bleed to death himself if we don't get his shoulder wound patched up."

"Good, loving God! He shot Haco?" said Warner, stunned.

"That's what he said," Madden replied. "Head and belly."

"I've never seen nothing go this bad this fast in my whole damned life," Sterling Warner said.

"How do we know it was Wilson Orez who took the two horses?" Madden asked. "Maybe he sent one of his men to throw us off. Maybe he's still inside there. Maybe he ain't left."

Warner just stared at him for a moment.

"You're right about one thing, nephew," he said with an air of regret. "He has not left. I'll bet on that." He looked all around warily in the blowing rain.

"Uncle," said Madden, "what if we—?" His words stopped short with a deep sudden grunt. He fell forward against his uncle with a stunned, pained look on his face. Warner saw the hilt of the big knife standing in his back between his shoulder blades.

"Damn it, brother Clarence," he said quietly. "Looks like I've gone and got your boy killed." He stooped and let his dead nephew fall to the ground. Standing, no longer paying attention to the adobe, he gripped his rifle in his wet hands and turned cautiously, looking back and forth, knowing he was next.

Hearing the sound of hooves splashing through the silvery downpour to his left, he swung his rifle quickly toward it. But when he saw the riderless horse splash past him, he realized too late that he'd been tricked. As he swung his rifle back in the other direction, three rapid shots hit him hammer-like in his chest, slamming him backward to the wet, muddy ground. He looked up, struggling for his last few breaths.

"Oh no," he gasped, seeing Orez step into sight. He watched him reach down and jerk his knife from his dead nephew's back. "You've killed me, Orez . . . ain't that enough?"

"No." Orez shook his head slowly, water running down the front of him. "You came to kill me. I have to show the next ones that coming for me is bad medicine."

# Chapter 11

In the pouring rain, a pale, grainy evening had begun to overtake an already dark day when the Ranger stopped the roan atop a stony bluff. Behind him he led a horse he'd found wandering the flood land with one of the men Orez killed lying tied down naked over its saddle. On the terraced land below him, he saw a ragged canvas tent pitched against the side of a hill above a wide yet shallow stream of runoff water. Beside the tent sat a buckboard wagon with a tarpaulin covering its load. A team of horses stood hobbled and huddled against a tall pine, their heads and front shoulders out of the rain.

As a new round of lightning glittered and twisted on the distant black horizon, Sam nudged the roan forward, his newly borrowed Winchester in hand, the dead man's horse staying close behind him. Descending the bluff, crossing the shallow stream, he saw the front fly of the tent open and two railroad men step out into the rain. They stared at Sam as they closed and buttoned their raincoats. One of the men held a shotgun at port arms.

"Hello the tent," the Ranger called out, slowing

the roan almost to a halt. He saw their eyes go over the dead man.

"Hello yourself," said the man with the shotgun. "What brings you out on a day like this?"

"I'm an Arizona Territory Ranger," Sam called out, nudging his roan forward at a slow walk. "I've been in pursuit of a wanted outlaw named Wilson Orez the past week. Ever heard of him?"

"A Ranger, huh?" said the man with the shotgun. He looked a little relieved. The shotgun sagged in his hands. He noted the top of the naked corpse's raw scalped head.

"Wilson Orez. I'll say we've heard of him," the other man said. He looked again at the rain-soaked body, its hands hanging pale and blue toward the ground. "That's not him, is it?"

"Jesus, Odell," said the man with the shotgun. "You think a Ranger would do something like that?"

"No, it's not Orez," Sam said, dismissing the matter. "It's a man who rode with him. They had a falling-out." He stopped the roan ten feet away.

"I'd say so!" said the man with the shotgun. "Why's his hands split nearly up to his wrists?"

"You'd have to ask Wilson Orez about that," Sam said, tired, slumped a little in his wet saddle. "It's some kind of Apache warrior sign. His feet have been cut the same way," he added. Seeing the man step closer and reach out to the corpse, he added, "You don't want to raise his face, take my word for it."

The man jerked his hand back from the body as if avoiding something venomous.

"Good Lord," he said, staring with a grimace at

the dead man's hands. They had been split between the man's second and third fingers, almost up to his wrists. "I would steer clear of any man who'd do another like that."

"I think that's the message he's supposed to get from Orez," said the other man. "Right, Ranger?"

"That's how I take it," Sam said, swinging down from the saddle in his swallow-tailed coat.

The two looked his clothes and footwear over, his floppy hat hanging wet with rain. Noting his youth, the man with the shotgun eyed him closer.

"Say, are you the young Ranger we've heard about?" the man with the shotgun asked.

"It's possible," Sam said. "I'm Samuel Burrack." He touched the brim of his soaked hat.

"Yep, it's you all right," said the man with the shotgun. He lowered the shotgun the rest of the way. "I'm Bob Ailes. This is Odell Colson. We were scouting the best place to stick a rail spur across the border before this wash blew in on us. The whole thing took us by surprise, even though we had time to see it coming."

"I understand," Sam said. "Did you happen to make any coffee between rains?" He looked over at a blackened, washed-out campfire.

"It's in the tent," said Colson. "We've got hot beans and sowbelly too, believe it or not. Rail scouts are well fed, if not well paid."

"It's nigh onto dark, Ranger," said Ailes. "Will you tent with us tonight? It's small and it stinks, but it's dry . . . so far anyway."

Sam could tell that even though good manners demanded they make the offer, he wasn't about to impose.

"It'll be dry enough for me under your wagon tarps," he said, gesturing toward the supply wagon.

"No, we won't hear of it," said Ailes. "You take the tent. I'll sleep under the wagon tarps. If it's dry enough for you, it's dry enough for me."

Sam shook his head.

"Obliged, but I can't let you do that," he said. "I need to be out here where I can watch over my dead man. I don't want wolves scenting him and coming in on us. The weather has them stirred up." He nodded at the torn shoulder of his coat. "I've had trouble with them already."

"Wolves? Jesus . . . ," said Ailes, trailing off. "We don't need trouble with them." He took on a look of consternation. "Maybe we ought to let you do what you know is best. There's extra rolled-up tarpaulins in the wagon bed with our supplies. You're welcome to cut a piece off one and wrap your dead man in it. Let us know what else you need."

"This will do it, thanks," Sam said, rounding his wounded left shoulder a little, feeling the stiff soreness of the doctor's stitches.

He led the roan and other horse, body and all, over to the pine, took out two short lengths of rope and hobbled the horses to keep from hitching them to a tree while lightning was still in the sky. He untied the body and swung it down to the ground until he could cut a length of canvas to wrap it in. The two railroad men stood watching as he walked back toward them, one boot, one dress shoe and the long, mud-splattered swallow-tailed coat.

"Wolves?" Ailes whispered.

"You heard him, pard," Colson whispered in

reply. "Let's hope he clears out of here first thing come morning."

"Lord, yes, let's hope so," Ailes whispered.

"Let's try some beans and coffee," Sam said, walking back toward them in the falling rain.

The railroad men looked at each other.

"Well, here we are," Ailes whispered.

They fell in beside Sam and splashed through the mud to the tent and went inside.

Over tin plates of beans and cups of hot coffee, the three men ate, while outside the buildup of wind, lightning and thunder began to roll in again.

"If you don't mind me asking," said Ailes, "why are you wearing one shoe and one boot, Ranger?"

Sam sipped his coffee and told the two how he had lost everything. He recounted the ravine flooding and the trail washing out beneath the stagecoach. The two men watched and listened intently.

After a moment, Colson ventured to ask, "With your shoulder wounded, why are you hauling the dead man around? You've got enough to look out for without worrying about wolves. Can't you stick him in under some rocks somewhere?"

"Yes, I can," Sam said, "and I will, first thing. I found him not far from here. I was looking for a good place to cover him up when I spotted your tent."

"The hillside gets rocky a mile or so around this trail," said Ailes. "I'll help you rock him over in the morning."

"Obliged, but I'll take care of him. I'll be leaving before daylight," Sam replied.

"Why?" said Colson. "Orez can't get along no

faster in this than you can. Besides, you've got no tracks to follow. The weather is all on his side as it is."

Sam wasn't going to explain what drove him on toward his prey. It was something most people would not understand. Instead he sipped his coffee and said, "The weather is on nobody's side except the man who won't stop for it. Orez doesn't stop for it. I can't afford to stop either."

"Seeing that man's handiwork, I'd stop altogether, go home and get me some other job," said Ailes, shaking his head. "This is gruesome work you're doing, no offense."

"None taken," Sam said, yet he turned silent, thinking about it. He knew everything Orez did was intended to turn back anybody following his trail. But it was going to take more than carving up a corpse to get rid of him. He had determined so much earlier when he'd found the stark blue-ivory body wandering the flooded badlands. What Orez didn't know was that Sam had been watching; he'd seen both the men die. He knew the man had been dead when Orez did the cutting. That sent him a different message altogether.

Carving up a dead man didn't impress him, didn't strike fear in his heart. He knew it was strictly for show. He had a gut feeling that something was wrong in Orez's world. Whatever threat Orez tried to send out wasn't working, he told himself. If he stuck close, he'd find out what was wrong, and whatever it was, he'd find a way to use it against him.

"I'm most obliged to you for the coffee and the

food," Sam said, standing in a crouch inside the small tent. "Now, if you'll both excuse me, I best get myself some rest."

The two men said their good nights and watched the Ranger turn and walk out into the wind and rain.

"Did I say something wrong?" Ailes whispered as lightning twisted and curled ahead of a loud clap of thunder.

"I don't think so," said Colson. "I think he's just got a lot on his mind—one of them driven men that won't rest easy until something's done and over with."

"Should I get on up an hour before daylight, help him with that body?" Ailes asked.

"He won't be here," Colson said in an assured tone. "He'll be up and gone before midnight, I'd bet on it."

"A strange fellow," Ailes said in a lowered tone, staring at the tent fly. "You never know what's going to blow in off these badlands."

Late in the night, when the new round of storms had come and gone, Sam unrolled himself from beneath the wagon's tarpaulin and stood up in the cold aftermath of drizzling rain. As he walked to where the horses stood huddled together under the big pine, a lantern came on inside the tent and Odell Colson stepped out and held the lantern above them as the Ranger readied the roan and the dead man's horse for the trail.

"I hate seeing a man take out in weather like this," Colson said, bunching his slicker at his throat.

He watched the Ranger step up into the saddle while silver rain angled sidelong in the lantern's glow.

"Obliged for your help and hospitality," Sam replied, drawing his wet coat collar up against his neck. The roan grumbled and chuffed at him as he turned it and nudged it forward, the dead man's bay huddled close to its side. "You'll feel better once we're moving," he murmured down to the testy roan.

After a few hundred yards of splashing mud and cold rain, the horse settled in under him in the moonless darkness and he didn't stop his two-horse contingent until a gray misty light shone long and low on the eastern hill line.

When daylight found him, he stood on the side of a rocky hill in the cold drizzle scraping out the thinnest of graves with an edged stone. As a renewed wind rose and rippled across stretches of shallow lakes of gray floodwater below, he rolled wet stone after wet rock atop the canvas-wrapped corpse until he convinced himself that any wolf or coyote strong enough to unearth the miserable sack of flesh and bone would be welcome to it.

Before stepping back atop the roan, he took off his soggy hat, folded his muddy hands at his waist and looked down at the mound of rock out of habit, even as he reminded himself that he felt no compulsion to speak on behalf of the sorely interred. That wasn't his job. Even so . . .

"I saw him kill you," he said grudgingly. "You hadn't done anything that I could see." He drew up in the swallow-tailed coat and glanced around the cold, wet and darkening flood lands. "Anyway,

I'm not sticking any more of your kind in the ground—not in this weather."

He eyed a lone coyote who sat in the rain atop a cliff watching him as he swung up into his saddle and put the roan forward at a walk, the bay moving along beside him. *Amen,* he said to himself in afterthought, looking back at the nameless pile of rock. Turning forward in his saddle, he took the two horses down to the edge of the shallow floodwater and rode on until the wind and rain grew fierce once again and the day blackened around him.

"Looks like a little more rain," he said wryly down to the roan. The roan chuffed and swung its head as if it understood him and took no solace in his words.

He stopped again two hours later when a new storm pounded in and forced him and the horses to take shelter inside a crumbling three-sided adobe. The abandoned timber and adobe house sat half-roofed, elevated on an island only a few feet higher than the floodwater surrounding it. Sam walked inside slowly, leading both horses behind him. As soon as he crossed a threshold of water and mud, he saw a spindly-legged paint horse staring at him from across a muddy floor.

Turning quickly, rifle in hand, he saw a wounded Mexican lying on a pile of rubble, staring dazed at him through a curtain of blood running down his forehead, soaking into a cloth headband. His chest and shoulders were covered with black, dried blood. A big Colt weaved back and forth in his weak bloody hand.

"Drop your gun, *hombre,*" the Mexican said in a raspy, broken voice.

Sam's thumb slid over his rifle hammer and cocked it.

"Drop yours first," he replied. "It looks like you've gone as far as you're going."

"I—I think . . . you are right," he said, relenting. His gun hand slumped down at his side. "You can go on . . . and shoot me. I don't mind. You're too late to kill me."

The Mexican saw the badge on Sam's chest behind his open swallow-tailed coat.

"What? You are a lawman?" he asked.

"Arizona Territory Ranger Samuel Burrack," Sam said, stooping down beside him. "I didn't come to kill you." He picked up the Colt and uncocked it.

"I am Haco Suarez. I am a . . . bounty hunter." He corrected himself, saying bitterly, "That is, I *was* . . . until I was shot in my head and my belly . . . by one of my own *compañeros*. By mistake, of course." He looked around, blood running down from his headband into his eyes. "Now I die here." He tried to make the sign of the cross on his chest, but he was so weak the Ranger had to take his bloody hand and help him complete the gesture.

Outside, wind howled. Lightning streaked.

"What were you and your *compañeros* doing?" Sam asked, picking up the headband just enough to see the gaping bullet hole. Dark blood surged with each beat of the man's heart.

Thunder exploded.

"We come to kill . . . a very dangerous man," he said. "Only I think we kill . . . each other instead."

"Who is this dangerous man?" the Ranger asked, his interest growing.

"Wilson Orez," the man said in a waning breath.

"Where was he? When did it happen?" Sam asked, getting even more interested.

"Only today . . . him and three . . . of his men. At the old *fortaleza*, the Apache *Matanza Motivo*," the Mexican said.

"Four of them, at the Killing Grounds Fortress," Sam repeated in English, familiar with the old Spanish fortress where the Apache had once slaughtered hundreds of Spanish conquistadors by hanging them upside down over fires and boiling their brains inside their skulls.

"*Sí*, the Killing Grounds. And so it was for me. . . ." The Mexican tried a weak smile. Sam looked at the battered Colt, and at the bandolier of ammunition around the Mexican's shoulder. He knew the wounded man was dying; he'd be dead any minute now. Sam knew he was taking the big Colt with him when he left.

As if reading the Ranger's mind, the Mexican said, "The gun is yours, Ranger . . . take it. So is the horse." He looked at the Ranger's coat and foot-wear. Even in his final moments he had to stifle a weak laugh. "I only wish to God my clothes fit you. . . ." His words fell away.

Sam stood up when he saw the last breath come out of the man's chest.

"*Gracias*," he said quietly to glazed-over eyes. He reached down, pulled the bandolier off Haco's shoulder and slipped it over his own.

"The Killing Grounds," he said aloud, adjusting the bandolier over his right shoulder and shoving the Colt down in his empty holster. He looked down at Haco Suarez's boots, gauging their size. But then he thought better of taking them and looked away, out the open doorway through the pouring windblown rain. He was getting closer every mile he pushed through.

*I'm coming, Orez,* he said to himself.

Lightning snaked down and twisted on the black horizon as if in reply.

# Chapter 12

After the Ranger had wrapped the Mexican in a soaked blanket he unrolled from behind the paint's saddle, he leaned the body back in place against the wall. While the brunt of the passing storm raged and howled beyond the adobe walls, inside, for the lack of a chair or dry place to sit, he leaned against the dusty stone face of a hearth and inspected the big Colt. He took the gun apart, rubbed each part clean with his thumb, reassembled it and rolled the cylinder one click at a time, holding it close to his ear, gauging the merit of the gun's crafting.

Satisfied with the precision and the voice of the gun's metal, he reloaded the big revolver, slipped it down into his wet holster and stepped over to the three horses, the Mexican's paint horse shied away from the other two as if uninvited.

"Come on in," Sam said wryly to the paint, picking up its dangling reins and ushering it over beside the two muddy wet horses. "We're all friends here."

When he saw the storm waning and moving away moments later, he gathered the three horses' reins and led them out into the mud outside the adobe. With the paint's and the bay's reins in hand, he stepped atop the roan and rode out at a walk, rain jumping like a field of crickets on the broad surface of muddy floodwater.

He'd realized how fortunate he'd been to come across the dying Mexican and hearing about Orez holing up at the old fortress. He would have liked to hear more, but the Mexican bounty hunter had given him all he could before slipping away. Anyway, he thought, the horses stepping up onto the lower edge of a long rounding hillside, he wasn't riding into four guns unaware, they with the cover of a fortress around them.

At the end of a wet two-hour ride, as the rain slackened and the wind and lightning fell away in the distance, he stopped the horses on a thin muddy trail and looked at the old Killing Grounds Fortress through a silver-gray mist. The old adobe fortress stood alone, surrounded by foundations and crumbled remnants of other buildings from the old, walled Spanish compound. The wall itself had been toppled and pulled down by a hundred years of bands of passing desert warriors.

Knowing himself and the horses to be partly obscured by the looming mist, Sam stepped down from his saddle a good distance back. He kept the barn between him and his horses and the front door and window gun ports of the old adobe. Watchfully he led the three horses through the foggy veil in a wide half circle around the large adobe building and to the rear of the ancient timber and adobe barn. Even as he walked along in the mud, rifle in hand, he saw the bodies of two men lying facedown on the ground beside a broken-down wagon, thirty yards from the adobe's front door.

At the rear of the barn, he shoved the door open and glanced around in the shadowy empty gloom. He looked down at a path of overlapping hoof-prints in the mud, all leading out to the rear door. He led the three horses inside and left the door open behind him. In the sparse gray light the open door provided him, he saw the body of a man leaning sprawled back against one of the barn's support timbers. The man's dead eyes stared straight ahead, a peaceful expression coming through the mask of deep gaping knife slashes that covered his face and chest.

Walking closer, the Ranger saw the man's scalp had been sliced from the top of his head and lay on the muddy floor beside him. The corpse's shirt had been stripped away, exposing a bullet wound in his shoulder. His torso had been split and lay hanging open from his breastplate to his crotch. Sam only looked at the maimed corpse for a long moment, inspecting it closely before averting his eyes and looking away. He noted that for all the cutting and stabbing the man had endured, his hands and wrists carried no wounds that a man would receive in defending his life. *Easy enough,* he told himself. The man had already been dead, just like the two he'd seen Orez kill.

*Why, Orez?* he asked himself. "Who do you think is following you? Who is all this for?"

He looked at the man's hands and bare feet, all split cleanly and severely straight up between the tendons, in the same manner as the dead man he'd found tied down across the bay's saddle. On the muddy ground beside the man's blue ivory feet stood a pair of boots, as if they had been left for him. But Sam refused the boots, took the dead man by his wrists and dragged him away inside a stall and covered him with loose straw.

"It's all I've got for you," he said quietly, stepping back out of the stall.

He gathered the three horses and walked out through the front door. In a wind lull, rain falling straight and steadily from a blackish sky, he kept a close watch on the old adobe's door and windows. Watching for any movement through the gun ports, he stepped behind the cover of the broken-down wagon, walked to the first corpse lying face-down in the mud and rolled it over. In a stark flicker of lightning, he saw blood-traced water run from the corpse's lipless mouth. In the mud beside the corpse, he saw two globs of gray muddy flesh, one wearing the mantle of a walrus mustache.

In this dead man's face he saw agony, terror. This one, he deduced, had been alive through most, if not all, of what Wilson Orez had inflicted upon him. This one's hands had been split, but not his feet. This corpse had three bullet holes in his chest. A rifle lay in the mud nearby; a Colt stood muddy and unused in his holster. Sam took it and shoved it down in the long deep pocket of his swallow-tailed coat. He stopped for a second and looked at all the material things the dead had divested themselves of.

He found it ironic, he thought, sloshing on through the mud, the horses right behind him. This harsh flood-swollen land that had previously denied him everything now lay rife and ready to fill his immediate needs—rain slickers, boots, guns, hats. All these things lay loosely on, or strewn near, the dead as if cast suddenly aside by souls who'd left in hurry.

*All yours for the pickings . . . ,* he told himself grimly. All it took was for men to die.

Without the wagon for cover, he sloshed past the next corpse and on to the adobe, walking between the horses until he stood in the mud and water outside the front door. His hand didn't ease in the least on the rifle when he saw the door standing ajar. But he did allow himself to draw an easier breath when he shoved the big door open, looked around inside and saw the body lying at the open door to another room.

Leading the horses inside, he dropped their reins, crossed the muddy floor and looked down at the body as he stepped over it and into the other room. The wet muddy horses stood midfloor nuzzling each other. This was one of Orez's men, Sam concluded, seeing none of Orez's knife mutilation on the corpse, only the gruesome wounds of countless gunshots the corpse had no doubt received while lying in the line of fire.

He looked around the room and went to the pallet of straw in the corner. Outside, thunder grumbled behind a harsh stab of orange-white lightning. He stooped beside the pallet and looked it over good, noting two indentations in the blanket. He picked up a short three-inch piece of dark thread that appeared to have fallen from an article of clothing. *A man and a woman here?* he asked himself, studying the thread. Then he noted how close the indentations were in the pallet—almost one, he told himself.

Beside the pallet he saw part of a small footprint

in the soft earth before the surrounding ground turned into mud. A woman's footprint, he was certain. Was it left there deliberately to be seen, to be found by someone like him? he wondered.

All right. He stood, looked around the room, out the open rear window. There had been people waiting here for Orez to arrive. One of them a woman, he surmised. Turning, he walked out of the room and to the hearth, stooped and laid his hand down above the ashes.

*Cold.*

But they wouldn't be for long, he told himself, eyeing the dry wood in a pile beside the hearth. He looked around and saw no sign of food supplies. But with the afternoon encroaching and no permanent letup in the storms, he would build a fire and warm and dry himself if nothing else, he decided. He stood again and looked at the wet, miserable horses.

"I'll check the barn for some grain or hay," he said aloud. The horses' ears pricked at his voice, then relaxed as their muzzles probed the damp air. He had started to turn and leave when his eyes caught something he had missed before. On the lower wall by the door where the dead man lay, he saw one word smeared in blood. Walking closer, he stopped to read the word aloud.

"*Ayuda,*" he whispered, knowing it was the Spanish word for *help*.

He turned his eyes back to the other room, to the pallet on the muddy floor. After a moment of consideration, he raised each of the dead man's hands and studied the tips of his fingers. The dead man was not a Mexican. Why would he ask for help in Spanish—or at all?—he asked himself, finding no coating of blood on the man's fingertips from writing the word.

This changed things, he told himself. He stood up and looked at the firewood and let out a breath of regret.

"Come on, fellows," he said to the three horses, walking over and gathering their reins. "No time to dry out. We'll rummage the barn and get you fed. Then we're back on their trail."

*What trail?* a voice asked inside his head. But he ignored the voice, turned the horses and led them back toward the ancient barn. He thought about the plea for help smeared in blood as he and the horses splashed through the mud in the pouring rain. There was a trail, and he would find it, he told himself with determination. This was the job at hand.

On the side of a rocky hill beneath a narrow cliff overhang, Freeman Manning huddled out of the rain as braided streams of muddy water ran on either side of them into a stream of floodwater below. Hardin, after relieving himself against the wall beneath the overhang, stepped over and stooped back down beside him. Rosa Dulce sat fifteen feet away in a drier spot where the overhang sank back a little farther into the hillside. She squatted on her haunches, Rudy Roach's rain slicker wrapped around her and held closed at the throat. Her free hand idly picked at loose pieces of thread at the muddy hem of her skirt. Rudy's slouch hat lay limp and dripping, pulled down over her head. Ten yards ahead of them, Wilson Orez stood straight and tall on the hill point, looking off through the rain in the direction of the border.

"Look at him," Manning said to Hardin, nodding toward Orez. "I believe he's crazy as a blind cricket." He shook his head. "If only I'd seen it before."

"It's never too late to turn away," Hardin replied quietly. "To tell you the truth, seeing what he did gave me the willies."

"Really? The willies?" Manning just looked at him curiously. "I wouldn't go so far as to admit that if I was you. Lucky for you nobody can hear it, except me."

Hardin looked a little embarrassed.

"I don't mean it gives me the wild, screaming, jerk-my-hair-out-by-the-roots *willies*," he said. "Just the plain ol' willies, is all." He shrugged.

"Just call it *unsettling*," Manning suggested, "and let it go at that."

Hardin nodded. He took in a breath and let it out.

"All right," he said. "It was *unsettling*."

"I knew a man who bounty-hunted Apache scalps for the Mex government back in forty-eight, forty-nine," said Manning. "He said the red savages would do stuff like this to the bodies when they got their hands on a white man. Even worse with a white woman."

"I've heard that myself," Hardin said. "But damn!" He shook his head and stared off at Orez.

"It's meant to scare people," Manning said. He gave a dark chuckle. "Looks like it worked pretty well in your case."

"All right, damn it, it was a mistake saying it gave me the willies," Hardin said beneath his dripping hat brim. "But I've never seen a white man do something like I saw him doing to those dead men, have you?"

"No," said Manning, "I admit I haven't."

"He looked like some blood-sated fiend out there," said Hardin in grizzly reflection, "cutting, hacking, slashing them corpses that way, throwing parts of them around like they were a slaughter beast." He drew up tighter in his wet rain slicker. "Oh yes, that was most *unsettling*. No sane white man would do something like that."

"That wasn't his white blood behind any of that," Manning said. "That was his wild bloodthirsty Apache side stirring him up, getting the best of him." Staring out, he watched Orez turn around and step down onto a slick path leading back from the lookout point he'd found. "I expect a man who has mixed blood, sooner or later the savage blood boils over, makes him as wild and as savage as the ones he sprung from."

"Yeah," said Hardin, pondering the matter, watching Orez make his way toward them through the pouring rain. "They say the moon has lots to do with it too," he said. A full yellow moon drives folks crazy. A blue moon makes them do things they would never do."

"What about a red moon?" Manning asked.

"A red moon brings out the killing," said Hardin. "They say folks commence to killing free and easy on a red moon, especially these frontier savages. They can't stop themselves."

"I've heard that but I've never believed it," said Manning.

"I'm afraid to say I *don't* believe it," Hardin said.

"Afraid?" Manning grinned. "I never knew you

was so easily unsettled and worrisome of mind. Now I'm hearing you're superstitious, to boot?" he chuckled.

The two watched Orez step in under the over-hang in a crouch and stoop down beside Rosa Dulce.

"I'm not superstitious," said Hardin. "I just don't like tempting fate against me."

"If you think fate can be tempted for or against you, that's about as superstitious as you can get," said Manning.

"Have it your way, Freeman," Hardin said, shutting up on the matter. "I don't like talking about fate either."

"Jesus," said Manning with a chuckle under his breath.

"Speaking of fate," Hardin said, "here comes ours right now."

The two watched as Orez stood and walked toward them on a slim path along the hillside. Neither of them said another word until Orez stopped and stood over them, holding his rifle cradled in the crook of his arm.

"Are you two ready to rob a bank?" he said flatly.

"Well, hell yes," Manning replied with a grin. "We're always ready to rob a bank. "Where? What have you got in mind?"

"Trade City said Orez. "It's less than a two-hour ride from here. Right across the border."

*"Comercio el Pueblo,"* Manning said, repeating the Mexican town's name in Spanish. "Sounds damn good to us," said Manning. He looked at Hardin.

"Ain't Trade City the Mexican town the rail spur set up last year?"

"Yes, it is," said Manning. "But it's more Texan than it is Mexican. That's why there's money there." He stood, brushing the seat of his damp trousers. "It's about time somebody nailed their bank. It's fat with railroad and cattle cash, trade money from both sides of the border."

Hardin stood up and grinned.

"Then we owe it to ourselves to rob it," he said. He looked at Orez. "I say let's do it first thing."

"Good," said Orez, "we'll be there by midafternoon if we ride hard."

"Whoa!" said Manning. "You mean rob it today, in all this rain?"

"Yes," said Orez. "They won't be expecting to get robbed in weather like this."

"I can see why they wouldn't expect it," said Manning, looking up and all around at the dark sky, the flicker of lightning in the distance. "I have to say I'm a little taken aback by the notion."

"It's not a notion," Orez said. "We're doing it. Both of you get your horses. We're headed there."

"What about her?" Hardin asked, nodding toward Rosa Dulce.

"What about her?" Orez asked sharply.

"Where is she going be while we're robbing the bank?" Hardin asked.

"Don't worry about her," said Orez. "She's with me now. She'll do what I say."

# Chapter 13

Riding abreast through three inches of lying flood-water, the four had ridden less than an hour when the black-streaked sky overhead turned dead calm. The rain stopped as fast as an off-turned water spigot. The wind seemed to be grabbed by some mighty and unseen hand and drawn backward across the wet tortured terrain. The change came so strong and sudden, Wilson Orez brought his bay to a short abrupt halt and stared at the black distant sky. Beside him, Rosa Dulce stopped too. So did Manning and Hardin.

"Now, this just suits the living hell out of me," Manning commented, taking off his wet hat, slapping it against his thigh. "What about you, Evan?"

"It pleases my soul plumb down to its sap," Hardin said, unbuttoning the top two buttons of his slicker and fanning air inside it. "It stopped so fast my ears popped."

"Mine did too, come to think of it," said Manning.

The two gunmen looked to Orez for a comment. But the leader sat staring straight ahead, stone-faced, his head cocked a bit toward a deep steady rumble in the distance.

Seeing his attention was drawn to a rising swirl over the curve of the horizon, Manning and Hardin listened too. Beside Orez, Rosa Dulce sat staring with a look of terror on her face, edging her horse away from Orez as if prepared to make a getaway.

"We must be closer to the new rail spur than I thought," said Manning. "I can hear a train from here."

"They haven't started building on the new spur yet," Orez said without looking around. Rosa's horse reared slightly, nervous, feeling the fear of its rider. Beneath Orez his big bay turned restless. He held it firmly by its reins.

"It ain't built yet?" Manning laughed and put his hat back on. His horse also grew anxious, agitated, and back-stepped against its reins. "Then somebody'd better tell that train," he said, turning his laughter to Hardin beside him. "Because it's bearing right at us."

"You see any rail tracks?" Orez asked him flatly, staring straight ahead.

"Well, no." Manning looked all around, confused.

"Damned fool," Orez said under his breath, sharply cutting his bay to his right. Beside him Rosa had already turned her horse. She batted her feet to its sides out of habit, but her horse had already sensed what was coming and bolted away, wanting no part of it.

"Now, where are those two going?" Manning asked with a bemused chuckle, looking at Hardin. "Are they afraid of trains?"

"Jesus, God Almighty," said Hardin, "look at

that!" He stared at the distant horizon, at a high rise of blackness swirling up into sight.

"*Tornado, tornado!*" Rosa shouted back at them in her native tongue. Her horse splashed water high around her as the animal ran for a line of hills and cliffs over a mile away, following the direction of Orez atop his horse.

"*Tornado?*" said Manning, still not catching on. "The hell does she mean?"

"She means *run*, Freeman!" Hardin shouted, jerking his horse around, batting his heels to its sides.

"Holy God, a twister!" shouted Manning, realization finally striking him like a hammer blow. He nailed his bootheels to the horse's sides even though the frightened animal needed no goading. The deafening roar of twisting wind tearing its way across flatlands and low hills was enough to send the animal into a full frantic run, splashing muddy water, nickering loudly as it sped away.

"Wait for me, Evan!" Manning shouted, the sound of the twister growing louder, closer, more terrifying behind him.

Ahead of Manning, Hardin barely heard him through the roar of the powerful wind. But he didn't dare slow down, and he didn't dare venture a look back over his shoulder. Lying low on his horse, he raced along through the shallow floodwater as if competing on a racetrack. He followed Orez and the woman, barely able to keep them in sight through the muddy spray they left hanging in their wake.

By the time he reached the low hills, the wind

roared and howled at his horse's heels as if pursuing them like some creature of prey. As he neared the shelter of the hills, he felt his hat whip off his head. Swirling wet sand chewed at his neck and his face and pelted his rain slicker like handfuls of tiny darts. Beneath him the horse whinnied as it ran. Hardin felt the wind try to lift him from his saddle; he felt the animal's rear quarters struggle to keep from flying sideways out from under him.

Somehow he managed to make it onto a thin path up into the rocky hillside, still with no shelter in sight. The wind twisted violently at his back, wrenching harder at him and the horse, the lower tip of the long spinning funnel drawing closer behind them.

"In here!" Orez shouted at Hardin as the fleeing outlaw's horse became overpowered by the outer perimeter of the twisting wind. It stopped in fear and confusion on the low hillside. Hardin leaped from his saddle but held the horse's reins. Orez appeared beside him and the two dragged the scared horse along with them behind a large, land-stuck boulder where Hardin saw the woman stretched out on the ground, her horse lying nervously flat beneath her. She held her other arm looped over the neck of Orez's flattened bay.

"Take your horse down," Orez shouted at the top of his lungs above the incoming wind.

Hardin felled his horse quickly and lay flat with his head lowered as chunks of cactus and lengths of tree limbs bounced across the top of the large boulder and flew off, twisting wildly up the hillside.

Hardin heard Freeman Manning cry out loudly

from the outer edge of the powerful wind, his voice barely audible above the whistling, grinding roar of it. Lying flat, he clung to his horse's neck and shoulder to hold them both to the ground. He squinted out through the black-gray swirl just in time to see Manning's horse go rolling and bouncing across the ground just below the hill path, twenty yards away. Following the horse came Manning himself, rolling and bouncing like some strange new species of screaming tumbleweed.

"Over here, Freeman!" Hardin shouted, but it did no good. Manning could neither hear him nor help himself. Hardin watched as his partner spun ten feet in the air, his slicker tails whipping wildly, and flew onto the hillside path. The twisting wind rolled him uphill along the thin trail, past the boulder and his hunkered-down partner.

Orez and the woman stayed flat over their horses, keeping the animals down, keeping themselves low, down out of the wind, Hardin noted. He debated with himself for about two seconds whether or not to try to help Manning. But he put the matter out of his mind, catching a glimpse of Manning bouncing and rolling, seemingly from rock to rock, on his rough tumbling path up the hillside.

"God, *no!*" Hardin bellowed, and shut his eyes tight, having just witnessed the wind's appearing to have ripped Manning's legs from his body against the side of a rock and sent them flying limply upward in the black wind funnel.

There was nothing he could do. He hugged down tight against his horse's neck, keeping the stunned animal flat to the rocky ground. The horse lay quivering, its legs jerking at times in reflex, as the wind pelted them both with rock, sand and debris. When Hardin ventured to open his eyes, he saw the woman and the two horses lying flat, Orez lying atop them, protecting Rosa from the debris and loose swirl of rocks.

Hearing a long, loud scream, Hardin turned his squinting eyes in time to see Manning rolling back down the hill, bouncing over rock and off the sides of boulders, his legs still in place, but his trousers missing beneath his flapping slicker tails. At the bottom of the hill trail, the wind picked Manning up four feet off the ground and bounced him in place like a child's rubber ball.

Hardin screamed and buried his face on his horse's side and lay as if in a trance until at length— he knew not how long—the roar of the wind fell away over the hill and moved on. As suddenly as it had come upon them, it had left, he realized, lying in a white ringing silence.

"Get up, get up, it's gone," shouted Orez, nudging his boot toe into his side. Hardin looked up and saw Orez standing over him, his hat gone, his long silver-black hair pressed in strands across his face. Beside Orez, his horse shook itself off. Next to his horse stood the woman and her horse, both of them looking badly shaken.

"Let's get Manning and get out of here before more twisters come calling," said Orez.

The three looked down at the bottom of the thin hill trail where Manning had miraculously struggled to his feet and stood turning in a complete circle, his arms outspread, his slicker tails split all the way up his back. His trousers were gone. He stood shakily in his muddy socked feet, his gun belt sagging down his thighs, held loosely by the tie-down string of his holster. When he stopped circling, he looked up at them in his long johns and staggered back and forth mindlessly.

"I'm near ruint here!" he called out in a rasping drunken-sounding voice.

"Jesus, he's alive," Hardin said in awe, rising, shaking off sand and gravel and bits of chewed-up cactus.

The three led their horses dizzily down the trail toward where Manning stood staring all around, as if having just arrived in a new and strange place. Fifty yards away his horse came splashing through the shallow floodwater, covered with mud, its saddle hanging half down its side, but looking otherwise uninjured.

"I'm ruint here," Manning repeated numbly as the three approached him, Hardin swinging wide to intercept his horse and bring it to him.

Straightening the muddy horse's saddle and adjusting its cinch, Hardin put the reins in Manning's hand.

"You're going to be all right, pard," Hardin said. He guided him up the side of his horse and onto his muddy saddle. "We've got to get out of here before another one comes along."

"Get moving, Manning. We've still got a bank to rob," said Orez, up in his saddle now and straightening out his reins.

"A bank to rob?" said Manning, as if having no idea what Orez was talking about. He looked around, struggling to make sense of things. Rosa sat atop her horse beside him, looking dazed and trembling.

"You heard him, Freeman. Let's go," said Hardin. "You'll feel better in a while."

The Ranger had kept himself and the three horses above the thin blanket of muddy floodwater covering the low lands and valley floors. When he'd left the old Killing Grounds Fortress, he'd searched along the wet hillsides until he found the partial, smeared and fading tracks left by the four horses headed south along the badlands border. Only by a stroke of good fortune did he find tracks and scrapings where the party had sheltered out of the rain beneath the cliff overhang. But how long ago had that been?

As soon as he had asked, he saw the dark arch of urine Evan Hardin had left on the inner stone wall. He could see it wasn't dark wet, but it was still wet enough to be seen. On the floor it had soaked in but left a round dark circle.

"Obliged," he said under his breath to whoever had stood there relieving himself.

As he turned away and walked the length of the overhang, he had stopped at the far end and stood looking around closely when he noted another short length of dark thread. *All right . . .* This was no coincidence. He stooped and picked it up and held it between his thumb and finger, studying it.

There was no doubt that the woman had left this unraveled thread intentionally for someone to find. She must have hoped against all odds that whoever saw the words smeared in blood would also find this short piece of raveling where she had dropped it. Sam turned the thread between his fingertips. She had dropped it so subtly that she could have denied doing so had anyone pressed her on the matter. He thought about it. The blood-smeared word on the low edge of the wall had been risky and desperate on her part. But the thread, first on the pallet, now here on this rocky hillside. Here was a woman leaving signs where she had little hope of them ever being found.

She was playing to win, he decided.

*Keep it up*, he said silently to her, gazing out across the black skies, the sodden, shadowy land. *This is how you'll get away. Keep playing whatever hand you're dealt. . . . I'll find you. You have my word.* He clutched the piece of thread in his fist.

He turned and walked back to where he'd left the horses. When he took up his reins and the lead rope and went to step atop the roan, the horse balked and pulled away from him.

"Easy, boy," Sam said. "What brought that on?" Even as the roan continued to resist on its reins, the Ranger noted the other two horses turning restless and hard to deal with on the lead rope. His first reaction was to look all around on the ground for any sign of a rattlesnake. Seeing none, he made a quick glance along the path beneath the overhang for wolves, or any other predators. *Nothing . . .* , he thought.

But as he turned back to the roan, he heard the first deep whir of wind on the far horizon and looked off toward it. He noted that the sky had settled; the wind appeared to have drawn its breath and held it. A yellowish pall lay beneath the low black sky—a suddenly dead and silent sky, he observed. Beyond the flat silence the whir of wind grew quickly into a roar. He felt his ears pop. The roan pulled harder against the reins in Sam's hands and chuffed and nickered restlessly. The other horses huddled but scraped their hooves and chuffed and grumbled along with the roan.

"All right," Sam said, "I hear it." He looked closer at the horizon and watched the whirling spinning black mass of air rise, twisting into sight on the edge of the earth like some mad monstrous being risen from the lower realm with old scores to settle. "I see it too."

He led the horse quickly to the deepest part of the overhang and looked all around. This would have to do, he told himself. He looked the horses up and down, seeing they had settled a little. There was no way he'd get all these three horses down at once, let alone hold them in place while the twister ran its course. He felt pain race through his wounded shoulder as he stripped off his swallow-tailed coat and ripped it into three pieces.

"Fellows, it's going to get rough as a cob any minute," he warned the horses as if they understood him. With no room to turn them facing the rocky wall, he huddled them side by side as close to the wall as he could. Then he slung a length of his ripped-apart coat around the roan's head, covering its eyes, and tied it snug behind its neck. "You're not going to want to see this," he said, giving a quick rub on the roan's muzzle while the roar of twisting, snarling wind grew louder, fiercer, moving closer from the distance.

"Easy, now, everybody gets one," he said to the next horse, stepping in with the makeshift blinder raised for its eyes. Keeping his tone low and even, as soothing as a lullaby, he said, "This'll all soon be over and you'll feel foolish for letting it scare you."

When he'd placed the blinder on the third horse, he kept a firm grip on the lead rope and the roan's reins and stepped back and forth, still talking, saying anything beneath the growing roar.

The animals jerked and twitched as the storm encroached with the crunching of trees and cactus.

In the worst of it, he stood braced, his hat off and clamped beneath his left foot, the horses' heads huddled and gathered to his as if in secretive planning, or desperate prayer. The horses jerked and twitched and nickered; the roan raised and cocked a rear hoof as if to threaten the wind away.

*There's a good chance you're gonna be sucked out of here and blown away,* a dark voice said inside him. The Ranger spoke to the horses in almost a whisper, feeling the twister pull at him, drawing his shirt so taught across his chest that he felt buttons pop off and fly away.

He disregarded that voice, staring down at his foot and the hat held beneath it. He held on to the horses and asked that dark voice in return what man or woman alive didn't run that same *good chance* of dying every waking day of his or her life?

*And there it is,* he concluded; he drew a breath and let it out, taking on a feeling of strength somehow, from the horses, from the ancient stone hillside, from the wind itself, and in some odd way the smallness and fragileness of his and all other life around him no longer mattered.

"Courage," he whispered to the roan's twitching,

nervous muzzle, as if sharing wisdom hard learned. He felt the horse's hot breath on his hand, reassuring him, while the twister howled and whistled and chewed and ravaged its way along the rocky valley floor below their perch under the narrow overhang.

# Chapter 14

————

At the town limits, a large wooden sign was propped in the ground, half-covered with mud. WELCOME TO TRADE CITY, it read.

A blast of a Mexican shotgun had taken out part of the phrase below, but one could still make out the words: IT'S DAMNED NEAR AMERICA. Floodwater running down from a hillside west of the town had formed a slow-moving creek across the trail that led to the town's main stone-tiled street.

In a straight-falling rain, Orez and his sore and disheveled contingent stopped at the muddy water's edge and stared across, along streets piled with downed roofs, strewn furniture and other less identifiable rubble the tornado had left behind.

"This answers the question of whether or not they got hit," Orez said, staring along the street. He handed Rosa an old unloaded revolver he carried in his saddlebags. "Carry this. You're one of us," he said. He chucked his horse forward into the shallow muddy water. "Stay close to me," he told her. "These folks see you with us, they won't likely be your friends anyway."

"I wasn't going to try to leave," Rosa said, putting her horse forward beside him, the big pistol in hand, resting on her lap.

Orez only glanced at her through caged eyes.

It was true, she told herself. She had not thought about leaving, not right then anyway. She was not one of them; she knew she wasn't. Yet, for reasons she could not even begin to understand, she felt drawn to this man, to some strange and silent pain that seemed such a deep-grained part of him. His darkness seemed to pull at her and close in around her. She felt safe near him, even as she warned herself that he held her life or death in his hands. She caught herself straightening in the saddle and staring definitely at the devastated town laid fallen before them.

Behind Orez and Rosa, Hardin rode forward into the shallow water at a walk, leading Manning's muddy horse by its reins. Freeman Manning sat wobbly in his saddle, a dazed look of uncertainty on his battered, blood-streaked face. Across the floodwater, a small red-haired boy and a spotted dog ran up to them. He and his dog passed Orez and Rosa in the street and fell in running, splashing alongside Manning and Hardin. The wet dog barked and snarled and snapped at Hardin's horse's hooves.

"My pa says if you ain't come to help, keep moving," the boy said up to the pair of beaten, muddy, battered gunmen.

Orez and the woman didn't even look around.

"Tell your pa to go straight to hell, you little son of a bitch, take you and your yapping dog with him," Hardin said flatly in a harsh tone of voice. Water ran from the sagging brim of his hat.

Hardin gave a quick jerk on his horse's reins, and the animal released a sharp, muddy kick that sent the dog rolling and yipping. Finally the boy was able to scoop the dog up in his arms. He ran shrieking into an alley between two piles of fallen rubble.

"Pay attention up here," Orez said back to the pair of bedraggled gunmen.

When the four came to a place where the new bank had stood only a couple of hours earlier, three townsmen with shotguns who stood watching stepped in closer and bunched in around a buckboard wagon. The wagon held four iron boxes with chains around them; big shiny locks kept the chains in place.

A man in a black, mud-smeared suit and a black string tie stepped into sight from around the side of the wagon. The rain held his hair plastered down to his bare head. His eyes looked vacant and stunned.

"We're closed," he said. He wiped his face with a palm of his hand.

"You look it," Orez said.

He and the woman stopped. Hardin and Manning spread out abreast of him. The four looked down at the pile of debris. All that was left standing was a large black safe, its door ajar to accommodate two more men who hauled out money and transferred it to another iron box. Two men stood by the safe's door, bags of cash in hand. Water poured freely from their hat brims.

"I'm the bank's manager, Lucas Turnbolt," said the man in the wet black suit. He looked at the canvas money bags similar to his own hanging over Orez's saddle cantle.

Orez only stared at him, his long hair plastered in strands across his face.

"Of course if you brought money here to deposit for safekeeping, I'll gladly take it and write you a receipt for it," said the bank manager.

"Safekeeping . . ." Orez looked away, off up the street where only a building had been left standing here and there. "Your bank does not look that safe to me," he said.

Along the street townsmen hurried back and forth clearing pathways through the debris to their respective businesses. Mexican and Anglo townsmen alike stood in rubble waist-deep, drinking in the falling rain at an oak long bar left standing after the saloon had blown away around it. Two doves wearing rain slickers sat in chairs at a table that had somehow gone undisturbed.

The manager gave a shrug, used to defending his bank's security and reputation under any circumstance.

"Oh, you're referring to all *this*?" he said, gesturing a hand toward the fallen building. "This can happen to any bank, anytime. It's true we never saw this coming, but your money is otherwise as safe here as it is anywhere on the border frontier. These men are ready to fight and die if need be to ensure our depositors' holdings."

"I bet they are," said Orez. He stared back and forth at the riflemen slowly.

"So, about that deposit?" said Turnbolt. He tried

to straighten his wet hair a little and offered a wide banker's smile.

"Do I look like a depositor to you?" Orez asked. He pulled his wet hair off his face and hiked it back behind his ear. Water dripped from the tip of his nose.

One of the riflemen's faces turned pasty and pale.

"My God, it's *Orez*," he said in a hushed tone.

"Yes, it is," Orez said, "and we're taking all this money off your hands before it all gets washed away."

The other gunmen braced, shotguns in hand, rain falling, splattering steadily around them. The two men at the safe door stood frozen, holding bags of money, their rifles leaning against the side of the safe. The bank manager started to say something, but before he could, a gruff voice called out from the middle of the muddy street behind them.

"What cowardly son of a bitch's horse kicked my boy's dog?" said a large man who stepped forward throwing his rain slicker aside and rolling his sleeves up over his thick forearms.

Turning in his saddle to face the big red-bearded man, Hardin swung a long-barreled Colt from its holster, cocking it, and held it out arm's length. Water dripped from its barrel.

"That would be *my* horse," he said. "He is a kicker." The dripping gun hammer dropped with an orange-blue explosion. Hardin's gun hand bucked high as the red-bearded man took the shot in his right shoulder and spun in a muddy spray of blood. The man splashed down flat so fast that

Hardin's next shot only whistled through the air above him.

"All right," said Orez almost matter-of-factly, his rifle already swinging around one-handed in front of him. "Kill everybody."

"Wait! Don't *rob us*!" Lucas Turnbolt shouted. "We've just got hit by a twister, for God sakes!"

"That ain't the half of it," said Orez, dropping him in the mud with his first rifle shot.

Around the buckboard, the riflemen moved against the robbers, but they didn't move quick enough. As bullets whizzed back and forth, they fell one at a time beneath Orez's and Hardin's guns. Buckshot from one of the shotguns sliced across Rosa's coat sleeve. When she let out a short scream, Orez singled out the man and dropped him with a bullet through his heart.

On the muddy ground the wounded man with the red beard shouted along the street, "They're robbing the damn bank! Come running, all of yas!"

"Damn it, are you still alive?" said Hardin, turning again in his saddle and firing at the wounded man as the man scrambled away while shot after shot kicked up muddy water at his fleeing heels.

Orez swung down from his saddle and handed Rosa his reins. He walked through a looming cloud of gun smoke, toward the two men who still stood frozen, the money bags in their hands.

"I'll take those bags," he said. But when he saw both men glance toward their rifles as if preparing to make a move for them, he shot each of them in the chest, then walked up and took up the bags no sooner than they hit the ground. Turning, he held the bags up and showed them to Hardin. "This is a nice place to rob," he said.

Hardin looked up the street through the smoke and saw men running toward them with guns.

"Uh-oh, here comes the town," he said, already returning fire as bullets began zipping past them.

"Keep them busy," Orez said to Hardin. He nodded at Manning. "You'd better get Manning to help you if he expects to get a share of this money."

"Come on, Freeman, you heard him," said Hardin, reaching over and shaking Manning by his arm. "Get to shooting! We've got all kinds of money, ours for the taking."

Manning seemed to perk up a little. He drew his Colt from his holster, aimed it in the direction of the townsmen and fired. In spite of his dazed condition, a townsman fell, the bullet slicing through his chest.

"I'll . . . do my best," Manning said.

On the ground, Orez jerked his horse over, then Rosa's, and hitched their reins to the rear of the buckboard.

"Climb down," he said to Rosa. "We're riding the wagon out of here."

Rosa jumped down from her saddle and climbed into the wagon while gunfire exploded back and forth between the townsmen and the three outlaws. Orez ran to the front of the safe and picked up the two money bags the riflemen had been holding. Running back through a hail of bullets, he threw the bags up onto the buckboard, jumped up into the driver's seat and slapped the reins to the backs of the two team horses.

"Stop them, shoot them! They are robbing us

blind!" a Mexican townsman shouted, firing a long-barreled Colt as the wagon circled out onto the muddy street. The wagon fishtailed sideways in the mud, straightened and raced away through the falling rain, splashing back across the muddy run-off water out of town.

Behind the wagon, Hardin and Manning turned their horses and started to race away, but the red-bearded man appeared out of nowhere, snarling like a bear. Enraged, his shoulder covered with blood, he grabbed Hardin by his leg and tried to pull him from his saddle.

"Need a little help here, Freeman!" Hardin called out, trying to get a shot down at the man as bullets sliced through the rain and past his head.

Manning seemed to snap out of his dazed trance. He circled quickly to Hardin's side and swiped a hard blow across the man's head with his pistol barrel. The man went down to his knees but was still conscious, cursing and snarling, fresh red and pink blood running down the side of his head.

"Get out of here!" Hardin shouted above the roar of pistol and rifle fire. The two gunmen righted their frightened horses, turned them hastily as one and pounded across the shallow water out of town. Riding in the muddy spray left behind by the fleeing wagon, the two rode hard through the pouring rain until their horses fell in alongside Orez, who sat bowed forward in the driver's seat.

Orez looked up at them, then stared back through the rain at the flooded trail ahead.

A mile farther along the trail, he looked around at the two splashing beside him.

"We have too much money," he said. He nodded toward a nearby line of low hills and reined the team of horses off the trail toward them.

The two gunmen looked at each other. Hardin grinned widely in the pouring rain.

"We've got *too much money*, Freeman," he repeated to Manning. "Can you imagine that?"

"I'm feeling queer all over," Manning said flatly, seeming to give no regard to what Hardin had said. "I'm going to stop and lie down a spell." He started to veer his horse away. But Hardin grabbed the animal by its bridle.

"Lie down a spell? Like hell you are," Hardin said. "Buck up, Freeman. Don't you go dying on me now. We've got too much money for you to do something like that." He looked Manning up and down. "Jesus, come on," he said, seeing fresh blood trickle from his partner's ear. He took the reins from Manning's hand and led him on through the rain in the buckboard's muddy wake.

On a jutting cliff made up of broken boulders sunken into the low hillside, Wilson Orez stood atop the tallest rocks and watched the two horsemen catch up to him and the woman. Before climbing down, he looked back in the direction of Trade City, seeing only a short ways before a swirl of gray rain cloaked the town from sight. Killing the townsmen guarding the buckboard had awakened a need for blood within him. His hand gripped and ungripped the handle of his big knife.

He clenched his teeth and fought down the urge to lift the knife from its sheath and slash out with it—cut something, anything. Hash something deep and mercilessly, he thought. But he calmed himself and thought about the money lying in the wagon below. A faint smile came to his rain-streaked face. He had money, he had a woman—everything most white men wanted, he told himself with a sense of disgust.

He looked up at the low swollen sky and felt rain fall into his open eyes. It was evening now. Soon it would be night. He needed the moon, he told himself. He had not seen it since the storms had moved in across the desert hill country. His *Apachean* spirit was of the water and of the moon. Water had cleansed and readied him; to be complete he needed the moon to course through him.

His white blood was finally gone; he could feel its absence from the core of him. It had been drunk up by the desert, just as the elder White Mountain warriors had told him it someday would. When he had become a Red Sleeve, he was told his purpose and his way in this world. When the last of his white blood was gone and a slayer of monsters was upon his trail, he knew that only the moon would save him. He knew that the time and place for these mystical things would come upon him, and soon.

He spoke the white man's language as well as the white man; he lived the white man's life, as much of it as he could stand. Yet he was now and forever bound to the life and fate of a Red Sleeve. *So be it.*

As he looked up, he saw no place in the swollen sky for the moon to appear, even if it sought him, even it had come to reveal itself to him. But that was all right. It would come to him as it should, when the time was right. Throughout his life, he'd heard in his inner ear the clash and ring of steel against steel—the voice of consecrated battle—and he had never heard it more clearly than he heard it now.

*Yes.* He believed it must be.

He shut his eyes to the falling rain and stood strong, letting it pour down on him. After a moment he took a deep breath and let it out slowly. He turned and climbed down from the rock in the pouring rain, seeing the two gunmen pull their horses up beside the buckboard wagon.

As Orez stepped onto the muddy ground, he looked through the rain and saw Freeman Manning sway in his saddle, then turn his bowed head sideways and vomit thin red blood down his horse's withers.

"Jesus, Freeman!" said Hardin, jerking his horse a step away still holding Manning's horse's reins. Seeing the hard look on Orez's face, he tried to lighten the matter by laughing it off a little. "Have you been drinking Mexican wine all day?"

"What's wrong with him?" Orez asked Hardin, staring at Manning as he spoke.

"What's wrong with him?" said Hardin. "Well, let's see. He's been caught in a twister, rolled up and down a rock hill, sailed through the air, beaten like a parlor rug, bounced like some kind of damned—"

"I'm all right," Manning cut in, stopping Hardin. "I just lost my bearings there for a minute."

"Lost them, huh?" Orez said, stepping in closer. He looked up at Manning and paused, then asked, "Are you dying on us?"

"Hell no," Manning growled, struggling to keep another stomach full of blood from surging up. He raised the Colt he carried across his lap. "I've got some fight left if I need it."

"Cock that gun at me," said Orez, rain running down him.

"Stop it, Wilson," said Hardin. "He said he ain't dying. Leave him alone."

"Go on, cock it," Orez demanded of Manning. "If you can't kill me, you can't kill nobody else." He poised his gun hand near his holstered Colt. "Cock it and shoot me, or I'll put a bullet in your head."

"That's enough!" said Hardin. He poised his gun hand toward Orez, but Orez paid him no attention.

Manning looked at the iron strongboxes sitting on the buckboard and the bags of money lying against them. His face turned regretful; his Colt slumped.

"Of all damn times to run out my string," he said. "Hell yes, I'm dying. I'm busted inside my head, my belly, I don't know where all else. Like I said, I'm ruint."

Orez turned his face to Hardin, who let his hand fall away from his holstered Colt. A fresh lick of lightning flicked on and off on the rocky, drenched hillside.

"Damn this weather!" said Hardin, looking away from Manning and Orez. "Damn it to *everlasting hell!*"

At that very moment, a new clap of thunder pealed on the horizon like encroaching cannon fire.

# Chapter 15

In the noisy clattering of rainfall on rock, the Ranger rode the roan across the flooded valley lands, below the same hill line where he and the horse had taken shelter. The center of the valley ran knee deep with silt-water that bobbed and pummeled chunks of cactus and twisted broken limbs of ironwood, cottonwood and pine. Approaching a turn in the valley floor, he saw the brown current turn frothy and break around an uprooted oak that lay bobbing on rock and gravel, half of its root ball still clinging to the bank, but ready to break free at any moment.

Drawing closer to the turn, Sam guided the roan and led the other two horses wide around the fallen oak, wanting no part of the huge tree should the muddy bank suddenly turn it loose and up the current, sending it barreling at them.

"I don't know about you," he murmured to the roan. "I've had enough of this to last me awhile."

Without understanding him, the roan all the same chuffed and blew and lifted its head at the sound of his voice.

Sam gave the horse a watery pat on its wet withers. The other two horses sidled as close to him as they could get.

Around the turn he stopped and sat staring for a moment at the sight of a mud-covered man sitting on a stone, dipping his dirty socks up and down in the silty water. It took Sam a few seconds to recognize the man. When he did, he put the roan forward at the same steady walking pace.

"Bob Ailes? Is that you?" he called out above the noisy rain and the braided, running floodwater.

The railroad scout rose shakily to his feet and looked up at the sky as if the voice of God had singled him out. Then he turned woodenly and followed the sound around to the approaching Ranger and spread his muddy arms in greeting.

"Lord Almighty, Ranger Burrack," he called out in an unsteady voice, allowing his emotions to get a little out of check. "We must be all of humankind left on this miserable wasteland. Would you suppose?"

"I hope not," the Ranger said, riding closer. "These horses are talking back to me as it is."

"Yes, yes, they do indeed, Ranger," Ailes said, staring strangely at him. Sam could tell the man did not know clearly what had been said to him. It didn't matter.

"Where's Colson?" Sam asked, drawing closer, stopping the roan and letting the other two horses sidle up closer to him.

"Why, he's dead, of course," Ailes said. He gave Sam a look that suggested he should already have known as much.

"I'm sorry to hear it," the Ranger said.

"Yes, well—" Ailes said, busying himself, inspecting the dripping socks in his hands.

As he spoke he wrung water from his socks,

shook them out and stuck them down behind his belt. Sam saw the muddy neck of a whiskey bottle peeking through the ripped-open front of the railroad man's muddy shirt.

"It was terrible," Ailes said after a pause. "One second there he was, struggling with the reins to keep the wagon horses settled, and the next second I saw him go flying straight up as if he'd never come down."

"Where were you, Ailes?" Sam asked.

"I—I was only twenty or so yards away," he said. "I saw the funnel cloud coming. We both did. I was still gathering equipment to take to the wagon. Odell had run ahead to get the horses calmed, they were carrying on so." He swallowed a hard knot in his throat. His eyes welled a little.

"Go on," Sam encouraged him.

"I saw I wasn't going to make it to the wagon in time, so I fell flat, wrapped my arms around a small pine and hung on. I could see around the tree just enough . . . " He paused, drawing the muddy bottle from inside his shirt and pulling out the cork deftly. "Just enough to see what I told you, Odell fly straight up into the black funnel and disappear." He took a long drink, as if to wipe the picture from his mind.

Sam refused the bottle when Ailes held it up to him.

"A moment later I saw the wagon, horses and all go flying up behind him," he said with a helpless shrug. "What could I do?" He took another swig of rye whiskey. "It was a full ten minutes later, supplies from the wagon come sailing down around me. It was raining spikes and hammers." He gave a strange stiff grin. "I was struck several times, but I didn't let it bother me."

The Ranger lowered his head and shook it slowly.

"You see much use in searching for him?" he asked Ailes.

"To tell you the truth, no, I don't," Ailes said. He corked the bottle with finality and shoved it back inside his shirt. "If he's alive after that, you can bet the devil owns his soul."

*What a strange thing to say,* Sam thought, staring at him. It was clear the man was badly shaken. But was there something more than that wrong with him?

"What do you mean by that?" Sam asked.

Ailes considered it for a second, trying to think of the best way to express himself. Finally he appeared to give up.

"What I mean is, he would never again be the same Odell Colson I knew," he said. "Not after going through all that."

Sam nodded and looked back and forth. As they had spoken, the rain had built back up and slanted on a rising wind. The blackness that had seemed to dissipate earlier was now coming back, noticeably moving in around them.

"Pick a horse for yourself. Let's get up out of here," the Ranger said.

"Where to?" asked Ailes, stepping over closer to the two wet horses, his muddy socks hanging from his belt.

"Trade City's our best bet from here," Sam said, nodding in the direction of the town.

"Trade City is where I was headed," said Ailes. He looked around, confused. "But I thought it was that direction." He pointed back the way the Ranger had come. "I should know, I've been there enough the past few weeks."

"No, Ailes," the Ranger said. "Trust me, it's that way." He nodded again.

"That's the way I just came," Ailes said. "I heard gunfire earlier. Are you sure you want to go that way?"

*Gunfire?*

"Yes," Sam said. "I'm very sure." He saw Ailes seeming to stall beside the horses. "You need a hand up?" he asked, wanting to get under way.

"No, I'm all right, Ranger," Ailes said, turning away from him to the nearest horse. "But I have to say, I have felt better. That's a fact."

Seeing him from behind, the Ranger winced at the sight of a long steel spike, finger-round, sticking directly through the back of his head. It almost looked as if it had been there all his life.

The Ranger froze, but only for a second. Then he swung down from his saddle and stopped Ailes from trying to climb atop the horse. He saw black blood down the railroader's back in spite of the falling rain washing down on it. He looked at the point of the spike sticking out an inch from his ear.

"Are you sure you're feeling all right, Bob?" he said. "We can rest here awhile. You can sip some more whiskey."

"If you're worried about the spike in my head, Ranger," he said, "I already know about it." He turned to the Ranger and carefully touched the steel spike head sticking from atop his skull. "I was going to mention it, but I must've forgot."

"I understand," said the Ranger, catching on quickly, knowing he had to go along with the man. What else could he do? "Are you hurting?"

"No, believe it or not," Ailes said. "I feel numb up there, and like I'm on the verge of one terrible headache. But no pain . . . none yet anyway. I keep getting glimpses of things that I know ain't real. Mostly I feel like I'm not entirely here."

"Tell me what to do, Bob," he said bluntly. "Is riding that horse going to kill you?"

Ailes tried to draw the whiskey bottle from inside his shirt again. Sam reached in and did it for him.

"I know only one way to find out," Ailes replied calmly, taking the bottle after Sam pulled the cork and handed it to him. "If it does, Ranger," he added, "I'm telling you now, it was my choice." He stared at Sam as he raised the bottle to his lips. "Just remember, I was dead before you found me here."

It was afternoon when the workers in Trade City looked up from clearing and piling debris and saw the Ranger and Ailes, their horses moving at a walk across the runoff water and rising onto the street through a silvery gray mist. When they had first started toward town, Sam had taken off his wet hat and placed it carefully down on Ailes' wounded head. The rain had ceased since then, but the distant sky was still low, black and threatening.

Along one side of the muddy street lay a dismal line of bodies, storm victims, male and female, young and old, Anglo and Mexican alike. At the end of the line of dead, nearest to the fallen bank building, lay the riflemen Wilson Orez and his accomplices had slaughtered. Wet towels, blankets and sheets lay partially covering the bodies, plastered ghoulishly to their faces from the day's drenching rainfall.

"My, my," Ailes whispered. "There appears to be more of us dead than there are of you living."

The Ranger never liked that kind of talk, but he knew the man was not responsible.

In the street, a group of workers stepped out in front of them, causing them to slow to a halt. The big red-bearded man stepped in front of the others. His right arm rested in a bloody sling; his head bore a high welt. The red-haired boy appeared at his side. The spotted dog limped forward and barked at the roan, but made no effort to snap at the roan's hooves.

"Who the hell are you, mister?" the big man asked, still feeling surly from the day's earlier attack. "I know that one is Bob Ailes, a railroad scout."

Sam stared at the big man for a moment before deciding to answer.

"I'm Arizona Ranger Samuel Burrack," Sam replied finally.

"This is Mexico," the man said gruffly.

"I knew that," Sam said, still staring hard. "I'm tracking some gunmen across the border under an agreement with the Mexican government—"

"If you're looking for four no-good sons a' bitches, one of them a bitch herself," the man said, cutting in, "they was here all right, you betcha."

"You don't know it's the same ones, Audie," said a mud-streaked townsman standing near him.

"It was them, sure enough," said the big man, Audie Murtzer. "I'd bet money on it. They robbed our bank and killed our bank manager and some others." He gestured toward the line of bodies. "Not all of them lying there," he corrected. "Just the ones with bullet holes."

Sam looked again at the bodies, noting the pinkish red spots on some of the sheets. The rain had washed away much of the blood.

"It was a *rootin'-tootin'* good time!" the red-haired boy cut in with a half-toothless grin.

"Shut up, Little Audie," said the man. He backhanded the boy a hard thump on the side of his head. The boy staggered to keep from going down. The dog jumped away sidelong, as if afraid he'd be next. "All this little jackass thinks about is *acts of violence,*" the man said. "I can't seem to beat it out of him."

"How long ago?" Sam asked, stepping down from the roan and walking around to Ailes' horse. The red-haired boy stood rubbing the side of his head.

"A couple of hours or better," said Murtzer. "We heard some shooting for a while. Then it all stopped."

Sam very carefully helped Bob Ailes down from his saddle as he asked Audie Murtzer, "How many townsmen rode out after them?"

"Six," Murtzer replied, watching how careful the Ranger was with Bob Ailes. "I'd gone too, except for this shoulder. Plus, the other night some horse thief made off on my Morgan. Some of us wanted to wait for the *federales* to show up. I said *hell*, like as not the *federales* will turn tail, they hear it's Wilson Orez. He's cleaved enough of their kinfolks' hair to stuff a large mattress." He grinned. "Cowardly sons a' bitches."

Sam helped Bob Ailes around to the front of the horse. He noticed how much paler Ailes had turned. A purplish cast had circled and formed under his eyes.

"What's *ailing* Ailes?" Murtzer grinned at his little joke.

"He got injured in the twister," Sam said. "I was hoping to find a doctor here for him." As he spoke, he carefully removed the wet hat from Ailes' head. It seemed larger than earlier, bloated on the rear right side, the Ranger noted.

"Somebody get Doc Menendez," said Murtzer. "Doc's a beaner, but not half bad. He fixed my arm and—oh *my God!*" he said, seeing the spike in Ailes' skull as Ailes half turned, looking more dazed than earlier.

The townsfolk drew back with a gasp.

"Doc rode out with the posse, remember?" said a townsman. He managed to pull his eyes away from Ailes' head and looked at Sam. "He was finished with the dead and wounded here. He's one of the best shots in town. We just figured—"

Murtzer cut in, "If I was you, Ranger, I'd take Bob out to him. He'll be along the trail with the others—got his medicine, his bag and all with him. But it looks like poor Bob could be dead before Doc and the posse get back. Besides, the doctor's house is blown away. I don't know what he's going to do for a place, especially for anybody in this kind of shape."

"I see," Sam said. He looked at Ailes.

"I'm still riding okay," Ailes said.

Sam considered it for only a second.

"Can I get a towel, a larger hat and a slicker or coat of some kind?"

"What are you going to do?" Murtzer asked.

"I'm going to wrap his head and take him with me," the Ranger replied.

"All right. It's all coming right up, Ranger," said Murtzer. He looked at Sam's footwear and at Ailes' bare feet. He turned and called out to people who were scrambling through the debris to get to some crates they had filled with muddy clothes, boots, shoes and other apparel. "Get them some socks— some boots too. Somebody grain these horses."

"Obliged," the Ranger said.

While the townsmen got busy gathering food and clothing for them, the Ranger guided Ailes to a battered cot someone dragged from the debris left from the doctor's house and helped Ailes down onto it.

"Close your eyes for a few minutes," Sam said.

"I don't mind if I do, Ranger," Ailes said, lying down stiffly. "If I go to sleep and don't wake up, *obliged* for all your help."

Sam patted his shoulder and helped position him in a way that looked less painful for him. Sam stepped back as Audie Murtzer sidled up to the cot. Audie looked over at the head of the spike standing atop Ailes' skull and winced. A few feet away came the sound of the horses crunching grain two men had poured on a canvas cloth laid on the ground before the hungry animals.

"I swear I can't stand looking at this man for more than a quick glance," Murtzer said in a lowered voice.

Sam only nodded.

"He's going to die soon, don't you figure?" Murtzer continued.

"I figure," Sam said quietly. The horses crunched their grain and chuffed in appreciation.

"You can leave him here," said Murtzer. "We can't do no more than this for him." He gestured toward the cot where Ailes lay. "But at least we'll make him comfortable."

"Comfortable?" said the Ranger. He glanced around. "Things as they are, a man in this shape decides his own comfort. I expect he'd sooner die riding to the doctor than waiting for the doctor to come riding to him."

"There it is, then," said Murtzer. He stood in silence until a Mexican townswoman hurriedly brought them an armful of towels from the barbershop with a tall hat sitting atop them.

"*Gracias,*" said the Ranger.

"What are you going to do?" asked Murtzer, watching the Ranger take two of the towels and step over to Ailes' cot.

"I'm going to wrap his head and hope it helps some," Sam replied.

Murtzer winced again, looking down at the protruding spike.

"Saint Jude . . . ," Murtzer whispered under his breath. Then he said to Sam, "Is there anything I can do to help, without touching Bob here, that is?"

"He feels like whiskey helps him some," the Ranger said.

"Whiskey, coming up," said Murtzer, turning toward the open-air saloon.

"Here, let me do that," the Mexican woman said, seeing what the Ranger was attempting to do. She stepped in, took the towels back and stooped down with them beside Ailes' cot.

"*Gracias*," Sam said, stepping back, gratefully letting her take over.

# Chapter 16

The rain still held off as the Ranger and Ailes rode out of Trade City, Ailes with his head thickly wrapped and insulated, spike and all, by a thick layer of white barber towels. Over the thick towels, he wore a large frontier-style hat with a tall crown. The Ranger had sliced the hat open from the band halfway up the rear of the crown, widening it to better accommodate Ailes' terrible injury. Across the rump of Ailes' horse hung a set of saddlebags, bulging with bottles of rye whiskey.

The Ranger looked over at Ailes every few minutes, checking on him. Surprisingly, now that the railroad man's head, as well as the rest of him, was warm and dry, his face took on a better color, Sam noted, almost wanting to flinch each time Ailes took a slight rise and fall with his horse's hooves.

"It doesn't hurt, you know," Ailes said, as if reading the Ranger's thoughts. He had reminded him several times throughout the day. Turning stiffly, he looked at the Ranger with a slightly whiskey-lit expression. "I realize I'm dying, but I am honestly in no pain at all." He paused and seemed to think about it, then added, "I mean, nothing like you'd think I'd be."

"That's good to hear, Bob," the Ranger said. "When we catch up to Orez, find cover and stay down."

"Why?" Ailes said flatly. "He can't hurt me."

Sam nodded, considering the matter.

"If I had a gun, I might even be of assistance to you."

"Obliged, but I don't think so, Bob," said the Ranger. He was glad to see that the wounded man appeared to be feeling better, yet he knew it was only temporary. He didn't want to see him wielding a loaded gun.

They rode on quietly until they reached a place where the posse had run into Orez and his men.

"Wait here," the Ranger said to Ailes. Bob Ailes only shrugged and did as he was told, although he couldn't see why.

Following a thick, layered path of horse's hooves and boot prints trampling up around a large boulder, the Ranger stopped and smelled the lingering odor of burnt gunpowder. Proceeding forward with caution, he paused again and let out a breath at the sight in front of him.

There atop a short rock that someone had rolled into place against the larger boulder sat the sprawling body of a man Sam took to be one of Orez's accomplices, riddled with bullet holes.

"One down," Sam said quietly to himself.

Stepping forward, he saw the dead man had been holding a gun in either hand. Or rather, each had been tied there by torn strips of cloth. One hand had shed its binding and lay hanging over the side of the rock, the long strip of cloth hanging toward the ground, the gun lying on the ground beneath it, cocked and ready to fire. When Sam bent to pick up the strip of cloth from the dead, bloody hand, he looked closer at the face, the gaping mouth, the wide-open eyes. Recognizing the man from an old wanted poster, he unwrapped the strip of cloth from around his hand and stood up with it between his thumb and fingers.

"Freeman Arridicus Manning," he said, from memory. "Jasper City, Texas. Fast gun, hired gun, a known associate of Tom Quinton, Barclay Owens and Evan Hardin—murderers and thieves to the man."

*Tom Quinton?* Was that who the initials TQ on the big Remington he'd found earlier belonged to? Of course it was. . . . *Another one bites the dust,* he told himself, dismissing the matter, inspecting the strip of cloth between his fingers.

*From the woman's clothes?* he asked himself, noting the same color of cloth as the thread he had found twice along the trail. He had a hunch it was. She had found a way to leave a trace of herself behind. *Good thinking.* He leaned down and saw more loose thread in the mud beside the rock, one piece still part of a short strip she hadn't used to tie the guns into Freeman Manning's hands. She hadn't given up, Sam told himself. That was good.

His thoughts were cut short by the sound of a horse behind him. He spun toward it, his Winchester coming up fast, cocked at his side, pointed at Bob Ailes, who had stopped short. He led the two horses behind him, Sam having left one of their three horses in Trade City.

"Whoa, don't shoot me," Ailes said, his eyes lit and bloodshot from the rye he'd been drinking steadily. "Don't waste a bullet on this discounted hide."

"Bob . . ." Sam let out a breath. "You should have waited back there with the horses. You didn't need to be climbing that path."

"It doesn't seem to have bothered me any, Ranger." He looked around. "Although I wouldn't mind sitting and resting a spell without a horse under me."

"Yes, let's get you seated," Sam said. He stepped over and took the horses' reins from him.

"Mercy," Ailes said, looking over at the bloody body sprawled on the rock. "Things can always be worse, can't they?" He staggered slightly in place; the neck of the rye bottle stood up from the pocket of his newly acquired coat.

"Yes, they can," the Ranger said. He led Ailes by his arm over to another rock, this one lying by itself off to the side. There was a muddy boot print on it and the stub of a cigar on the ground beside it, where one of the posse men had sat smoking earlier.

Seating Ailes, the Ranger stepped back and looked down at him for a moment. Ailes swayed in place.

"Bob, I say we camp here for the night," the Ranger said. "We've got food. I'll build us a fire and cook us a meal. What do you say to that?"

"Yum," Ailes said with a slight whiskey slur.

Keeping an eye on him while Ailes weaved slightly on the rock with his huge bandaged head bowed, the Ranger took down the canvas bag of food the townsfolk of Trade City had packed for them. Without the benefit of dry wood for a fire, the Ranger opened two tins of beans and gave one to Ailes. They ate by raising the tins to their lips and drinking in a mouthful of beans. Ailes washed his beans down with sips of rye whiskey; Sam sipped tepid water from a canteen the townsfolk had given him.

When they had finished eating, the Ranger took off Ailes' hat while he sat slumped over on his side. Seeing no fresh bloodstains, Sam set the hat aside and stepped back quietly. He drew the horses in closer for the night and sat watching over Ailes until he was convinced he was asleep. When Ailes lay on the rock on his side with the whiskey bottle in hand, the Ranger relaxed in the pale light of a half moon showing through a break in the dark clouds and allowed himself to drift to sleep as well.

On the grainy silvery cusp of dawn, the Ranger awakened to the loud squall of a big cat somewhere on the hill above them. A moment later as he stood, rifle in hand, he heard the sound of padded paws moving swiftly over rock and wet brush across the hillside, traveling upward and farther away from him every passing second until the shadowy hillside once again turned silent. No sooner had the sound of the fleeing cat diminished into the distant hills than another sound took its place.

From the trail below, he could make out horses moving along, sloshing through mud and puddles of water. In a moment he listened as the horses stopped. As he heard what sounded like two horses split away from the others, he stepped over to Ailes and shook his shoulder gently.

"Bob, wake up," he whispered.

He waited for a second and shook him again when he saw he didn't stir.

"Bob?" he whispered, looking closer at Ailes' face in the pale grainy light. "Are you all right? Bob?" He shook him a third time as he heard the horses move toward the thin path leading up toward them. He saw the bottle of rye slip from Ailes' hand and land softly on the ground.

Detecting no sign of life, he stooped and looked at Ailes' shadowed face.

"Adios, Bob Ailes," he whispered softly. But as he stood up and let out a sigh, Ailes raised his bandaged head an inch and looked up at him.

"Are you leaving me, Ranger?" he asked.

The Ranger quickly placed his hand over Ailes' mouth, catching a strong smell of rye.

"Quiet, Bob," he whispered. "Somebody's coming up the path."

Ailes nodded and remained silent. He stood when the Ranger removed his hand from his mouth. The two left their horses standing but walked quietly over and took cover out of sight around the edge of a sunken boulder.

In the darker shadow of the boulder, they waited as the footsteps of man and horses rose along the path and started to walk past them. As one man leading two horses froze at the sight of the two horses staring at him in the grainy darkness, the Ranger stepped out beside him and stuck the Winchester against his side.

"Make a sound, I'll drop you where you stand," the Ranger whispered near his ear. "Are you with the posse?"

"Uh-huh," the man said quietly, nodding.

"What's the name of the doctor riding with you?" Sam asked, testing him.

"That's—that's Dr. Menendez," the voice whispered. "They sent me to gather the body we left here—"

"I'm Ranger Samuel Burrack, from Arizona Territory," Sam said, cutting him off. "Tell them I'm here, introduce us, real easy-like."

"Bradford," the man called out.

"Yeah, Holden, what?" a voice called up from the trail below.

"There's a Ranger here by the name of Burrack. He's got a rifle against my side."

A tense silence fell around the hillside and the trail.

"Oh? Why is that, Holden?" the voice said, sounding suspicious.

Sam called out, "Because I didn't want everybody to start shooting first and feeling bad about it later."

"Makes sense," said the voice. "What do you want from us, Ranger?"

"The folks at Trade City told me Dr. Menendez is riding with you. I've got a man here who was hurt in the twister. He needs a doctor real bad."

Another tense silence passed. Finally the same voice called out again, "We're coming up. You'd better be an Arizona Ranger and there'd better be a man there needing the doctor's help."

"I've got a spike stuck in my head," Ailes called out in a strange, half-drunken voice.

"You've got what?" said the voice below.

"Let it go, Bob," said the Ranger. "They won't believe it until they see it." Then on Ailes' behalf,

Sam called out, "Never mind, come up and see for yourself."

Even as the sound of horses moved onto the path, the voice called out, "Holden, what's it look like up there?"

Sam gave the man a nod, letting him know it was all right to answer.

"I can't say how bad he's hurt, Bradford," the man said. "But his head is bandaged up bigger than any pumpkin I ever saw."

Sam listened as the men stepped down from their horses. A lantern light came on and Sam watched as it lit the path and the men led their horses up the last few yards and stopped again. In a moment the posse leader, Gans Bradford, stepped into sight. Light from the lantern he carried filled the small clearing around the boulder and shone harsh and gruesome on the body of Freeman Manning.

"All right, let's see what we've got," the posse leader said, looking the Ranger up and down, then seeing Phil Holden standing stiffly with a rifle aimed loosely at him. Looking at Ailes, he asked, "Don't I know you?"

"I've been in Trade City many times," Ailes said.

"Yep, I've seen you. You're one of the scouts for the new rail spur," Bradford said.

"That's me," said Ailes.

The posse leader relaxed a little.

"It's okay, Doc," he said. "I know this one from town. It's all right to take a look at him."

Sam relaxed too. He lowered his rifle as a middle-aged Mexican stepped forward, carrying a medical bag. He looked around, holstered his revolver and examined the bandages on Ailes' head.

"You are in no pain, I take it?" the doctor asked him in perfect English.

Ailes looked taken aback at the doctor's voice and appearance.

"None to speak of," he replied. Then he said, "You look Mexican, but you don't sound like it."

Menendez only smiled thinly in reply. The posse leader stood watching as the doctor seated Ailes back on his rock, unwrapped the towels from his head and turned him around into the lantern light. Two other posse men stepped into sight leading their horses. One wore a bandage much like Ailes', only not as thick. A red circle of blood shone through on the side of his head.

"As you can see, Ranger," Bradford said, "we've got some wounded of our own—" His words stopped short. "Good Lord God in heaven!" he said, seeing the spike sticking out from the top and bottom of Ailes' skull. The rounded spike head glinted in the lantern light an inch above the railroad man's blood-matted hair. The two newly arrived posse men almost reeled at the sight. Dr. Menendez looked curious and attentive, yet otherwise unimpressed. The posse men tightened their breath, seeing the doctor's hand reach and touch the spike on both ends and examine Ailes' head all around the wound.

"What say you, Mexican doctor?" Ailes asked in a cynical whiskey-blurred tone. "Can you yank this thing right out? Should I expect to pull right through this?"

The doctor was having no part of his wry, flip manner.

"No, you shouldn't expect to," he said. "But you can live. You don't have to die from it."

Sam looked doubtful. So did the posse men.

"What we've got to do is get you back to town. I'm without facility at this time, but we'll get settled into a tent where I can observe this wound for a day or two, decide whether I need to remove it or let it stay."

"Let it stay?" said Ailes.

"Yes," the Mexican doctor said in perfect English. "If I start to remove it and the blood and fluid begin to disclose too greatly, it will be best to leave it in place for the time being and continue observation."

"I'll never have to pay for another drink as long as it's stuck there," Ailes said.

"The drinking stops now," the doctor said firmly. "I'm going to wrap this back up and we're going to get under way to Trade City immediately."

"My life is in your hands, Doctor," Ailes said with a shrug.

The doctor stepped back from Ailes and left him staring away from the gathered posse men. He motioned the Ranger to his side and spoke to him under his breath.

"Were you with this man when it happened, Ranger?" he asked.

"No, Doctor, I found him washing his socks in some floodwater not long after the twister came through."

"Has he acted the same since you've been with him?" he asked.

"Pretty much," Sam said. "At first he was confused, but he soon got over it." He paused, then asked, "Did you mean it, that he might live?" he asked.

"I have Civil War medical journals showing accounts of others having lived through similar injuries," the doctor said. "He's up and around. There appears to be no brain damage at this time. We'll have to get him to Trade City and wait and see. But yes, he may very well live."

"I'm turning him over to you, Doctor," Sam said. "I'm in pursuit of Wilson Orez, same as you are." He gestured a nod toward the body of Freeman Manning, then at the wounded posse man. "I see your paths have crossed."

"Yes, and to dramatic consequence," the doctor said. "We stopped here to pick this body up on our way home."

Gans Bradford stepped over, joining them.

"We have two wounded of our own, and a prisoner to take back with us," he said.

"A prisoner?" The Ranger looked surprised.

"Yep," said Bradford. "He claims he wasn't with them, but I'm not convinced."

"Where is he?" Sam asked. "I'd like to see him."

"Right around the boulder there," Bradford said. "With one of my men's shotguns staring him in the face." Without another word on the matter, he called out around the boulder, "Doody, bring our so-called *detective* around here for the Ranger to look at."

"Detective?" Sam said.

"That's what he claimed," said Bradford. He fished a small badge form his vest pocket and held it out to the Ranger. "Found this on him. Probably robbed it off a railroad detective somewhere."

Sam looked at the badge for only a second, then looked up as a powerful-looking horse stepped into sight, a handcuffed man sitting slumped bare-back on the animal. A posse man with his arm in a sling rode right behind him, shotgun raised one-handed and pointed at him.

"He could pass for Mary Shelley's Frankenstein monster, if you ask me," Bradford said.

Sam stared closely as the man lifted his head, revealing his face beneath a mud-streaked bowler hat. Sam saw the many stitches lining the man's bat-tered face, recognizing them to be his own handi-work.

"The drummer, Tunis Weir," Sam said in sur-prise.

"A drummer?" said Bradford. "We found no musical instruments of any sort—"

"A *hardware drummer*," said the Ranger, cutting him off. "I'm the one who sewed his head up. We were on a stagecoach together. That's one of the coach horses he's riding."

"Told us his name is Foster Tillis," Bradford said. "Detective for the Pinkertons assigned to rail-road security."

He looked to Sam as if for confirmation; Sam offered none. Instead he said, "Let me have him. I'd like to question him. If he's wrong, I'll see to it he cools his heels in a Mexican prison."

"We were wanting to hang him in Trade City," Bradford said. "But the Mexican government here frowns on some of our American customs. We didn't see him with Orez when they robbed our bank—our *buckboard* bank, that is." He sighed. "I'll give him to you if you want him. Question him, then let him slip and fall off a cliff, far as we care.

If there happens to be rope around his neck, that's good too."

"Obliged," Sam said, staring over at Tunis Weir, aka Foster Tillis.

The battered-faced man sat slumped atop the big coach horse and looked away from him.

# PART 3

# Chapter 17

When the doctor had finished rewrapping Ailes' head, and Ailes sat easily in his saddle, the posse finished strapping Freeman Manning's body across the posse's spare horse.

"Keep a close eye on that one," Bradford warned the Ranger, eyeing the battered face of the prisoner with suspicion. The prisoner sat slumped, still cuffed, on the same rock Ailes had sat on earlier.

"I will," Sam assured him. Looking at Ailes, he said, "Best of luck to you, Bob. I'll be checking on you on my trip back through."

"Best to you too, Ranger. I'm obliged for all you've done for me," Ailes replied, Dr. Menendez holding the reins to the injured railroader's horse, leading it forward behind him.

The Ranger stood watching as Ailes gave him a short wave of thanks and good-bye over his shoulder. Then the contingent rode out of sight down the path to the muddy trail. In the east, a low curtain of black clouds gave way sparingly to a streaked and red sunlight.

"I'm glad that's over with," said the man with the battered, sewn-up face, also known as Tunis

Weir. He stood and held his wrists out toward the Ranger. "I expect you'll be taking these off me now?"

Sam only looked him up and down, then looked away, back toward where the riders had descended the narrow path.

"How is your face healing up?" he asked.

"Very well," he said. "Even though the Mexican doctor said he would have done a much better job. Said whoever did the sewing should not be allowed near a needle and thread."

"Well," said the Ranger, "he wasn't there. I was."

The man added quickly, "I don't mean that to sound like—"

"What's your *real* name, mister?" the Ranger said quietly, not giving him a chance to finish.

"All right." He let out a breath, as if giving in. "For the sake of simplicity, it's Tillis. Foster Tillis, just like I told Gans Bradford."

"For the *sake of simplicity*," the Ranger said, "I'll call you Tillis, then, until I find out your real name." He turned facing the man and held out the badge Bradford had given him. "Tell me all about this," he said.

"I really am a Pinkerton detective, assigned to the Southwestern Railways," he said. "Had we met under better circumstances, I would have told you so the night you sewed me up." As he spoke, his fingertips touched his stitched face carefully. "Obliged, by the way. I meant nothing a while ago. I know I was in bad shape that night. Hadn't been for you and that dove, Jenny . . . something or other." He taxed his memory, then gave up and shrugged. "Anyway, I likely wouldn't have made it."

Sam listened and observed.

"Jenny Lynn was her name," Sam said, refreshing his memory. "What happened to her anyway?" he asked.

"She's dead, Ranger," Tillis said, shaking his head in regret. "After all she did for me, I had to watch helplessly as the floodwater swept her away."

"That's too bad," the Ranger said quietly.

"Yes," said Tillis. "She was a dove, but she was a truly giving, caring person. I only regret not getting to know her better."

"I understand," said the Ranger. He noted that Tillis gave a guarded look at the two horses, the big coach horse as well as the roan.

"Suppose you take these cuffs off me, Ranger?" he said. "My wrists are getting sore from them."

Sam ignored his request and changed the subject.

"How well do you know Wilson Orez?" he asked.

"As a detective, I know him better than anyone else who carries a badge," Tillis said. "I know his habits, his methods, where he likes to hide out, his tricks for throwing off posses—"

"No," said Sam, cutting him off. "I mean how well acquainted are the two of you? How well do you know him personally?"

"Personally? Why, not at all," said Tillis, looking taken aback at the question. "As for us being *acquaintances . . . huh-uh.*" He shook his head. "I should take offense at you suggesting such a thing."

"Why do you suppose he beat you so bad?" Sam asked.

"When I catch up to him, I'll be sure and ask him, Ranger," said Tillis. "Right before I kill him."

Sam stared at him for a moment, looking him up and down.

"See," he said, "I figured it was so when the stagecoach men showed up looking for their late stage, they'd have to take you back for treatment instead of going after him."

"Well, then, there you have it," Tillis said. He looked a little relieved.

"Except," the Ranger said, "why not just put a bullet through your foot, or your shoulder? It would serve the same purpose."

"Beats me," said Tillis. "I guess he just wanted to beat the living hell out of somebody and there I was."

"Seems personal to me," Sam said. Again he looked the man up and down. He wasn't going to mention that Dawson, the shotgun driver, had told him he saw Tillis walk right up and start talking to Orez; then Orez began beating him. Sam couldn't make that right in his mind. But he wasn't going to push the matter any further right now.

"Well, it wasn't," said Tillis. "And who knows why a man like Orez does what he does, in any case? Maybe to him it *is* something personal. Something you and I would never understand."

"Maybe," Sam said, letting it go.

Tillis raised his cuffed hands for the third time.

"I know you're hearing me ask, Ranger," he said. "Are you going to take these cuffs off me or not?"

"No, I think not," the Ranger said. "I think I'll let you wear them awhile."

"But I'm not your prisoner," said Tillis. "Am I?"

"Not yet," Sam said, "but I'm considering it."

He turned and walked over to where the townsmen had left a fire striker and a small travel lantern with a full tank of fuel oil. One of them had left a small pile of dry kindling he'd taken from his saddlebags. As he looked the items over, a small cloth bag of coffee beans caught the Ranger's attention. He picked it up and squeezed it a little, then laid it back down.

"For God's sake, I'm a servant of the law, the same as you! We're fellow lawmen," Tillis said, walking over to him. He held up his cuffed wrists. "Why are you doing this?"

"Because so far, I don't believe one word you've told me is the truth, including your name," the Ranger said. "Until I start to believe you, I'll feel better seeing your hands cuffed." He sniffed the bag of coffee beans. "It's for your own good too," he said. "If those cuffs came off, there's not a doubt in my mind you'd make a run for the horses." His look turned cold and hard. "I'd feel bad for a week if I had to kill a *fellow lawman.*"

"You're mistaken, Ranger," said Tillis. "It didn't enter my mind that I might try to make a run for the horses."

The Ranger ignored him as he gathered the items the posse had left for them and stored them in his saddlebags. As he prepared for the trail, he looked up at the breaking sunlit sky above them, yet off in the direction the storms had been coming from he noted the same low, swollen darkness on the horizon.

"You have no legal reason to keep me handcuffed or held here against my will, Ranger," Tillis said.

"On the U.S. side of the border, that would be true," Sam said. "But this is Mexico. I think the rule is, don't get yourself cuffed to begin with."

Tillis shook his battered head.

"I had hoped you'd be a man who listens to reason," he said.

"I will. As soon as I hear some from you," Sam said. "Meanwhile, get that coach horse between your knees. I want to get some ground covered today before these storms jump down our shirts." He turned to the roan, gathered its reins and waited until Tillis climbed atop the bareback coach horse. Then he swung up into his saddle and motioned Tillis ahead of him onto the path leading down to the main trail.

When they stepped down from their horses at noon, they sat on a low bundle of rocks alongside the trail. The Ranger looked back, studying the oncoming dark sky that seemed to have followed them all morning.

Tillis looked up along a hillside to their right where large, land-stuck boulders loomed above broken stone ledges, shading piles of rocks that would be considered large by any other comparison.

Sam passed an open canteen of tepid water to Tillis, who took it gratefully and sipped from it, then wiped a hand over his mouth. As he held the canteen in his cuffed hands, he swirled its contents in contemplation for a moment.

"You know, Ranger," he said quietly. "It makes no sense, us being at odds with each other."

The Ranger continued to study the far sky and listen.

"You want Wilson Orez, and I want him too. We should be looking for ways to work together on this, make sure it gets done. The Southwestern Railroad has a bounty on his head. So will this stage company he robbed. I know you don't work bounty, but whatever I get, I'm willing to split with you."

"And how much would that be?" Sam asked.

Tillis smiled to himself, thinking he'd struck a nerve.

"Well, it would be half of whatever I get," he said.

"I didn't know Allan Pinkerton's men worked for bounty," the Ranger said.

"Public knowledge says I don't," said Tillis. "But the agency always gets a large portion, sometimes *all* of the bounty on an outlaw's head. Being the agent who brought Wilson Orez to justice, *dead or alive*, I would receive a generous bonus out of that reward money."

"Really, now?" the Ranger said, sounding interested.

"Absolutely," said Tillis, scooting over a little closer, handing the canteen back to him. "And half of that nice fat bonus will be yours."

Sam appeared to consider it.

"Let's break that down," he said. "We take Orez, *dead or alive*. Allan Pinkerton gets a bounty fee. He shares part of it with you, and a part of what he gives you comes to me?"

"There it is," said Tillis. "What could be sweeter?"

"This could be sweeter," the Ranger said. "I deliver you to the *federales* in Picate, tell them to hold you there and question you until I come back for you. But instead of coming back for you, I go take down Orez on my own, collect all of the bounty money for myself and go on about my business." He stared at Tillis. "Sooner or later, when they decide I'm not coming back for you, they might turn you loose. By then you'll be tripping over your own beard."

Tillis sat staring at him.

The Ranger shook his head and capped his canteen.

"If that's what it took all morning for you to come up with, I'm disappointed," he said. He stood up and gestured toward the horses.

"All right," Tillis said, standing, giving a shrug. "But this is a mistake, us not working together. I know where Orez is headed. How do you even know you're headed in the right direction?"

"I know," the Ranger said confidently.

"Yeah? How?" said Tillis. "What makes you so sure you're headed where he's going?"

"Because you haven't stopped me," the Ranger said, gathering his horse's reins.

Tillis stood slumped in defeat.

"Let's go," the Ranger said. "You've got all afternoon to come up with something worth listening to. If not, we'll be headed through Picate come morning. I'll show you around your new home."

They mounted and rode on, the Ranger noticing Tillis scanning the rocky hillsides every few minutes. Ready to cut the horse away and make a run for the rocks? Sam asked himself. No, he didn't think so. Tillis, or whatever his name might be, wasn't the kind to cut and run with handcuffs on. This man was smarter than that. He had more up his sleeve than a break-and-run, Sam decided.

The Ranger had something up his sleeve too. Tillis had no idea that Dawson had told him what he'd seen before the pistol whipping took place. Sam couldn't picture the man walking up and talking with Orez. Talk about what? Only one thing that he could think of—money.

But that was all right too, he decided. If this was a detective gone wrong, it wouldn't be the first time, and it wouldn't mean he couldn't work with the man. But before that happened, the Ranger was going to have to hear the truth come out of his mouth. *The truth, the whole truth and nothing but the truth . . .* if Tillis believed there still was such a thing.

Behind them, as they rode along throughout the day, the dark sky continued to advance until, by late in the afternoon when they stopped for the night, the grumble of thunder and the flash of lightning had returned, preceded by a fine wind-blown rain. "Up there," the Ranger said, nodding at a flat undercut ledge supporting the receding hillside above it. "The angle this wind is blowing, we might even stay dry for the night."

"I sure hope you're talking about a warm fire and some hot coffee," Tillis said over his shoulder.

"I am," the Ranger said. He looked at Tillis as they turned their mounts onto the rocky hillside.

They let the horses find their footing and climb toward the ledge, both animals appearing to know instinctively where shelter lay waiting for them out of the rain.

"Did we get lucky or did you know this place was here?" Tillis asked over his shoulder as they managed to ride their horses all the way up and under the overhang. Behind them the wind grew stronger, the lightning brighter in the failing evening light as the two stepped down from the horses and led the animals farther away from the edge.

"We got lucky, I suppose," Sam replied. He wasn't going to reveal anything about himself or his trail-craft by telling Tillis he had spotted the overhang an hour earlier, searching it out for shelter when it was little more than a black spot on the hillside.

"Sometimes luck overrules knowledge," Tillis said. He stood looking at his cuffed wrists while the Ranger took out the lantern and the dry kindling the townsmen had left with them. The Ranger nodded toward a blackened circle on the dusty stone floor where others had made camp under the overhang. Beyond it lay some limbs and brush.

"Get us some wood while I strike up this kindling," Sam said. He watched Tillis walk over, gather the limbs and return with them. He laid the wood down and stepped back and looked at his wrists again.

"I don't want to sound like a worrier," he said. "But I hope Gans Bradford did give you the keys to these cuffs. I didn't see him do it."

"He did," Sam said, listening closely and offering no more on the matter than what he'd been asked.

"Good," said Tillis. He paused for a moment, then said, "And I suppose you have that key in a safe place, of course?"

"Of course," the Ranger said flatly, listening, weighing Tillis' possible reasons for asking such questions.

"Okay, I can see you don't want to talk about it," Tillis said. "So I'm not going to ask you *where*, because

I know you'll take it the wrong way. But suppose, *through no fault of mine*, something happened to you. Things being as they are, look at the fix I'd be in."

"If I were you, I'd do my best to make sure nothing *does* happen to me, things being as they are," the Ranger said, giving him a look.

# Chapter 18

The Ranger had laid the blanket he'd gotten in Trade City just outside the small circle of firelight, into the darkness farther back in the overhang. On the other side of the fire, Foster Tillis had done the same thing, a common caution among lawmen, Sam noted to himself. But after an hour, still awake, he waited and listened until he heard snoring from Tillis' side of the fire. Then he left his blanket folded against his saddle, crawled away—in case Tillis was feigning sleep—and took up a position standing back along the inner stone wall.

Before another hour had passed, he heard the roan grumbling and grousing under its breath. Beside the roan, the coach horse stood still and quiet without a care in the world as a silhouette stepped silently into sight against the gray night. The Ranger watched coolly as a hand reached out and tried to settle the roan. But the roan would have none of it, and the silhouette moved away, circled wide around the fire toward his blanket on the stone floor.

Sam watched and eased forward from the shadows as a hand holding a gun rose, the black silhouette moving closer toward his saddle and blanket.

But all at once the silhouette froze, seeing the empty blanket outside the circle of firelight.

"Uh-oh," the voice said quietly, seeing the mistake. But it was too late.

Sam sprang forward, threw his arm around the silhouette's neck from behind, stuck his Colt against the side of the person's head and held tight.

"Drop the gun or go down with it," he said.

The seriousness of his voice left no room for question. The big gun fell to the stone floor with a loud clank.

"Don't shoot, Ranger! It's me, Jenny Lynn!" the silhouette said fast, her voice shaking. "The gun is dropped, see?"

Sam, hearing Tillis thrash and rise quickly to his feet, swung the woman around to face Tillis.

"Here she is, Tillis," Sam said, making it up as he went. "Just like you told me she would be."

"Foster, you bastard," Jenny Lynn shouted. "You told him I was coming?"

Tillis slumped and shook his head.

"Jesus, no, Jenny Lynn! I didn't tell him, but you just did," he said, sounding disappointed in her. "He was lying, reaching for anything he could."

"He didn't tell you I was coming for him, Ranger?" Jenny Lynn said, sounding confused.

"Not in so many words, ma'am," said the Ranger. "But he told me." He lowered the gun from her head and uncocked it. "He's been telling me all day somebody's coming for him. I just didn't realize it was you."

He turned her loose after running his hand up and down her rain slicker for any other gun. As she stepped away with her hands raised, Sam stooped and picked up the bone-handled Colt he'd last seen in the satchel along the edge of floodwater.

"Well, well, look who's here," he said, looking at the Colt, turning it in his hand.

"I don't want you to get the wrong idea here, Ranger," said Tillis, moving quick, trying to salvage whatever he could from the failed attempt at freeing him. "She wasn't going to shoot you. Were you, Jenny?"

"No, I wasn't," the woman said straight-faced.

The Ranger just watched and listened, hefting the bone-handled Colt in his hand.

"The gun is nothing more than an inducement—a stage prop if you will," she said. "What I was getting ready to do was awaken you, threaten you with the gun and make you take the cuffs off him. But I wouldn't have shot you, I promise."

"That's comforting to know," said the Ranger.

"Ranger, I know there's no way for me to prove it now," the woman said. "But I so hope you'll take my word for it."

"What's your play in all this?" the Ranger asked.

"Well—" she said, fishing for a place to start explaining herself. "I'm not a dove, as I was pretending to be." She gave Tillis a glance, then looked back at the Ranger. "I'm what Mr. Pinkerton calls a lady operative. We sort of fill in where—"

"How'd you get here?" Sam asked before she finished.

"I arrived by horse, Ranger," she said, looking at him as if he should already know that answer.

"A buckskin horse?" he asked, sounding confident in what he said.

She looked trapped, worried.

"Well . . . yes, in fact it is," she said.

"You stole it from Trade City right before the twister hit there," the Ranger said.

"Actually, she did not," said Tillis. "I acquired the horse."

"Stole it," the Ranger corrected.

"*Acquired*," Tillis insisted. "But have it your way." He dismissed his actions with a shrug. "What else could I do? We're in pursuit of a robber—a killer, in fact. We had to have a horse. We had no money to purchase one. I would have returned it afterward, or given the owner a purchase voucher on behalf of—"

"So you're horse thieves," Sam said bluntly, getting tired of hearing him justify what he'd done.

"I wouldn't say we're horse thieves, per se," said Tillis.

"But the man in Trade City whose horse you stole would say you are," the Ranger replied.

"Please, Ranger, let's not split hairs over this," said Tillis.

"I can take the two of you there so you can settle whether or not you're horse thieves, *per se*," the Ranger said. "Mexico doesn't hang horse thieves. Instead they horsewhip you and stick you in prison for a few years, let you think about what you did, decide how you might have done it different."

The two looked at each other. Tillis took a breath and tried to release the tension in the air.

"My goodness, I ask you," he said, "how did things ever get so messed up? Where did we go so far apart on things?"

"I can tell you." Sam looked at them, not about to let them off the hook. "It all started when you posed yourselves to me as a hardware drummer and a saloon dove instead of being honest."

"All right," said Tillis. "I admit it was a mistake, not being honest with a fellow lawman. But we had spent so long, worked so hard. I had gotten so close to Orez, I couldn't risk letting anyone know who we are."

"How close were you, considering he nearly beat you to death?" Sam asked.

"Something went wrong, Ranger," Tillis said. "Things that wouldn't concern you."

"Good enough," the Ranger said with finality on the matter. "Come morning I'll hand the two of you to the *federales* at Picate, and I'll pick up Orez's trail and track him down."

"You'll never find him," Jenny Lynn put in quickly. "We know where he's going. You don't. You need to keep us with you."

The Ranger shook his head. "I don't usually partner with people who come at me with guns in the middle of the night, then start seeing who can lie the quickest when I get the drop on them."

"But, Ranger, we're not lying to you now," Tillis said. "We've told you who we are, what we're doing here!"

"You haven't told me everything, Tillis," the Ranger said.

"We have told you everything!" said Tillis. "I swear we have."

"Be careful what you swear to," the Ranger cautioned him. "If you swear you've told me everything, how are you going to convince me when you decide to add some things to it?"

---

In the night, the Ranger sat in the shadow of the over-hang watching Foster Tillis' and Jenny Lynn's every move without them seeing whether or not his eyes were open. He'd purposely left the two seated beside the fire talking quietly, sorting things out between themselves. The Ranger had escorted them both to where she had left Audie Murtzer's stolen buckskin Morgan hitched along the trail. Now the Morgan stood comfortably beside the roan and the coach horse that Tillis rode.

With his ear tuned to the roan, the Ranger managed to doze on and off, knowing that any attempt they made toward taking the horses and riding off in the night, the cross-natured roan would let him know right away. Besides, he reasoned to himself, Tillis wasn't going anywhere without first getting rid of the handcuffs.

Near dawn when the Ranger straightened and noted that the whispering conversation between the two had ceased, he stood up and walked to the fire.

"Time to go," he said.

The two went about preparing their horses for the trail. Taking their silence to mean they had decided to leave the situation as it stood and say nothing more on the matter, the Ranger saddled the roan, gathered his belongings and stood waiting until the two led their horses onto the path down the side of the rocky hill.

Once mounted on the trail, they rode toward the hill town until the Ranger spotted the overturned buckboard lying off the trail down the steep hillside to their right. Strewn along the rocky slope, the iron strongboxes lay empty, their tops flung open. No sooner had the Ranger seen the wagon and the iron boxes than Tillis and the woman saw them too. They reined their horses up in front of the Ranger and stared down with solemn expressions.

"It looks like Wilson Orez decided to lighten the load," the Ranger said. "He must've been getting ready to climb up into the Twisted Hills and disappear up into the Blood Mountains."

Tillis and the woman looked at each other. After a moment, Tillis turned to the Ranger.

"It's foolish, the three us not working together to get Orez, Ranger Burrack," he said, his stitched and puffy face appearing to be healing slightly.

"I agree," the Ranger said, crossing his wrists on his saddle horn. "From everything I've seen of Orez, he'd be hard enough even for three of us." The Ranger saw Tillis and Jenny Lynn give each other a guarded glance. He saw Jenny Lynn shake her head ever so slightly.

*All right,* Sam told himself. He could wait.

He turned the roan back to the trail and gestured them forward in front of him. They rode on until, over an hour later, they stopped at a trail that turned off to the right and snaked across a flat stretch of desert floor to a long row of foothills leading up into a rugged mountain range. Behind them, the familiar black cloud had begun creeping forward at a quicker pace than it had traveled the night before. Pale lightning flicked at the far end of the earth.

"Here's the trail to Picate," the Ranger said. As he spoke, in the near distance the three of them saw a column of uniformed Mexican soldiers riding in their direction. "If I'm lucky, maybe this patrol will take you off my hands. I can get back under way. Either way, you'll both be in Picate before evening. Odds are you'll both be in a cell waiting for beans and goat meat before nightfall." He turned the roan toward the trail and gestured the two ahead of him. "They can send for Audie Murtzer in Trade City and have him come claim his stolen horse."

Without a word, Jenny Lynn gave Sam a defiant look and started to turn her horse. But Tillis looked at the cuffs on his wrists and slumped on his horse's back.

"Hold it, Jenny," he said. "I didn't come this far to end up in a Mexican prison for horse theft."

"You've told him all we can tell him," Jenny Lynn said.

"We both know that's not true," said Tillis. He turned to the Ranger. "All right, Ranger, you want the truth, here it is."

As Tillis spoke, the woman looked away, toward the storm closing in from the distant horizon.

"We both *really* are detectives with the Pinkerton Detective Agency," Tillis said. "We both started searching for Wilson Orez over a year ago—a year and seven months to be exact." He gave Jenny Lynn a glance. She only stared away more intently.

"I was working under cover," Tillis said, "posing as a hardware drummer whose scheme was to sell stolen army guns and snake-head whiskey to the Indians. I managed to get closer to Wilson Orez than any lawman so far," he said. "So close that he began paying me big money for information I could get on valuable rail and stage shipping coming across the border under the new trade agreement."

Sam quietly watched him and listened, feeling as though the words out of Tillis' mouth this time would be the truth, the whole truth and nothing but the truth.

"At first even taking money from him and setting up the jobs seemed like a surefire way for me to nail him any time I felt like it. Meanwhile I was hanging on to the money he gave me, telling myself, I should say *convincing* myself, that when the time came I would take him down, turn the money over to my superiors. My intentions were honorable. At first, in any case."

The woman turned in her saddle, looked at him, then looked away.

"What he means is, until he started trusting me," she said.

"I never said that, Jenny Lynn, and I wasn't going to," said Tillis.

"It needs to be said," the woman replied. "I was the one keeping tabs on the money, Ranger. I was the one to start spending it. At first, just on things I thought we needed to keep the case going—better food, better lodging. Then new clothes for myself. . . ." She let her words trail as she shook her head slowly. "It soon started adding up. I lost control of it."

Sam drew in a deep breath and let it out slowly, gazing off at the Mexican soldiers riding toward them, getting closer now. He shook his lowered head.

"Two detectives gone wrong," he murmured.

"You took sides with the thief and murderer you were sworn to bring to justice. That's as low as it gets in this occupation."

"I know that, Ranger," said Tillis.

"So do I," said the woman. "We had both realized what a terrible thing we'd done. We were out to fix it when things went wrong and Orez turned on us for no reason."

"That's right," said Tillis. "We'd already decided to make things right before they went any further. I could have salvaged the whole operation with what I would have coming for these last robberies I set up for him, the stagecoach and Trade City Bank. But it turns out, Orez had already decided he was through with me. I tried to talk to him when he and his men were robbing the stagecoach." He gestured at his face. "This is what I got."

"And now," said Sam, "you want me to believe you're both after Orez and the money you know he has, so you can clear everything and make yourselves *right* again?"

"Yes, we'd like you to believe that, Ranger," said Tillis, looking him squarely in the eye. "It happens to be the truth."

Sam looked at the *federales* drawing closer, recognizing the young captain at the head of the column.

Tillis and Jenny Lynn looked at the soldiers too, their expressions turning tight and grim.

"Don't you believe people can see their mistakes and change, Ranger?" Tillis said.

Sam didn't answer. Instead he sidled his horse over to him as the soldiers drew within a few yards of them.

"Stick out your wrists," he said. "I'll be taking back my cuffs now."

The two sat crestfallen. A tear ran down the woman's face.

Putting the cuffs away, Sam turned to her.

"Get off the stolen horse, Jenny Lynn," he said. "Get up behind Tillis. "You're riding double now."

She and Tillis gave each other a puzzled look as the column slowed to a halt and the young captain recognized the Ranger.

"Ah, Ranger Burrack," he said. "What do you bring us this time? More prisoners, I bet?"

"This time I bring you a stolen horse," Sam replied. He took the Morgan by its reins and led it forward. One of the men broke ranks, rode forward and took the horse from him. "It was stolen from a man named Audie Murtez, in Trade City. I know he'll be happy to get it back."

"*Sí*, and we will get it to him immediately," said the captain. He gave a grin and said, "Now that you have turned to chasing down horse thieves, soon both of our countries' horses will be safe." He looked around to make sure his men appreciated his joke; then he turned back to the Ranger.

The Ranger nodded amiably to show he was a good sport. Seeing the questioning look on the captain's face as the man eyed Tillis and the woman, Sam said, "These two *acquired* the horse." He shot Tillis a look. "Knowing it was *stolen*, the woman brought it to me—woke me in the middle of the night to take it from her." He shot Jenny Lynn a glance, then looked back at the Mexican captain.

The young captain eyed the three of them each in turn, curious at the sight of Tillis' bruised and sewn-up face, wolfish at Jenny Lynn, her bare knee and calf dangling down the big horse's side, showing below her muddy, hiked-up skirt.

"Is everything else good, Ranger?" he asked, looking Sam up and down, his battered hat, the swallow-tailed dress coat, a pair of scruffy miner boots the townsfolk at Trade City had given him.

The Ranger nodded and touched his fingers to his hat brim.

"Good as ever, Captain," he said. "If you'll permit us, we'll ride with you into Picate, try to get to shelter before this storm gets to us."

"Blast these storms for the devils that they are," the captain swore toward the black distant sky. "*Sí,* ride with us, Ranger Burrack," he said with a dismissing toss of his hand. "I know our horses will all be safe with you along."

# Chapter 19

───────

At the town livery stable in Picate, Tillis and the woman traded in the big coach horse for two saddle horses complete with tack and saddles. Sam paid the forty-dollar difference in the trade with a gold coin from his saddlebags. While thunder slammed and the storm moved in behind the familiar hard-blowing rain, he and Tillis stood in the open door of the livery barn. They looked out at a silvery gray rain blown sideways beneath a black sky. The roan and the two new horses stood eating grain from a long wooden trough.

"I won't forget this, Ranger," Tillis said between the two of them, feeling better without his hands cuffed, without looking through the black iron bars of a jail cell the way he'd anticipated doing once they arrived at Picate. "I'm going to pay you back the forty dollars, every penny," he added, still rubbing his freed wrists.

The Ranger only nodded, staring out into the horizontal darts of rain, his rifle hanging in his hand.

"I want you to know that I hadn't forgotten everything you did for me." He gestured toward his stitched face. "Had it not been for the storm, I like to think I would have told you the truth about everything as soon as I got my senses back. The beating took a lot out of me."

"I understand," the Ranger said.

"I can't say what I might have done had I managed to rest a couple of days and sort things out in my mind. But then the hillside washed away and I had time to figure out what to do. All Jenny and I could think about was staying alive. For all I knew, we were the only two who survived. I found my gun, I found a coach horse still alive. All I could think of then was going after Orez, getting the money and making things right."

The Ranger looked him up and down.

"And now that's what you're doing," he said, capping Tillis' story off for him.

"Yep," Tillis said with satisfaction. "And I can't tell you how good it feels, doing the right thing. I got knocked off the right path there for a while. But now I've got things right in my head, and I'm back on the job."

"That's good to hear," the Ranger said.

Across the barn, Jenny Lynn sat resting on a blanket thrown over fresh straw.

"I don't know about you two, but I'm starving," she called out to them.

The Ranger and Tillis looked at each other.

"I could use something to eat myself," Tillis said.

"There's a restaurant right down the street," the Ranger said. "We can eat early, get a good night's rest and be on Orez's trail before daylight."

"I'll put the horses in their stalls," said Tillis, turning, heading for the horses at the feed trough.

The Ranger started to follow, but he saw Jenny reach a hand up toward him for assistance.

"Ranger, would you, please?" she said. "Since it appears you're the only gentleman here."

"Of course," the Ranger said. He stepped across the barn floor and bent slightly, his hand extended to her.

Jenny smiled and took his hand. In the instant she did so, the Ranger saw in her eyes the image of Tillis looming behind him, his hand raised, a wooden rope fid in it.

*Uh-oh . . .* It was a trick. Sam tried to jerk his hand away fast, but Jenny Lynn held on to it with a powerful grip. The Ranger tried to brace himself, realizing he was past stopping anything.

On the blanket, Jenny winced as the fid hit the back of the Ranger's head and sent him falling toward her. She managed to catch him just enough to soften his fall. Then she rolled him aside and sprang to her feet. When she saw Tillis draw back for another blow with the tapered, top-heavy fid, she grabbed his wrist with both hands.

"No, Foster, that's enough!" she said.

Tillis hesitated, looking down at the Ranger lying slumped on the blanket.

"Just one more, for good measure?" he asked.

"Give me that," Jenny Lynn demanded, taking the wooden fid from his hand. She pitched the tapered wooden tool away. "Get his handcuffs. We'll cuff him to a stall."

The Ranger moaned on the blanket, already trying to regain consciousness. Through a watery veil, he saw the woman hovering over him. But he only saw her for a moment; then a heavy fog moved across his senses and she vanished. A moment later he came to, lying on the blanket, feeling his wrists being cuffed. He heard Tillis and the woman talking, but they might as well have been speaking a foreign language as far as he was concerned.

Through the watery veil, he saw the horses clop past him, their hooves awfully close to his face, he thought. He wanted to raise himself from the blanket and make a lunge for Tillis, but no, he told himself, that wasn't the wise thing to do. He had expected something like this to happen. Now here it was. *Lie still, be patient,* he demanded of himself.

The roan stopped beside him for a moment and reached out with its muzzle to investigate. The Ranger felt it sniff his face all around. He felt it chuff and blow out a hot breath in his face. Then he saw it raise its head and walk away behind the other two horses.

*This is going to be all right,* the Ranger reminded himself, relaxing as he heard heavy rain splatter from the roof edge as someone opened the livery barn door. At least this was one night he wouldn't have to ride in a storm.

When the Ranger awakened again, gray dawn light seeped slanted through the barn windows and the plank barn door as a child's small hand gripped his healing shoulder and shook him. Pain coursed through the stitches in his shoulder. He opened his eyes and stared at the barn post his wrists had been pulled around and cuffed to.

"Ranger! Ranger, wake up," said a grown-up's voice standing over the young Mexican boy, who was doing the shaking. "You must wake up and have for yourself some coffee to clear your head."

Sam batted his eyes and looked first at his cuffed wrists. As he stared, he saw the owner of the livery barn and his young son, Julio, standing over him. He watched the man stoop down with a handcuff key, unlock the cuffs and pitch them aside. Young Julio looked on.

"Why were you cuffed, Ranger?" Julio asked.

"Shhh, Julio," his father said. "It is not something you ask a man the first thing in the morning."

"It's all right, Raul," the Ranger said, sitting up, rubbing his wrists. "Did you mark those horses' shoes good and clear like I asked you to? I didn't get a chance to check them."

"Ah yes, of course, Ranger," said the livery owner. He reached a strong hand down and helped the Ranger pull himself to his feet. "You can see the file marks here." He pointed a long finger at the hoofprints on the soft wet floor. "I file one X on the man's and two Xs on the woman's."

"Good job, Raul," Sam said, looking at the floor, seeing clearly the Xs the liveryman had filed on the front hoof of each horse. As he spoke, his head pounded with each pulse of his heart. "You mentioned some . . . coffee?" he said in a quiet, pained voice.

"Sí, come sit down," said Raul. To Julio he said, "Go get coffee, my son, and a wet cloth. The Ranger needs to clear his head. I can be sure you will be going after the people who did this to you, *mas pronto*, eh, Ranger?"

"Oh yes, Raul, you *can be sure*," he said, following

Raul to a wooden stool, where he sat down and cupped the back of his head. He took the wet cloth when the boy reappeared and handed it to him. He accepted a heavy coffee mug and sipped from it as he held the cool wet cloth against the knot on the back of his head.

"How bad did it rain last night?" he asked the livery owner.

"It rained bad, like it has rained every day and night," Raul said. "You will have a hard time finding the tracks they left in the night."

The Ranger only nodded and sipped his coffee. That was all right, he told himself. He had a good idea which way they had traveled in the night. They would ride right up onto the high hills trail. He had no doubt about that. It was up there that he would need to identify their prints, once the rain had ceased, or at least slowed down for a while. Sipping the coffee, he stood up and steadied himself. Still holding the wet cloth to the back of his head, he walked toward the rear barn door.

"Let's see what kind of riding stock you've got for sale," he said over his shoulder to the livery barn owner. "The longer I sit, the sorer my head's going to be."

"Ah, it is always the case with these things, Ranger," Raul said, following him to the rear door, hurrying ahead and holding it open for him. The two walked outside in a light rain left over from the night before. As they walked to a corral where seven muddy horses stood huddled together under the roof of a lean-to shelter, Raul reached out a hand toward the animals. The horses stared through the gray morning rain.

"Here are the beauties I have on hand for you today, Ranger," he said.

Sam walked along, looking the horses over one at a time, until he spotted a black-speckled gray desert barb with a muzzle and jawline full of brush scars. The hard-boned little barb stood off to itself in the rain, just out from under the shelter. The horse took a step back from him as the Ranger put a hand out toward its muzzle.

"He's not a friendly sort, is he?" the Ranger observed. The barb stopped retreating and stood still and silent for the Ranger to rub his muzzle.

"No, he is not friendly, Ranger," Raul said. "He does not like people or pets or other horses, I think." He raised a long finger for emphasis. "But he is from these desert hills. These storms have not bothered him. Perhaps he has been in storms like this before."

Looking at the speckled barb as he spoke, rubbing its muzzle, the Ranger said, "I don't know that there's ever been storms like these before. If so, I've never seen them."

"I have seen them like this," Raul said. "They come and go and when you know they are gone is when you see a red moon."

"A red moon?" the Ranger pondered, the wet cloth against the back of his head.

"*Sí*, a red moon," Raul said. "It scares the old women and makes them weep. It makes the young ones act loco until it is gone. The Apache warriors say it is big medicine." He made a tight fist.

"Big medicine in what way?" Sam asked.

"They believe all spirits, both good and bad, await to rise on a red moon," he said. "Great men fall on a red moon. Other men become great in their place. Good men are harder to die. Bad men die easier. But all men who stand in a red moon will change, some for the better, some for the worse."

The Ranger only stood staring at him, as if waiting for him to get the story out of his system.

Raul shrugged. "But listen to me, I talk about the moon and the storms when I should be selling you a horse. Anyway," he said, "I believe this barb is a good horse for fifty *americano* dollars, eh?"

"He's a better horse for thirty-five," Sam came back.

"But still a real bargain for forty-five?" the livery owner said. He knew he was going to sell the Ranger a horse; it was just a matter of settling on the price.

"A *real* bargain for forty," Sam said.

"Yes, or an even better bargain standing under a saddle and bridle for forty-five?" Raul said, knowing it was coming—waiting for it, waiting—

"Forty-five, and trail ready," the Ranger said.

There it was. Raul smiled.

"Ah yes, *trail ready*, of course," he said. "Follow me, Ranger. I have just the saddle for you."

"Good," the Ranger said. "I need to get on up into the Blood Mountains. The man I'm after is up there."

"Oh, *Montañas de Sangre*?" Raul said. He gave the Ranger a wary look, but offered no more on the matter.

As they walked back toward the barn, the Ranger, holding the wet cloth to his head, said, "Tell me more about the red moon."

"I hope I have not made you think I am foolish, talking about these old Apache beliefs," Raul said.

"Not at all, Raul," Sam said. "Lately I've taken a sharp interest in anything Apache."

"Oh, you mean you are interested in Apache because you are hunting Wilson Orez?" Raul asked.

"How'd you know I'm hunting Orez?" the Ranger asked.

"Who else would you be hunting up there?" he said, gesturing in the direction of the distant hills and mountains obscured by miles of silvery rain. "Above the Twisted Hills, everything belongs to Orez. To him and the renegade *Apachean* Red Sleeve warriors." He paused, then said, "Anybody who goes there will die, unless Wilson Orez says otherwise. It is his lair. Everybody who knows of him knows not to go there."

"I'm going there," the Ranger said.

"And the man and woman who stole your horse, they are going there too?" Raul asked.

"Unless something stops them," the Ranger said. "I'm sure they're already on their way."

"I see," said the livery barn owner. "That explains what I saw in their faces."

Sam looked at him as they walked along.

"What did you see in their faces?" he asked.

"I saw only death," the man said grimly, staring straight ahead.

"Look long enough, you can see death in anybody's face," said the Ranger.

"This is true," said the Mexican. "But I didn't have to look very long to see it in theirs." He looked sidelong at the Ranger. "Be careful that their deaths do not become your death too."

"I'm going to try my best," the Ranger said.

When he'd wiped the wet, mud-streaked barb down with an empty cloth feed sack, he pitched a worn and well-attended California-style saddle atop its back and cinched it. The speckled barb stamped a hoof in anticipation and shook out its wet black mane.

"Don't start right off rushing me," the Ranger said, giving a quick rub on the horse's muzzle.

Stepping into the saddle, his Winchester in hand, he buttoned his swallow-tailed coat and pulled a brown rain slicker over it, buttoning the slicker all the way closed and flipping up the collar beneath his hat brim. He pulled on a pair of leather trail gloves the Mexican liveryman gave him and tapped the barb forward toward the open barn door.

Rain from the roof splattered across his shoulders as the barb walked out of the barn into the blowing rain. Sam leaned in the saddle and followed the three deep sets of hoofprints with his eyes, seeing them fade away in the mud and rain less than five feet away. But that was all right for now, he thought, already knowing the direction the two would start off in.

The pair of detectives would go back along the same trail out of Picate that they'd ridden in on. At the main trail they would turn right toward Twisted Hills—toward the Blood Mountains, *Montañas de Sangre*, as the Mexican had called them.

Putting the barb to a light gallop in the rain, splashing through the mud, he noted that the animal made no more than a short reflex response to both the flicking slice of lightning and the rumble of thunder following it.

"Good boy," he said down to the barb. He pulled his hat tighter onto his forehead and rode on, not stopping or slowing the barb until he reined it up at the T in the trail and looked off to his right, where he knew the Twisted Hills lay obscured in the silver-threaded rain.

Turning the horse in that direction, he touched his bootheels to its sides. But as the horse started to advance, he reined it up sharply.

"Wait a minute," he said aloud to himself, holding the barb in check.

*It is Orez's lair. Everybody who knows of him knows not to go there,* he heard the Mexican say to him only a few minutes ago.

*What were you thinking?* he admonished himself. Maybe the wooden fid had knocked him off his usual game. He reined the barb around quickly on the trail and looked off in the opposite direction. There was something about the wagon being where they'd found it that wasn't right, he thought—Tillis and Jenny Lynn had seen it too, he was certain.

Beneath him the barb pawed at the mud and blew out a breath.

"All right," Sam said, straightening the animal back on the trail to Trade City where they had found the empty wagon. "I hope you like running in the rain."

# Chapter 20

In the pouring rain, Tillis and Jenny Lynn had struggled with the large rock until it had finally come free from the mud with a loud sucking sound and lay half over onto its side. Some of the stitches on Tillis' forehead had popped open. Pink-red blood ran down his face in the rain. His hair was plastered to his bare head. But he still managed to let out a chuckle of delight when he saw the bank bags piled under the rock where Orez and his two men had buried them.

"And here we find it, lying in wait for us!" he said. "Just like we knew it would be!" Laughing, he shuffled his feet a little on the wet muddy ground.

"Shhh, take it easy," Jenny Lynn said in a low-ered voice, trying to quiet him down. She looked around warily through the rain. Lightning flick-ered in the black sky.

"Take it easy, hell!" said Tillis, still laughing. "It's ours, and there is nothing or nobody going to take it away from us, Jenny. Do you hear me? Nothing or nobody!" he shouted on the hillside above the trail where the Trade City posse had found the body of Freeman Manning with his guns tied in his hands.

Jenny Lynn shook her head and picked up the shovel Tillis had brought along from the Picate livery barn. She began digging a wider space under the overturned rock to better reach the bags of money stuffed beneath it.

Tillis watched her dig for a few minutes, standing with his collar held snug around his neck, the bone-handled Colt stuck down in his waistband behind his coat.

Seeing her stop digging and start tugging at one of the bags to get it freed up beneath the rock, Tillis sighed and shook his head in exasperation.

"Here, get up out of there," he said, reaching a hand down to help her up. "Let a man do it."

Jenny gave him a spiteful look but didn't reply. She sank the shovel blade into the dirt, took his hand and stepped up away from the rock. The rock swayed back and forth a little as she pushed against it on her way to her feet.

Tillis gave a short smirk and stepped down where she'd been standing.

"We'd be here all day and night, as slow as you were going," he said, stooping down, taking a hold on one of the bags and pulling hard on its string-tied top. "Jesus," he said. "The rock's got it pinned under it."

"Why do you think I was digging?" Jenny said coldly.

"Blast it!" said Tillis. He put a hand on either side of the rock and shoved hard back and forth to get its weight moving and tip it the rest of the way over. As he rocked it back and forth, he grunted, saying, "What the hell is it going to take to get this thing to—" His words stopped as the big rock tipped slowly over toward him. "Oh no!" he shouted as he shoved the rock with all his strength.

Jenny let out a short scream and tried to reach over and help him shove the rock. But it was too late.

"Holy God!" she shouted as she saw the rock turn over against all of Tillis' efforts and flop on top of him, smashing the helpless man down into the mud and the bags of money beneath it. The weight of the rock jarred the soft earth and settled atop Tillis with a deep thud, pinning him from his waist down.

"Get it off me! Get it off me!" Tillis shouted, near panicked, the weight crushing him below his waist.

"What can I do? Tell me!" Jenny shouted, tearful, near panic herself.

Behind her, a man stepped into sight, walked over near the rock and looked down at Tillis.

"If I was you," he said calmly to Jenny Lynn, "I'd use a rope and horse." He smiled. "Hope I'm not butting in."

Jenny Lynn gasped, turning to face Hardin.

The gunman smiled and touched his wet hat brim, a long Colt hanging in his hand, his thumb over the hammer. He wagged the gun barrel, gesturing to where more rocks of similar size lay strewn on the ground a few yards away.

"That's what we used, Orez and me," he said. "To get the rock from there over to here? We roped that big boy, tied our horses to it, yanked it up right out of the ground." He turned his smile down to Tillis. "Once it was unstuck, it rolled for us like a big ol' croquet ball."

"Who—who are you?" Tillis asked in a halting

voice. He tugged on his gun handle, trying to free it up. Hardin looked at what he was doing but didn't seem concerned.

"I'm Evan Hardin," he said. "Part of that money you're trying to steal belongs to me. The rest belongs to my pal Wilson Orez. I expect you've heard of him?"

"We're not stealing it," Jenny said. "Part of it rightfully belongs to us. We set up some big-paying jobs for Orez."

"I see," said Hardin, water dripping from his hat brim. "So you were going to only take some of it? Leave the rest of it, make sure we all got what was coming to us?" He chuckled. But then his chuckle stopped abruptly, his friendly smile vanished, as he swung a pointed finger at Tillis.

"If you get that gun pulled, you'd better shoot yourself instead of me. Because without me, you're going to die right there, half in, half out of your grave. Nightfall, when the critters come for you, guess how good you'll taste to them, all fresh and screaming while they chew out your eyes and dig their way inside your skull through the empty sockets." He licked his lips as if imitating a wolf or a coyote.

Jenny Lynn stood staring, mesmerized by his vivid words.

Tillis lay crushed down into the money bags, his Colt mashed beneath his coat just at the edge of rock lying atop him. He'd managed to get his hand inside his coat and around the gun handle, but he hadn't been able to pull it free. His hand fell in submission.

"Please!" he begged, nearly hysterical. "Get me out of here, mister! For the love of—"

"Hush, now," said Hardin, cutting Tillis off as if he were an unruly child. "Blaspheming never helps, especially not at a time like this."

"Please help me get him out of there!" Jenny said, finally coming around. "Do you still have the rope?"

"Come to think of it, yes, I do still have it," said Hardin. "It's on my horse, just around that big boulder there." He lowered the Colt into his holster. "Why don't I just get it for you?" He pointed in the direction of the path around the big boulder.

"Plea-please," she said.

Hardin started to turn and walk toward where he'd left his horse. But he stopped in second thought.

"Oh, before I go get that rope, we need to talk about what's in this for me," he said, rubbing his thumb and fingers together in the universal sign for greed.

"Anything! *Anything!*" shouted Tillis. "Hurry, please. I can't feel my legs! You can have my share, all of it, *please!*"

"Hear that?" Hardin asked Jenny Lynn, a bemused expression on his face. "Can't feel his legs. Wants to give me *his* share." He stepped in closer to Jenny Lynn. "Does that mean you're willing to give me your share too?"

Jenny Lynn stalled and didn't answer.

"Well, does it?" Hardin said.

"I don't know," said Jenny Lynn. "I mean, I hadn't thought about it." Her eyes darted back and forth between Hardin and Tillis like a trapped animal. "I—I need my share of that money. Isn't his share enough? He's the one stuck with a rock on his belly."

Hardin laughed and shook his head as he raised the Colt from its holster again. Jenny Lynn's eyes widened.

"I swear, you people kill me," he said. "You're both bargaining with money that doesn't even belong to you." He cocked the Colt and raised it.

Following the main trail as far back as where he, Jenny Lynn and Tillis had found the overturned buckboard, the Ranger slowed the barb to an easy gallop and cut up a steepening trail running alongside a stream of runoff water. Beneath a familiar black sky, blowing rain and thunder and lightning looming low above him, he rode the desert barb along a higher, more treacherous route that would lead him to the place where they had found the dead outlaw atop the bloody rock.

Higher to his right lay the southern end of Twisted Hills, a line of rugged rock hills so named by the Apache long before the lathed boot of the white man had stamped its imprint on the desert lands. Above the Twisted Hills stood Blood Mountains, where Orez would have them believe he'd fled to. But the Ranger wasn't falling for it. *Huh-uh.* . . .

Orez wouldn't have attempted to carry all that money by horseback with a posse breathing down his neck. Neither would he have ridden off and left it unguarded, taking a chance on its being gone when he returned for it. Orez was still here, the Ranger told himself, pushing the barb on through the driving rain.

By midmorning the fierceness of the storm had only lessened a little as the Ranger rode upward diagonally away from Twisted Hills, away from the longer, safer switchback trails and took a shorter, rougher route that would have staggered most horses. He noted that the hard-boned desert barb didn't seem to mind.

When he knew he had ridden well past the switchbacks below, he rode back down through the rain on a steep narrow path to the main trail—a trail that he knew would have cost Tillis and the woman twice as long to travel.

No sooner had the barb's hooves touched the main trail than he heard gunshots in the distance, six of them, slow, steady, the timing seeming deliberate. Turning the barb sharply toward the gunfire, he tapped his bootheels to its wet sides and put it forward in a run along the muddy trail. He could almost picture in his mind what had just happened at the boulder where he'd found Freeman Manning's body. The money would be there; he was sure of it.

Jenny Lynn stood wide-eyed in front of the rock where Foster Tillis lay helpless and spent. He'd had to give up on drawing his gun from under the weight of the heavy rock for the moment. He lay catching his breath, the rock crushing down on him. Jenny Lynn felt her nose burn from the smell of gunpowder drifting around her in the falling rain. On the ground in front of her, Hardin was writhing in the mud, his Colt only inches from his fingers as he gasped and struggled, dark blood spewing from his bullet-riddled lungs.

"I—I was coming back," he managed to say, trying to push himself up, his palms sinking into the mud. "I swear . . . I was."

"I don't believe you," said Orez, stepping forward, drawing his big knife from its sheath. He reached down, gripped Hardin by his hair and raised his head at a sharp angle.

"No, no!" said Hardin.

But his words turned into a gurgling sound as the edge of cold steel sank deep and sliced hard, leaving a dark streak of blood spewing out from the beard stubble on his throat. Jenny Lynn half covered her face and winced at the quiet deadly sound of steel cutting through human flesh and tendon again and again until she shuddered as she heard the thump of Hardin's head splash in the mud.

"There, it's done," Jenny heard Orez say. She opened her eyes and watched him stoop and wipe his knife clean on the muddy ground. A flash of lightning cast him in a stark gray-purple light.

She closed and opened her eyes again, this time looking at the young, strange Mexican woman who stood ten feet behind Orez, her face a mask of terror, the gun she'd used to shoot Evan Hardin still smoking, hanging in her trembling hand.

"You done well, Rosa," Orez said to Rosa. He stepped over to the stunned, shaking young woman and took the gun from her hand. "That wasn't so bad, was it?" he said to her.

She trembled so hard she couldn't answer. Instead she shook her head as best she could and stood, her left arm across her midriff, gripping her right arm at the elbow. She managed to look at Jenny Lynn, whose eyes pleaded with her as Orez dropped the spent cartridges from the big Colt, reloaded it and put it back in Rosa's hand.

"Now her," he said evenly, giving a short nod toward Jenny.

"Her too?" said Rosa, her face pale, ashen.

"Yes, her, too," said Orez, stepping forward, staring at Jenny Lynn as he helped her point the Colt at the helpless woman. "Today is the day for everybody to die." He cocked the Colt for Rosa.

Behind Jenny, pressed under the rock, Tillis was struggling again to raise his Colt, knowing it was the only chance he had to save himself, as slim as he knew that chance might be. But it was no use; the pistol wasn't coming out. He would die here, he told himself, helpless, with a loaded gun in his hand.

"Take your time, Rosa," Orez coached her, stepping away from Rosa, closer to Jenny Lynn. "Take good aim and squeeze the trigger, the way I showed you."

*Please,* Jenny Lynn said silently, her lips forming the word, but unable to say it aloud. She saw the young woman standing behind the gun, ready to pull the trigger. But in a flash of hope, Rosa turned the gun away and aimed it at Orez's back. Jenny gasped aloud at the explosion as the hammer fell.

Orez winced and jerked in place, then straightened and turned around, walking stiffly back to Rosa Dulce, his hand on the bone handle of his big knife.

"You must have misunderstood me," he said in a soft, even tone. "I meant for you to shoot her, not me."

# Chapter 21

———

The worst of the storm had passed when the Ranger arrived at the path leading up to the big boulder. He stepped down from the California saddle and led the speckled barb the last few yards, his Colt in his left hand, his Winchester and the horse's reins in his right. When he eased his way around the boulder, he saw the young Mexican woman sitting in the mud.

"He's . . . gone," she said, barely above a whisper.

Still, the Ranger looked all around before stepping any closer. He saw the scalped and decapitated heads of two men and one woman, standing in a row across the top of the overturned rock where the gunman Freeman Manning had spent the last minutes of his life.

*More warnings?* he asked himself, staring at the heads, rain pouring down their sightless, open eyes, pink blood still running down the rock into the mud. Beside the rock, he saw the empty hole and a short shovel lying in the mud. That's where the money had been buried, he told himself.

When the posse was on Orez's trail and Orez knew that much money would only slow him down, he had his men roll a rock over beside the boulder, scratch out enough dirt to bury the bags, then roll the rock back atop everything. *Smart thinking*, Sam had to admit.

He let the barb's reins fall from his hand and walked over to the woman. Looking all around to make sure it was clear, he then stooped down beside her and examined her bloody, mud-streaked face, her wet, filthy clothes and the rope lying in a pile on the ground beside her.

"Are you wounded anywhere, ma'am?" he asked, looking at a splotch of watery blood on the wet ground, another a few feet away. He wasn't about to ask if she was all right. She clearly wasn't, wound or no wound.

"I—I'm afraid if I stand up, I'll fall in half," she said in a raspy voice.

The Ranger raised a cold arm from across her waist and looked closely at her. He saw no blood.

"I see no wound," he said.

She didn't respond to his words. Instead she let her arm fall back limp across her lap when he turned it loose, and she looked all around slowly.

"I killed them all, you know," she said quietly. "I shot them dead."

"No, ma'am, I didn't know that," Sam said. "Did Wilson Orez make you do it?"

She shook her head slowly, as if having to consider it for a moment.

"Make me? No," she said. "But I already knew that I had to do whatever he wanted me to do. He told me *today everybody dies*." She took on an uncertain look. "Is that the same thing as him making me?" she asked.

Sam didn't answer right away. He laid his rifle

across his wet knee, reached out and wiped a fleck of mud from under her eye. Finally he said quietly, "There's all kinds of ways of making folks do things, I expect. Who are you?"

"I'm Sweet Rose," she said with a slight but painful-looking smile.

Sam just looked at her.

"My name really is Rosa Dulce," she added.

"You've been leaving me signs along the way?" he said. "String, pieces of your skirt hem?"

She looked surprised.

"You found them," she said. "You knew I was here." She stiffened her expression a little. "Did you come for me, or the money?" she asked.

"To tell you the truth, I came for both," Sam replied. "But mostly I came for you," he said. "Whatever you did, I know he must've made you do it. So, if it comes down to anybody questioning—"

"I shot him too," she said bluntly.

"You did?" said Sam, looking back at the splotch of watery blood on the ground.

"I did," she said, barely shaking her head. "It didn't bother him. He took the gun from me, replaced the bullet and put it back in my hand. He said, 'This time, get it right.' So I went ahead and killed them both."

"Don't talk about it now," the Ranger said. "Just keep telling yourself that you're safe, that it's over. That's enough for now." He looked around. Orez had taken all the horses to carry the bags of money. "How bad is he bleeding?" he asked.

"He's bleeding a lot," she said. "But it doesn't bother him. I don't think he can be killed."

"He can," Sam said. He took her hands in his and stood up, helping her to her feet. "There, see? You didn't fall apart."

"He knows you're tracking him," she said.

"He does? How does he know that?" the Ranger asked. Even as he asked, it dawned on him that Orez hadn't left a horse for her.

"Because he's seen you now," she said. She gave him a strange, thin smile. "He said he would know for sure when he sees you come here. I think he knows everything, about everything."

*Sees me come here?* Sam looked all around warily, his eyes going up along the cliffs and ledges above them.

"He knows about the string and the cloth I left for you," she said. "I told him everything last evening."

"Come with me," he said quickly, realizing Orez had meant what he'd told her. Today everybody dies. He had only left her alive to keep him standing in the open. Orez was up there, behind the breaking clouds, waiting for his shot.

Still scanning the cliffs and the hill line, Sam took her arm and started to lead her to the shelter of the large boulder. But before they moved a step, she gave a loud grunt and slammed against him. He caught her in his arms as he heard a distant rifle shot resound from somewhere in the swirl of rain on the barely visible hill line above them.

Without a second between shots, Sam dragged the woman to the shelter of the boulder as mud from the next bullet sprayed up, followed by the explosion. Quickly he leaned her back against the boulder and looked at the gaping wound in her chest.

"See?" she said, choking, gasping for breath. "He was right, today everybody dies," she said. "Just like he . . . said we would. . . ." Her head fell over onto her shoulder and she seemed to relax in the mud and the falling rain.

Sam closed her eyes with his wet gloved hand, then turned and looked around the edge of the boulder in the direction the killing shot came from. *Who in the world could make such a shot as that?* he asked himself, feeling the icy reality of just how deadly this man was. He looked up as thin breaks in the black sky drifted across the obscured ledges and cliffs.

*Don't let him throw you,* he warned himself. If Orez had gotten his way, one of those two shots would have left him lying dead in the mud beside the young woman.

*You wanted me to fear you. All right, you've got that,* the Ranger told himself, looking over at the three heads standing drenched in the pouring rain. "But so what?" he murmured aloud to himself. He'd felt fear before, more times than he cared to recall. He forced himself to his feet, his back against the boulder, and stood there for a moment.

He understood fear. He'd learned that fear wasn't the lack of courage. Indeed not, he told himself. He'd come to know that there could be no courage without fear being the challenge it had to overcome. He took a breath, stepped out from the boulder and walked to where the barb stood in the open, staring at him through the rain.

Why hadn't Orez shot the horse if he didn't want to be followed?

He didn't know; he didn't care. Whatever Orez had in mind, it was getting ready to play out, he thought, gripping his rifle tight in his wet, gloved hand. He felt whatever fear he had fall away under the icy current that swept through him. He gathered the barb's reins, stepped up into the saddle and touched his heels to the horse's sides.

*Today, everybody dies,* he said silently to himself, looking back up at the gray-silver mist hiding the hill line. *Today, everybody dies. . . .*

In an ancient dugout on the wall of a high bluff at the mouth of the Twisted Hills, an old Red Sleeve warrior named Yehicho, or Iron Belly, awakened with a start and looked up at Wilson Orez, who sat at the front of the high cliff dwelling looking out on the slow, steady rain falling into the canyon below. Neither man acknowledged the other.

After a long silence, Orez said over his shoulder, "Before I cut the face off the man who fathered me, and burned his trading post down around him, I told him it was Iron Belly who informed me he was my father." Orez paused for a moment. "He didn't like it. He said you were supposed to be his friend."

"No, he did not like it." Iron Belly gave a thin, flat smile.

He had heard the story so many times he didn't have to pay close attention. Instead he reached up with his knife, cut a slice of dried antelope from a shank of meat hanging from the ceiling of the dwelling and cut it into smaller pieces on his bare knee.

"I was never his friend," he said. "A Red Sleeve has no white man for a friend." He took a bite of the meat for himself and held a piece over to the nose of a blind, aged dog who lay curled up beside him on the stone floor. The dog took the piece of antelope in his toothless mouth and gummed it slowly, savoring the taste of it.

Iron Belly pitched the largest of the pieces over against Orez's thigh.

"Eat with me," he said. "You smell like a long journey."

"It *has* been a long journey," said Orez, picking up the meat and tearing off a mouthful of it with his teeth. Without looking around at the old warrior, he chewed the meat and reflected. "In the last moon, twenty white men came to kill me, to collect the bounty on my head." He paused, then said, "But I killed them, one and two and three at a time, until now they're all dead—all except one." He shrugged. "I'll kill him before the day's gone and the moon rises for the night."

"The one still coming is not after bounty, is he?" Iron Belly said.

"No, he's not," said Orez. "A man I killed today told me this one is an Arizona Ranger. He doesn't scare easily. These kinds of lawmen don't stop. They don't hunt for the sake of bounty. They hunt for the sake of the hunt. This one is a warrior, like we are."

He sounded pleased, Iron Belly noted. He saw the blood ooze down Orez's side. But he wasn't going to mention it. A man knew when he was wounded, and how bad. It was not his place to say anything.

Instead he said, "What more do you want from the white man, Wilson Orez?"

"I don't know," Orez replied. "I've killed his kind, violated his women and stolen his money." He paused, then added, "Still, it's not enough. I'm not satisfied."

"It's the white man's blood in you that keeps you from being satisfied," said Iron Belly. "You are as much white man as you are Apache. The war you fight inside you never stops." He shook his head slowly and passed another small piece of meat to the blind dog's frost-colored muzzle. "When you were a boy, you used to cut yourself, to punish yourself for having the white man's blood. When you grew up, you cut everybody else for it."

"I cursed my white blood. I still do," Orez said, tearing off another bite of meat with his teeth.

"You curse it, but you can't change it," Iron Belly replied.

"The other day I thought I had gotten rid of it," Orez said. "I stood naked in the storm and felt it leave me."

"But it was back inside when the storm passed, wasn't it, Wilson Orez?" said the old Apache.

Orez only sat slumped, chewing the dried antelope.

"Tell me, old man," he said, "what would the Red Sleeves think of me, if they knew I'm one of the last of us alive?"

"Don't wonder what the dead think," said Iron Belly. "They knew you as a warrior. Your white blood didn't matter to them."

"You're wrong, Iron Belly. It did make a difference," Orez said. "I proved myself the best of us warriors, time and again. Still, I knew they thought less of me for my white blood."

"You did prove yourself a great warrior to the Red Sleeves, Wilson Orez," said Iron Belly. "But you never proved it to yourself." Again he shook his head slowly and gave the blind dog another small cut of antelope. He scratched its bony head as it gummed the meat. "And that has cost the lives of so many people whose paths crossed yours on this earth," he said with regret.

"I have four horses carrying bags of money," Orez said. "How many bags can I give you?"

"I have no use for the white man's money," Iron Belly said, brushing the notion aside. "I once used it when I had no wood to burn. It made my fire burn greasy, and smelled like fish that were too long dead." He paused, then said, "Does their money always smell that way?"

"Yes, I believe it does," Orez said. "They don't smell it, though. At least I've never heard them complain." With much effort he rose to his feet, his hand pressed to his bullet wound behind his right side.

"No wonder you hate them, then," Iron Belly said in reflection, still scratching the blind dog's head. "How can they not smell something so bad?" He gave a look of disgust.

"They've grown used to it, like they have many other things, Iron Belly," said Orez. He turned to the open stone doorway and stared out at the rain falling deep to the canyon floor. "I became a Red Sleeve at a time when the Red Sleeves' world was dying. Now there are two of us, you and me." He breathed deep. "When we're gone, they'll say good riddance. The Apache were too savage, and the Red

Sleeves were too cruel and brutal to live." He stood in silence, then said, "They'll be right, won't they?"

"What will we care? I am out of this place as soon as this old dog closes his eyes for the last time," Iron Belly said. "What about you, Wilson Orez?"

"What about me?" Orez asked.

"Did you come to tell me good-bye?" said Iron Belly.

Orez let out a breath and stood for a moment longer, listening to the sound of the dog sucking on the meat. Then he straightened in the stone doorway and stepped forward, his hand still pressed back on his wound.

"Good-bye, Yehicho," he said over his shoulder without looking back.

# Chapter 22

The Ranger didn't step down from his saddle when he reached the cliff where Orez had left his two brass shell casings lying in the mud after killing the woman. Instead Sam leaned slightly in his saddle, his Winchester in hand, and studied the hoofprints on the wet trail. His eyes followed the prints from the gravelly floor to the soft inner edge of a path leading up to the trail above the cliff.

Above the path lay a taller, wider world of steep stone and deep, bottomless canyons. It was a place where any man with a mind to could easily vanish, hide himself from the world. Yet Wilson Orez had done nothing to hide himself, Sam thought, the empty cartridge shells, the hoofprints—two of the horses with Xs filed on the front edge of their iron shoes. If he saw these things, Orez saw them too, he told himself, nudging the barb forward in the hoof tracks, up onto the wider trail.

All right, he understood. Orez wasn't making himself hard to follow or hard to find. Not anymore, Sam realized. No more gruesome warnings left behind, no more captives, no more killings— well, only *one more killing*, he reminded himself.

But as soon as that thought entered his mind, he quickly dismissed it and rode on.

The barb climbed a series of narrow paths in turn, each one winding higher upward into the Twisted Hills, standing like sentinels along the Blood Mountain Range. He knew he was now in the old hiding place of the Red Sleeves band, and he cautioned himself, although he realized he needed no cautioning. It no longer mattered what awaited him in the end. He would go where Orez's trail led him, no matter the outcome.

He knew that at the end of that trail, one of them would die. That was the kind of thinking a man like Wilson Orez could appreciate—so could he, Sam had to admit to himself.

The storm had lost more of its fierceness as man and horse climbed higher. All that remained of it now was falling rain and distant rumblings of thunder moving away on the far edge of the earth. This time, there could be felt a finality to the dissipating storm that he had not noticed before.

Was it over? *Yes . . . yes*, he believed it was.

"Good riddance," he said quietly to himself, seeing the barb's black-tipped ears rise at the sound of his voice, then relax again as they rode on.

Even the dark lingering rain cloud now lay in the silver sky below them as the Ranger gradually put himself and the barb up into a steep misty world of split boulder rock and twisting valleys and draws. Here, he and the barb both stopped on their own and stood for a moment, met by massive, towering bodies of upturned plate stone that had broken off from the earth's fiery belly and over time eternal had risen and fallen and now lay slantwise at angles reaching above a thousand feet.

"My goodness," Sam whispered as if in awe, seeing the spot for the first time. "Heaven must've been born here."

Below him the barb nickered quietly under its breath and scraped a hoof.

"Shhh. . . . You don't have to say a word," Sam whispered, patting the barb's damp withers. They stood gazing at the land before them for a moment longer, and then the Ranger tapped the horse's sides and put it forward, up and around a steep, smooth stone plate that appeared to hold back a whole rocky hillside.

Wilson Orez had taken a position on a high hillside and fitted his rifle with a long brass scope. He'd watched from afar while the Ranger and the barb stopped, staring up at the mountainside rising above them. With the scope to his eye, Orez had been able to observe the Ranger's face close up. He saw powerful strength in the young Ranger's face, in his eyes. Yet, lowering the scope for a moment, Orez noted how small and insignificant both man and horse suddenly become to the naked eye against the backdrop of the mountain range.

He raised the scope again and stared into the Ranger's face as the Ranger steadied the barb and swung it toward the upper path around the long sloping wall of plate stone.

Orez knew he didn't need the scope to make a shot like this any more than he'd needed it to make the shot that killed the woman. But with the scope, he had seen the bullet rip through the woman's back. He'd seen her lifeblood form a red-pink mist and loom in the air as she buckled forward into the Ranger's arms.

He enjoyed watching his kill—what man wouldn't?

With the scope, he'd managed to see the woman clearly and closely, even through the veil of rain and low drifting cloud cover. Now, with the weather clearing quickly and being in a position to take a front shot, he would see everything. Through the scope he would see the impact on the Ranger's body when the bullet hit him—see the expression on his face. Watch him die . . . if he wanted to. Taking a breath of satisfaction, he lowered the rifle from against his cheek and laid it across his lap.

As he looked down at the rifle, it dawned on him. He could have taken the shot just then, but instead he'd waited. *Why?* He ran a hand along the rifle stock wondering, feeling warm blood running down the small of his back.

It didn't matter *why*, he told himself, looking all around. The Ranger's life belonged to him now. Up here in his realm, his lair, he knew he could take that life any time he chose to. Anyway, he decided, he didn't like this spot. There were much better places for him to kill a man than here, he told himself, standing, pressing his free hand to the bloody wound in his side. There were much better ways to kill him too.

He walked up to where he'd tied his horse and the horses carrying the bags of money draped over their backs. As he took up the lead rope, the roan sidestepped, pawed at the dirt and slammed its hoof down as if in protest.

"No more trouble out of you," he said to the roan, jerking on the lead rope close to its muzzle. "Tonight I'll find out if your meat is better than your disposition."

The roan grumbled but settled in among the other horses as Orez drew his big knife and walked over beside it. The roan stared at him nervously and blew out a hard breath. Orez swung the blade around fast toward the roan's side and sliced through a short rope holding a bag of money. The roan nickered and swung its head around, but Orez shoved it away. He stooped down, cut the bag open, picked it up and shook it.

Loose money fluttered out over the hillside like moths waning in flight. Orez sliced the bag into two pieces, wadded each piece of soiled white canvas cloth and stuffed them both inside his shirt, front and back, against his bleeding side wound. The roan and the other packhorses stood watching.

"You're right, Iron Belly," he said quietly, watching the paper bills float and flutter away off the hillside. "It does smell like fish gone bad."

Orez stepped back to his horse and pulled himself upward into his saddle. He felt deep sharp pain in his side as he turned his horse up a narrow path toward the rocky trail, lead rope in hand, the string of packhorses in a line behind him.

He rode for over a half hour, through mazes of sloping plate stone and boulder, and across long spills of overlapping stone, where liquid had once boiled up from deep inside the earth and cooled layer upon layer down an ancient hillside. On the other side of the rocky hill, he rode upward onto the trail he had taken earlier, knowing the Ranger would take the same trail following the X-marked shoes of the horses.

He stepped down from atop his horse and hitched the animals in full view, to a spill of large rocks that had broken free and lay across the trail. The roan sawed its head and grumbled at him again. But Orez ignored the horse and stepped up onto the rock spill, rifle in hand. He sat down on one of the larger rocks facing in the direction the Ranger would be coming from.

While he sat waiting, he felt his strength coming back to him in spite of the blood and pain in his wounded side. Holding the rifle propped beside him in his left hand, he reached his right hand up and slipped the big knife from its sheath. He rested it along the top of his thigh, his hand feeling at home, gripped around the knife's handle.

When the trail winding high above the stone plates grew too steep and narrow, the Ranger stepped down from the California saddle and led the barb upward another three hundred yards. He stopped at the only place he'd come to where the trail turned sharply out of sight, around a large boulder. For a moment he only stood, rifle in hand, looking up, seeing where the mountain itself twisted behind a blanket of cloud, gunmetal gray, streaked with long rays of breaking sunlight.

Quietly, he led the barb to the edge of the trail and hitched its reins loosely to a jut of rock—*loosely*, just in case, he reminded himself. He rubbed the horse's wet muzzle and walked away. He followed a thin, steep game path up around the back of the boulder, a path worn deep by centuries of fleeing hooves and pursuing paws, legacy of both the hunted and the hunter.

At the top of the worn path, where it began its circle back down and off the hillside onto a high cliff, the Ranger lowered himself onto all fours and crawled out atop the boulder. He lay there out of sight, looking down at the trail below. He scanned the rock spill, the horses, the money bags, then, *Wilson Orez . . .* , he whispered even in his head, as if a man such as Orez might hear even his silent thoughts. Without a moment's hesitation, he eased his Winchester around, seated its butt into the pocket of his shoulder and drew the hammer back so slowly he barely heard the metal cocking sound of it himself. He took aim down at Orez, fielding the bullet first, drawing its flight pattern and strike in his mind before squeezing the trigger.

A head shot, he told himself, seeing Orez almost in profile, seated atop a rock spill facing what turned out to be a horseshoe turn in the trail.

Yes, a head shot would do, he thought, lifting his rifle sights off Orez's chest where the bullet would cut diagonally at such an angle that with Orez's least movement, or a fluke surge of wind, the shot might graze only across his breastplate. At that point he would have to relever, reaim and fire again.

No, he told himself, raising the sights to the front right side of Orez's head—diagonal, through the temple. Here, even with a last-second movement of any sort, the bullet would still take out the largest portion of Orez's forehead. There would be no second shot, he told himself, just the ringing silence of sure and sudden death.

*So be it.*

The Ranger calmed his breathing and settled into his shot, taking his breath in and out evenly, slowly, each one measured to the same length, same rhythm. He felt his finger begin to squeeze the trigger.

*Wait. . . .*

He let his finger uncoil from around the trigger and lowered the rifle an inch. What bothered him about this? He looked back and forth, down at the horses hitched to the rocks below Orez, the bags of money tied across their backs. He looked back up at Orez, noting for the first time that had Orez seated himself only a few inches farther back on the rock spill, he would have been at an angle that would have cut off any shot from atop this boulder. It would have put Orez behind the cover of an edge of stone protruding from the inside wall of the trail. Sam lay staring, running the scene through his mind.

Orez was no fool. He had to know this boulder would be the first one standing along the trail. He had to know the Ranger was savvy enough not to walk blindly around it. What was he doing sitting there? Was this a trap, a trick of some sort? Why was he sitting in the open when only a foot deeper on the rock spill he would have been invisible?

Yes, why indeed? the Ranger asked himself, letting out a breath. But he already knew why. Orez had done this for the same reason he had left the shell casings, and not tried to hide his tracks. The same reason he had shot the young woman and let her fall dead in the Ranger's arms while his second shot missed the Ranger altogether and fell short in the mud.

As silently as the Ranger had cocked the rifle, he uncocked it and lay for a moment looking down at Orez. In the west, he saw the sunlight leaning deeper into the clouds on the peaks of the mountain line. *All right*, he said to himself; then he belly-crawled backward over the boulder, dropped onto the game path and climbed back down to the trail.

# Chapter 23

---

Wilson Orez let go of his rifle, allowing it to fall back against the rocks when the Ranger walked into sight around the turn in the trail. He stood up slowly, his big knife hanging in his hand. He noted the Ranger wasn't leading his horse or carrying his rifle, and he saw no sign of surprise in the Ranger's face or demeanor as the Ranger looked up at him. Orez watched quietly until the Ranger stopped on the trail a full thirty feet back from the rock spill.

"You're the Ranger the railroad sent to kill me," he said.

"The railroad didn't send me, Orez," the Ranger said. "It doesn't work that way."

"How does it work?" he said with contempt, looking the young Ranger up and down. "You tell me. How do you decide who lives and who dies?"

The Ranger stood staring at him.

"I keep it simple," the Ranger said. "I carry a list of names. If your name gets on the list, you're half-way there already." He paused, then added, "Your name's been on that list over a month."

"A month, huh?" Orez said. "What took you so long?" He took a step down on the rock spill as he spoke. The Ranger saw the Colt standing in a holster on his right hip. But Orez's right hand held the big knife.

*This is how it is, a knife fight. Watch for a trick,* he warned himself.

At the rock spill the roan stared, its ears raised in interest toward the sound of the Ranger's voice. Its nostrils flared and probed the air, taking in the scent of him. The Ranger heard the horse nicker and caught a glimpse of him jerk and rear against the hitched lead rope. The other horses shied away from him as far as the rope would allow.

"When I'm through killing you," Orez said, "I'm cutting his throat. What I don't eat of him tonight, I'll dry and take with me into the mountains." He reached his left hand behind his back, took out another knife and pitched it handle-first at the Ranger's feet. He took another step down the rocks, then another, and another, each one quicker than the one before.

*Here it comes,* the Ranger told himself. He stopped and picked up the knife, but he remained crouched, braced, seeing Orez leap the last step out of the rocks onto the trail and charge forward in a run, no regard for the big Colt holstered on the Ranger's hip.

The Ranger responded quickly; he raced forward into Orez rather than take the full force of his charge straight on. Crashing together, each instinctively grasped the other's wrist with his free hand. Each withstood the other's attack as they both stood their ground to the inch. But then Orez made the next move, striking fast.

The big half-breed twisted forward right to left,

swinging his weight between himself and the Ranger. With one swift flip, he tossed the Ranger over his back and onto the firm, wet trail. The Ranger landed hard, but he had no time to spend there. He saw Orez's knife slashing down at him, a full swing from left to right; all he could do was roll away and keep rolling until he caught himself and sprang to his feet. He crouched again, facing Orez.

Orez gave a short, sly grin and tossed his knife back and forth hand to hand, flashy, showing off, a dangerous thing to do, the Ranger thought.

That was all right. Sam needed a second to recatch the breath that the fall had taken from his lungs. But he didn't get much more than a second before the two of them were facing each other again, crablike, hands and knives out, each ready to anticipate the other's move.

"You were fast, Ranger," Orez said. "I once killed a cavalry sergeant with that same move."

The Ranger didn't reply. He had nothing to say, and no breath to waste saying it.

"It was your own fault you died here today, Ranger," Orez said. "I left signs all along my trail, warning everybody." He shook his head. "I painted my trail with blood. Still, here you come."

"If that's why you killed those folks, you wasted a lot of human life for nothing," the Ranger said. The two circled back and forth, watching, searching, each ready for the other to leave himself open for a split second, just enough to allow the other in to kill. "The law doesn't stop because one crazy murderer warns it to."

"Crazy murderer, huh-uh. I'm a Red Sleeve warrior," Orez said, as if defending his sanity.

"Call it how it suits you, Orez," said the Ranger. "It's too late to stop fooling yourself anyway—"

Before his words left his mouth, Orez was upon him, his big knife swinging back and forth too fast for him to defend against. All the Ranger could do was jump back away from the bite of slashing steel. Still, Orez kept coming. He stopped his attack only when the Ranger stepped sidelong and brought his own blade through the air so fast it sliced across Orez's forearm.

"You drew first blood," Orez said flatly, glancing down at the long flowing strings of blood running from his arm, splattering on the wet ground.

The Ranger stood crouched, ready, not replying. He knew what to expect now that Wilson Orez saw that his own blood was the first to spill. In an instant, like the strike of a snake, Orez slashed forward, again so fast that the Ranger could only jump backward away from the deadly steel. This time Orez's strike was so swift and vicious he couldn't move backward fast enough. Instead he only managed to spin away from the blade at the last second. As he did so, he felt the white-hot burn of steel streak across the small of his back.

He was cut and he knew it. But he shook it off, not wanting to think about how bad, not now. Not while he felt the warm blood spread down over his hip from just above his belt line.

Orez stepped back, crouched less than before, not seeming as intense as before. There was almost a swagger to him.

"It's the ones you don't see coming that do the most damage," Orez said, staring at him. As he spoke, he ripped his sliced and bloody shirtsleeve down off his arm and wrapped it hastily around his wound.

Sam realized the man could have killed him just then. Why hadn't he? Instead of slicing the blade across his back, he could just as easily have sunk it between his shoulder blades or driven it deep and rounded it through his heart. That would have ended it, Sam told himself. But no, Orez didn't want to end it.

Before he could think any more on the matter, Orez lunged at him again, this time the knife blade streaking close to his throat, only missing by an inch. The Ranger backed away again. This had been a mistake; he realized it. He'd had Orez dead in his rifle sights. Why hadn't he himself ended it right then, right there?

Now it came to him what Orez was doing; he was flaunting death. He was ready to die, but he wasn't selling his life away cheaply. The warrior in him wanted to die as bloody as he could make it. Somehow Sam understood that. Suddenly it was all making sense in this small dark world of killing.

Orez came in again; this time the Ranger didn't jump back. He was through jumping back. As Orez's big blade came swinging across him, he swung back with his own big blade. The sound of steel on steel clashed loudly. The Ranger crouched again, ready to go back to circling, getting the fight back under his control. But as he crouched, he heard a ring and clatter of steel on the rocks behind him. He glanced down at his hand realizing that the sound he'd heard was his own broken knife blade flying in a high arc and landing in the rock spill.

Orez stared at him with an almost disappointed expression and shook his head slowly.

"I gave you every chance," he said. He lunged forward, this time with the seriousness of a man finishing a job he had to do.

Sam could do nothing but drop the useless knife handle and fall back step after step as Orez's big blade swung to and fro with increased intensity. When he tripped backward over his own boot and fell to the ground, Orez stopped for only a second. But then he regripped the big knife in his hand and made his final lunge.

The Ranger, on the ground, brought the big Colt up just above his holster, not a second too soon. He felt the gun buck in his hand, shot after shot, each bullet tearing a hole through Orez's chest, leaving a red mist in the air behind him. Suddenly the hillside turned dark and silent, and Sam lay back slowly on the hard wet ground. He holstered the Colt that rested smoking his hand.

In the silent graying evening light, the speckled barb, stirred by the scent of something on the prowl on a rocky hillside above him, sawed his head and tested his reins until at length they fell from around the jut of rock. Still, the horse waited and probed the air back and forth, then nickered to himself. Finally, as if giving the matter no more consideration, he trotted out around the turn in the trail without stopping until he saw the Ranger lying flat on his back in a dark puddle of blood.

Hearing the slowing clop of the barb's hooves, the Ranger turned his face to the side and stared into the glazed eyes of Wilson Orez lying flat on the ground beside him. A moment passed and he felt the warm breath and the dampness of the barb's muzzle against his cheek. From the rock spill, he heard the nickering of the roan and looked over and saw the animal jerking and picking at the hitched lead rope with its teeth.

*It's been a rough one, but it's over.*

He breathed in relief, shoved himself up and sat slumped on the ground, letting himself come back slowly from some dark place where he'd been. He felt a stiffness where the wound across his back had dried over against his shirt. He could hear the lingering ring of cold steel blades colliding in mid-air as he saw Orez's knife lying near his boot. At first sight he stuck out a boot and shoved it away. But then he reached over, unlooped the knife's sheath strap from around Orez's shoulder, picked up the knife and pushed himself up to his feet. He shoved the big knife firmly into its sheath and hung the strap over his shoulder.

His first step was halting, hard to get started. Then he staggered, righted himself and walked, the barb following close behind him, to where the roan stood nickering amid the other horses.

"Easy, boy," Sam said, watching the roan settle as he drew nearer, reached out a hand and rubbed its muzzle. The barb stepped in beside him, as if to not be left out of anything. The horses watched with interest as Sam took a bandanna from the roan's saddlebags, wadded it and stuffed it inside his shirt and back against his bloody wound. "That'll do for now," he said.

In the failing evening light he gathered the string of horses and looked them over, taking in the bags of money across their backs. He shook his head and glanced at Orez's body, noting how much smaller the man looked in death than he had in life. Overhead, above a thin bank of remaining cloud cover, a streaking red glow loomed large and round. The Ranger saw something black, something wide of wing batting upward. He watched it rise and cut across the Mexican hill and mountain line and move up out of sight into the black heavens above.

He walked to Orez's body, dragged it to the edge of the trail and rolled it off the side. He stood listening to the sound of it falling for a moment, but never heard it land.

Walking back to the horses, he saw the roan and the speckled barb standing close together, staring curiously at him. He rubbed both their muzzles, the roan pushing forward a little, demanding more than the barb. He'd gone through a lot of horses this trip, Sam reminded himself.

"I'm obliged, to both of you." He looked back and forth at the two tired, wet, mud-streaked animals and said, "Fellows, let's go home."

Taking up the lead rope, he stepped into the California saddle atop the barb. He put the barb forward, leading the string; the roan sidled in close at the head of the string, its nose almost against his leg. The Ranger tried pushing its muzzle away gently, but the roan would have none of it.

"I liked you just as well when you were a little standoffish," the Ranger said. The roan persisted, keeping its nose close to him, and chuffed and blew and shook out its damp tangled mane as they walked away around the turn in the trail. The soft clop of the horses' hooves fell gently on the ground. Overhead, the sky lay as quiet as a whisper.

Arizona Ranger Sam Burrack is back!
Don't miss a page of action from
America's most exciting Western author,
Ralph Cotton.

## *LAWLESS TRAIL*

*Twisted Hills, the Mexican Badlands*

The wide dirt street of Paso Alto lay beneath a veil of dry wavering heat as Arizona Ranger Samuel Burrack rode the black-speckled barb at a walk past the Gatos Malos Cantina. From under the brim of his sweat-stained sombrero, he eyed three men seated along a blanket-cushioned swing on the cantina's front porch. Each man held a rifle; each man wore a bandolier of ammunition hanging from his shoulder across his chest.

The three men returned the Ranger's stare, keeping the porch swing moving slowly back and forth with the slightest effort of their scuffed boots.

"That's right, gringo. You just keep moving on along," the man in the middle growled under his breath, more to his two *compañeros* than to the Ranger.

On the man's right, a broad-shouldered Mexican gunman known only as Pesado gave a single grunt of a laugh, finding irony in Ross McCloud calling the stranger a gringo. McCloud was from Missouri, after all—less than three months in Paso Alto, where he'd taken refuge from Missouri law.

"You are one *loco bastardo*, Ross," Pesado said with a sharp grin, his dark eyes following the Ranger for a few yards before turning away.

Ross McCloud stared straight ahead and spoke to the gunman on his left, an on-the-run murderer called Little Richard Fitts.

"Did he just call me a *crazy bastard*, Little Richard?" McCloud asked quietly, menace in his voice.

"Yes, I believe he did," Little Richard replied, eyeing a busty young British woman who stepped out of the cantina and lighted herself a thin black cigar.

Ross McCloud nodded.

"Good," he said, also watching the woman draw deep on the cigar and let out a stream of smoke. "For a minute there, I thought he was insulting me."

Ten feet away the British woman untied the strings holding her blouse shut across her breasts.

"I hope you fellows don't mind," she said with only a trace of a British accent. "It's hotter than Hades at high noon." She fanned the open blouse, then left it hanging agape; her pale freckled breasts stood firm, exposed and glaring in the white-hot sunlight.

"We *don't* mind, do we, Little Richard?" McCloud said without taking his eyes off the woman.

"Not too awful much," Little Richard replied, staring at her, his lips hanging slightly agape. "It is high noon," he added.

"And this is hell," McCloud said to her. "Leastwise it was, until it got so hot, the devil moved out." Without taking his eyes from the woman, he stood up and held his rifle out sidelong to the Mexican beside him. "Pesado, hold this for me. I'm going to go count this young lady's freckles."

"Oh, are you now, luv?" the woman said. She turned facing them, a hand cupped at the center of her naked breasts. "And what might I be *counting* whilst you amuse yourself?" She turned her cupped hand enough to rub her fingers and thumb together in the universal sign of greed, then clasped her hand back over herself as if overcome by modesty.

"I can't stand this," said Fitts, leaning his rifle against the end of the swing, stepping forward. "I'll give you something to count," he said to the woman.

"Easy, luv. Your fangs are showing," the woman said to Fitts.

"Wait a minute, Little Richard," said McCloud. "Who invited you?"

"When she turned them puppies loose, that's all the inviting I needed," said Fitts. He started forward.

McCloud hurried alongside him, shoving him away.

"We've been pards awhile, Little Richard," he warned. "But I swear to God—"

Behind them, Pesado stood laughing under his breath. But something in the corner of his eye caused him to turn suddenly toward the empty street. When he did, he found himself staring at the Ranger, who stood less than two feet from him, his big Colt cocked and aimed at the Mexican's broad belly.

"*Día bueno, Pesado,*" the Ranger said quietly.

In reflex the Mexican started to swing his Spencer rifle around, having to drop McCloud's

Winchester to do so. But before he could complete his move, the Ranger poked him with the gun barrel, just hard enough to make himself understood.

"If I wanted to kill you, you'd already be dead," the Ranger said menacingly. "Drop it."

McCloud and Fitts both turned upon hearing the Winchester hit the ground. Now they saw Pesado's Spencer rifle fall from his hands. They saw the Ranger standing with his Colt jammed into the Mexican gunman's belly.

They started to make a play for the revolvers holstered on their hips.

Pesado saw the look in the Ranger's eyes.

*"Don't!"* he shouted at the other two gunmen. "This one will kill me. I know he will!"

"Who are you, mister?" McCloud asked, his and Fitts' hands rising chest high in a show of peace. "What the hell is your game here?"

"I'm here to see Fatch Hardaway," Sam said flatly.

"Hunh-uh. We can't let you do that," said McCloud, in spite of the Ranger catching the three by surprise and getting the drop on them. He and Fitts took a cautious step sidelong toward the cantina door as if to block it. The British woman stood back, cigar in hand, watching intently.

"Sure you can," said Sam. "He knows I'm coming."

As he spoke, he pulled the cocked Colt's barrel back an inch from the Mexican's belly and pulled the trigger. All three men braced, their eyes widened—especially Pesado's. But the Ranger caught the gun hammer with his thumb in a split second and eased it down. Pesado let out a deep sigh and cursed the Ranger under his breath.

"You dirty, rotten gringo . . ." He let his words trail.

The Ranger, his Colt hanging in his hand, slipped the Mexican's revolver from its holster, pitched it down beside the rifles and stepped away from Pesado toward the door.

"I already said we can't let you do that," Mc-Cloud said in a stronger tone, his and Fitts' gun hands dropping down so they were poised beside their holstered revolvers.

The Ranger's thumb cocked the big Colt again. He stopped and raised the barrel calmly, smoothly, before either man made their move.

*Damn it!* McCloud raged silently. Again this stranger had the drop on them. *Damn it to hell!*

The British woman shook her lowered head. She let out a stream of smoke, dropped the thin cigar and crushed it out under her foot.

"By my stars," she said, "aren't the three of you just *the berries*—"

Her words fell away as a tall man in a black sweat-stained suit coat stepped into the doorway and looked back and forth. He held a sleek long-barreled Remington Army revolver in his right hand. He raised his free hand and removed a long, thick cigar from his mouth.

"Well, well, Ranger Samuel Burrack," he said. "Here you are, just as I'd hoped."

"I said I'd be here, Hardaway," the Ranger replied.

"So you did," said Hardaway. "And you've

strolled through my bodyguards without so much as a shot fired, I see." He gave each of his three gunmen a scorching look. "I can't tell you how pleased that makes me, as much as I'm paying these gun monkeys."

*Ranger?* McCloud, Fitts and Pesado looked at one another as if dumbstruck. McCloud stepped forward, embarrassed, and gestured toward Sam.

"Boss, it's lucky for him you showed up just now," he said. "We came very near to killing this fool, not knowing you was expecting him, that is."

"Yes, lucky him," said Hardaway with a searing stare at Ross McCloud. "All of you *bodyguards* best pick your guns up before someone carries them off."

The British woman gave a short playful chuckle; Hardaway shot her a hard glance, too. Seeing her pert round breasts, he took a deep, patient breath.

"Edy, put those away before somebody walks into a post and knocks his damn teeth out," he said seriously.

"I certainly wouldn't want that, now, would I?" she said, loosely closing her blouse front, but not attempting to retie the strings.

"There you are, Ranger," said Hardaway. "See why I want to go back to Texas without getting hanged? Life gets awfully trying around this bunch."

"I'll bet," Sam said. "You need to remember that the next time before you shoot a man and burn his saloon with him inside it."

"I realize that I may have acted a little rash and hastily, both in killing him and in burning his saloon down," said Hardaway. "But what has become of forgiveness these days?"

Sam just stared at him.

"At any rate"—Hardaway looked the Ranger up and down, then motioned him inside out of the sun—"welcome to the Bad Cats Cantina," he said.

The Ranger stepped inside and looked around the cantina's dingy dark interior. "This is your place?" he asked Hardaway.

"Let's just say I've acquired a substantial interest in it," he said, guiding the Ranger across the dirt floor toward tables standing beneath rings of circling flies. "I do hope you've got some good news for me."

Ready to find
your next great read?

Let us help.

**Visit prh.com/nextread**

Penguin
Random
House